WARHAMMER
AGE OF SIGMAR

Collections

The Realmgate Wars: Volume 1
Various authors
Contains the novels *The Gates of Azyr, War Storm, Ghal Maraz, Hammers of Sigmar, Wardens of the Everqueen* and *Black Rift*

The Realmgate Wars: Volume 2
Various authors
Contains the novels *Call of Archaon, Warbeast, Fury of Gork, Bladestorm, Mortarch of Night* and *Lord of Undeath*

Legends of the Age of Sigmar
Various authors
An anthology of short stories

Rulers of the Dead
David Annandale & Josh Reynolds
Contains the novels *Neferata: Mortarch of Blood*
and *Nagash: The Undying King*

Warcry
Various authors
An anthology of short stories

Champions of the Mortal Realms
Various authors
Contains the novellas *Warqueen, The Red Hours, Heart of Winter* and *The Bone Desert*

Gods & Mortals
Various authors
An anthology of short stories

Myths & Revenants
Various authors
An anthology of short stories

Oaths & Conquests
Various authors
An anthology of short stories

Novels

• HALLOWED KNIGHTS •
Josh Reynolds
BOOK ONE: Plague Garden
BOOK TWO: Black Pyramid

Eight Lamentations: Spear of Shadows
Josh Reynolds

• KHARADRON OVERLORDS •
C L Werner
BOOK ONE: Overlords of the Iron Dragon
BOOK TWO: Profit's Ruin

Soul Wars
Josh Reynolds

Callis & Toll: The Silver Shard
Nick Horth

The Tainted Heart
C L Werner

Shadespire: The Mirrored City
Josh Reynolds

Blacktalon: First Mark
Andy Clark

Hamilcar: Champion of the Gods
David Guymer

Scourge of Fate
Robbie MacNiven

The Red Feast
Gav Thorpe

Gloomspite
Andy Clark

Ghoulslayer
Darius Hinks

Beastgrave
C L Werner

Neferata: The Dominion of Bones
David Annandale

The Court of the Blind King
David Guymer

Novellas

City of Secrets
Nick Horth

Thieves' Paradise
Nick Horth

BEASTGRAVE

C L WERNER

BLACK LIBRARY

A BLACK LIBRARY PUBLICATION

First published in 2019.
This edition published in Great Britain in 2020 by
Black Library,
Games Workshop Ltd.,
Willow Road,
Nottingham,
NG7 2WS, UK.

10 9 8 7 6 5 4 3 2 1

Produced by Games Workshop in Nottingham.
Cover illustrations by Rezunenko Bogdan.

A CIP record for this book is available from the British Library.

ISBN 13: 978 1 78999 056 0

See Black Library on the internet at

blacklibrary.com

Find out more about Games Workshop
and the worlds of Warhammer at

games-workshop.com

Printed and bound by CPI Group (UK) Ltd, Croydon, CR0 4YY

For Hannah, who helped me see the forest through the trees.

From the maelstrom of a sundered world, the
Eight Realms were born. The formless and the divine
exploded into life.

Strange, new worlds appeared in the firmament, each one
gilded with spirits, gods and men. Noblest of the gods was
Sigmar. For years beyond reckoning he illuminated the realms,
wreathed in light and majesty as he carved out his reign. His
strength was the power of thunder. His wisdom was infinite.
Mortal and immortal alike kneeled before his lofty throne.
Great empires rose and, for a while, treachery was banished.
Sigmar claimed the land and sky as his own and ruled over a
glorious age of myth.

But cruelty is tenacious. As had been foreseen, the great
alliance of gods and men tore itself apart. Myth and legend
crumbled into Chaos. Darkness flooded the realms. Torture,
slavery and fear replaced the glory that came before. Sigmar
turned his back on the mortal kingdoms, disgusted by their
fate. He fixed his gaze instead on the remains of the world he
had lost long ago, brooding over its charred core, searching
endlessly for a sign of hope. And then, in the dark heat of
his rage, he caught a glimpse of something magnificent. He
pictured a weapon born of the heavens. A beacon powerful
enough to pierce the endless night. An army hewn from
everything he had lost.

Sigmar set his artisans to work and for long ages they toiled,
striving to harness the power of the stars. As Sigmar's great
work neared completion, he turned back to the realms and saw
that the dominion of Chaos was almost complete. The hour
for vengeance had come. Finally, with lightning blazing across
his brow, he stepped forth to unleash his creations.

The Age of Sigmar had begun.

CHAPTER ONE

The stink of burning flesh slammed against Ludvik's senses and drove the last wisps of sleep from his head. He was roused from exhausted slumber by the blaring of the watchtower's trumpet, and the foul stench was enough to snap him into full awareness. No mistake, no idiot's jest. Calamity had befallen Locmalo, and every inhabitant of the town was being called to action.

As he rushed from the earthen barracks he shared with twenty other men, Ludvik saw flames leaping up into the night. They threw eerie shadows across the clustered timber buildings. Several of the structures were alight, with fire flashing from their windows and doorways. Plumes of smoke rushed up from beneath crumbling sod roofs – long grey fingers that spilled upwards into the sky.

More than the roar of the flames and the blare of the trumpet assailed Ludvik's ears. Screams rang out from the burning homes. He saw a ragged figure emerge from Marek the cooper's house. The fire-wrapt shape took a few stumbling steps and collapsed in the muddy street. Steam sizzled off the dying frontiersman's smouldering clothes.

Ludvik's first instinct was to run for the nearest well and seize one of the buckets laid there against the threat of fire. As he turned to do so, another sound impressed itself on his awareness. A sound more frightful than the shrieks of people trapped in burning houses. Inhuman howls and bestial war-whoops rose from beyond the log palisade that encircled Locmalo. Ludvik felt cold horror rush through him. He knew the sort of creatures that made that savage din, just as he knew the doom that now reached out for the settlement. A doom the humans had long thought to defy.

The children of the forest had come. Come to punish this invasion into their domain. Come to sweep away the creep of civilisation into the wild places and stamp out the human trespassers.

Ludvik's hand fell to the long-bladed hunter's knife that was always strapped to his arm. The frontiersmen had learned to their cost to never be without some means of protection, even when in the safety of their own beds. He had seen Udalrich's body. He had been murdered in the night by a stealthy prowler. The inhuman killer had cut him open to eat his liver, all without waking the other dozen men in the barracks.

'They have broken through the outer wall!' The shout carried down from the frantic sentinel up in the watchtower between blasts on the trumpet. The reaction of the men around Ludvik was a mixture of despair and anger. For himself, he felt only a kind of sickness in his belly, a sour churning of the soup he had for supper.

Two palisades defended Locmalo – an outer and an inner fence of sharpened logs. Between these was a cleared pasture where the people grazed their herds. Ludvik himself had two cows out there, animals he had purchased with the pelts he had captured through the autumn. It was his first step towards becoming independent, establishing himself so he would not have to brave the forest and the beasts that yet lurked beneath its boughs.

Ludvik heard the agonised wailing of the cattle. The attackers were in the pasture and slaughtering the livestock. For a moment, all he could think of was his own loss. Then a cold chill swept through him. If the attackers found a way through or over the inner wall, it would be men not kine that would be massacred.

Ludvik ran towards the walls. He saw the beadle with a cartload of spears handing weapons to anyone who came near him. Men and women, old and young, anyone with the strength and heart to carry a bow or swing an axe, were hurrying to the palisade to take up the fight. Ludvik hurried to the beadle and snatched a spear from the cart. He took only a heartbeat to judge its quality before he was moving again. The muddy streets of Locmalo were a bedlam of fright and confusion. As the defenders ran towards the walls, fiery objects came hurtling down into the settlement. Ludvik saw one of them splash in a puddle of mud. It was an old skull stuffed with dried dung and sealed with pitch. He saw the crude glyphs daubed on the skull in streaks of blood. He trembled. Their enemies had called upon witchcraft to aid the attack.

More of the skulls came flying over the wall. They burned with an ugly orange glow as they sailed through the air. One of them struck the roof of the tannery. It shattered like an eggshell and splashed its contents across the roof and the nearby walls. Timbers were instantly set alight. Ludvik felt there was an unholiness about the way the flames spread. The fire's hunger was more than natural.

'To the wall! To the wall!' The command was shouted by Squire Dytryk himself. He stood near the main gate, Locmalo's five militiamen arrayed around him in a compact bloc. Only one of the soldiers wore his armour. The others had been stirred from their sleep with barely enough time to grab helmets and shields. The squire himself only had a bearskin robe on, though he'd picked up his sword before dashing out into the street.

'To the wall!'

The cry was taken up. The direction gave the defenders focus, something to fixate upon before fear and confusion could break their resolve. Ludvik joined the line of spears that formed about the base of the wall. He jabbed upwards at the dark shapes trying to climb the palisade. He felt grim satisfaction when a horned figure fell back into the shadows and a thin rivulet of blood trickled down the shaft of his spear.

A few hunters with bows moved among the spearmen, adding their arrows into the mix. Ludvik wished he had gone back for his own bow as he watched his comrades ply their deadly skill. Whenever an enemy presented itself, an arrow would speed towards it. Even when they missed, the threat from the archers was enough to make the attacker drop back.

Behind the line of spears, those settlers with axes and swords clutched their weapons with anxious fingers. As much as Ludvik envied the hunters with their bows, he was thankful he had at least a spear to drive the attackers back. If all he had was an axe or his knife, he'd be forced to stand idle with the others. Watching and waiting. Dreading the moment when he would be called into the fight. The moment the beastkin forced their way into Locmalo.

Ghroth watched the fires rise, their glow illuminating the inner palisade. The herdchief wiped the string of saliva that dripped from his fangs. The smell of cooking human was almost intoxicating, far more than the scent of slaughtered cattle. It did not take much to goad the brays and ungors of his warherd into charging the wall. The real test of his authority was getting the larger gors to restrain themselves. Few beastkin understood patience or had the discipline to plan for the future, however immediate it might be.

Ghroth was one of those few. His craftiness and his ability to delay gratification, were what set him apart. It was why he had supplanted the old herdchief, waiting until after a vicious fight with the tree-fiends of Thornwyld before challenging him for his position. He wore the horns of his rival, bound around his left hand like a spiked gauntlet. It was a reminder to the rest of the beastkin of his strength. When the warren of humans was crushed under his hooves, that too would serve as a reminder to the warherd. It would be a display of his wisdom. An example of his power.

The ungors and brays threw themselves at the walls. Smaller and slighter than the more bestial gors like Ghroth, their lack of bulk was something of a benefit to them as they tried to clamber up the logs. Covered in fur, with hoofed feet and nubby horns, these beastkin were closer to humans in appearance than others in the warherd. The brays in particular had manlike faces and builds – Ghroth even employed them to decoy humans in the forest by making them think the brays were men like themselves.

With their present task, there was no question of the brays being mistaken for humans. The frontiersmen were attacking anything that tried to get over the walls. At the edge of panic, their desperate efforts were fending off the beastmen. Many of the ungors fell into the pasture with ugly gashes and cuts. A few of the brays collapsed with arrows through their chests.

'Small horns never get in.' The comment came as a sullen growl from the armoured brute that stood beside Ghroth. A full head taller than the herdchief, Kruksh had adorned his black-furred girth with metal plate looted from dead humans and orruks. Even his goat-like face was banded with strips of mail. The grotesque greenskin cleaver he carried would have been impossible for most gors to wield.

Ghroth glared into the bestigor's beady yellow eyes. Kruksh

grunted in contempt. There was no cunning in his gaze, only the impertinent confidence of a creature that relied solely upon his brawn. 'Small horns not need get in,' Ghroth stated. He gestured at the injured ungors and at the tips of the spears that could be seen waving behind the wall. 'Small horns fight. Show where man-flesh fight. See where manflesh strong.' He gave Kruksh a piercing look, trying to find some awareness there. 'See where manflesh strong, see where manflesh weak.'

Kruksh slapped his chest and snorted. 'All manflesh weak,' he asserted.

Ghroth bared his fangs at the implied insult. He raised his arm, ensuring Kruksh could see the sharpened horns of the old herdchief. The bestigor lowered his head and averted his eyes. There was no challenge there. At least not yet. Ghroth resisted the impulse to tear out Kruksh's throat. Right now killing the humans was more important. Besides, it was more practical to kill a rival in front of the entire warherd. That way all of the beastkin would know their place.

The sharp tang of smouldering dung made Ghroth turn. He watched a pair of ungors run towards the palisade with smoking skulls in their hands. Loops of dried gut were wound about the skulls and, as the beastmen drew close to the wall, they swung the weird missiles in an arc. When the arc reached the right speed, the ungors let go and sent the skulls flying over the wall. A moment later there was a loud whoosh and flames erupted from the settlement.

Ghroth stalked over to where the ungors had received their macabre weapons. His nostrils flared in revulsion at the unnatural scent of the creature crouched beside a stack of skulls. Useful as magic might be to the warherd, none of the beastkin liked to be near something as steeped in the arcane reek as the shaman Sorgaas. The cloaked mystic was daubing glyphs on the skulls with the severed head of a serpent. He dipped the reptile's blunt nose into a bowl of blood and painted the sorcerous signs on the bones. Normally the smell of blood would excite Ghroth, but the shaman's activity had corrupted the scent, made it somehow rancid.

'More flame for manflesh,' Ghroth growled, trying to make the words more of a command than a question. He was chief of his warherd – even the giant bullgors obeyed him – but he still felt a tremor of fear when the smell of Sorgaas was in his nose.

The shaman looked up from his labour, the hood of his cloak drawing back to expose a lupine muzzle covered in blue-black fur. A single horn rose from above his nose, branching out into two sharp points. The entirety of the horn was stained with glyphs, and talismans dangled from its bifurcated tips. Cold eyes, yellow and slitted like those of a serpent, stared up at Ghroth. Sorgaas lifted a hand that was scaly, with black talons at the tip of each finger, utterly unlike the slender gloved member that held the snake's head.

'All will burn,' Sorgaas said. He turned his talons towards the pile of skulls. 'Magic enough for all of these. This is why I tell you to wait.' He thrust his claw skyward and pointed at the stars. 'Now is the time when my magic is strong. Now is when the gods of men are weak.'

Ghroth glowered at the shaman. 'Ghroth herdchief,' he stated. 'Victory mine.'

Sorgaas tapped the snake's head against the skull he was painting. 'Yes, and these will bring you victory. You will be a mighty herdlord. If you listen.' The ophidian eyes strayed from Ghroth and focused on the two ungors who had come creeping back to retrieve more of the fiery skulls.

Ghroth followed the direction of the shaman's gaze. The ungors cringed away from him. He grunted his satisfaction and motioned for the beastmen to continue. Whatever awe they might feel for their shaman, they did not forget it was their herdchief who ruled.

'Burn the manflesh,' Ghroth snarled. 'They know fire. They know fear.' He turned and looked at the palisade, drawing the smell of humans from the wind. 'They know death,' he declared. 'Good feast for warherd.'

Ghroth studied the way the ungors and brays were driven back. He fought against the impulse to simply charge the fortification. There had been other attacks against the humans before, attacks that had failed because the beastkin did not restrain their blood-lust. Ghroth would show the warherd. He would show them why he was their leader. This attack would not fail.

The packs of ungors and brays rushed the walls, pressing the defenders to divert fighters to oppose them. The gate itself was only lightly challenged, just enough so that the humans would not become suspicious. If they were too wary they would try to reinforce it, but if they could be gulled into believing the warherd was threatening the whole of the palisade it would cause them to move where the danger was greatest.

After a few moments of study, Ghroth turned to Sorgaas. 'Give signal,' he told the shaman.

Sorgaas set down the snake head and rose to his feet. He clasped his mismatched hands together, pressing them tight against his chest. The slithery eyes rolled back, the pupils vanishing beneath the orbits of his skull. An eerie chill gripped Ghroth as dark energies were drawn into the mystic's body. The dangling talismans clattered against the bifurcated horn as Sorgaas shivered.

'*Urugu*,' Sorgaas suddenly shouted. He thrust both arms into the air and from between his hands a stream of green light flared up into the night.

Ghroth did not need to see the dark shapes that scurried up the side of the watchtower, the slinking spies that had entered the settlement hours before the attack. He could tell they had accomplished their purpose when the blare of the trumpet was silenced.

The only men who could have seen far enough into the pasture to warn of what was coming were gone.

'Gate!' Ghroth shouted. 'Bash gate!' He swung the brutish axe he carried overhead, its jagged blade reflecting the fires of the burning town. Out from the darkness a score of goat-headed gors charged towards the palisade, each helping to bear the weight of an immense log. Tied to the front of the log were half a dozen of Sorgaas' incendiary skulls. Ghroth pointed his axe at the gate as the gors ran past.

The log slammed into the iron-banded timbers of the gate. The skulls fitted to its front exploded in a dazzling burst of flame. A pillar of fire, forty feet high, licked across the gate and threw smouldering drops into the town beyond. The gors nearest the explosion bleated in agony, their bodies engulfed. The others hastily dropped the log and retreated.

Ghroth could imagine the humans inside the town were even more shocked by the explosion. Some were certain to abandon their places at the wall to defend against an attack on the gate. As they did, they would confuse those who tried to hold the palisade. Fear and confusion – the allies that would bring the warherd victory.

'Kill!' Ghroth howled. The vicious cry rose above the crackle of flames and the screams of the dying. It was taken up by dozens of bestial throats, repeated with the savagery of warriors finally set loose upon their foes. Until now only the smaller beastkin had assaulted the walls. The larger gors and bestigors flung themselves into the attack. Driven amok by their pent-up bloodlust, they rushed the walls with berserk fury. Their impetus carried them over the sharpened logs and they plunged down to the confused defenders below.

Ghroth savoured the sight. He enjoyed the shrieks from the humans as his warriors fell upon them. He relished the smell of blood that wafted back to him on the wind. His fingers tightened on the haft of his axe and all restraint left him. He charged towards the wall, froth dripping down his fangs. No longer did he think of victory or maintaining his place as herdchief. He did not think of ploys and tricks or the magic of Sorgaas. There was only room in his mind for hunger and wrath, the scent of blood and the taste of flesh.

It took Ghroth only a few heartbeats to reach the wall. Like a charging tiger, he leapt at the palisade. His axe came flashing down between two of the sharpened logs. Using the weapon for leverage, Ghroth pounced down into the settlement. All around him was bedlam. Humans lay butchered in the mud. Beastkin were spitted on spears. Unchecked fires roared, their flames an orange glow. The stink of smoke assailed his senses, blotting out all other smells. Screams and moans, the desperate cries of men and the murderous growls of beastkin formed a savage medley.

Ghroth rose from the mud and stamped his hooves in eagerness as a spearman lunged at him. He twisted aside as the weapon stabbed at his stomach. A chop of his axe broke the shaft and left the man gaping at him in horror. Before he could flee, Ghroth sprang at him. The sharpened horns tied about his left arm raked across his enemy's face, turning it into crimson ribbons. He collapsed into the mud, screaming in pain.

Ghroth moved to bring his hoof stamping down on the maimed human, but as he did another defender came charging at him. Like the first foe, this one bore a spear, but unlike his ill-fated comrade he was not so easily disarmed. He avoided the downward sweep of the herdchief's axe and raked the edge of the spearhead across Ghroth's ribs. It bit just deep enough to draw blood, slashing through the shaggy hide.

Instead of stamping down, Ghroth brought his leg cracking against the prone man with such force that he was kicked into the path of the spearman. His assailant reeled back to avoid being tripped by the very comrade he had thought to protect. As he did, Ghroth sprang at him. A sideways sweep of the sharpened horns tore the spear from his enemy's hands.

The foeman stumbled back and drew a long knife from the sheath lashed to his arm. He whipped the blade back and forth, forming a deadly circle between himself and the herdchief. Even with the longer reach of his axe, Ghroth knew he would not be able to penetrate that defence with impunity.

Ghroth glared at his enemy and spat in the human's face. For an instant the man was blinded. The knife wavered. It was all the advantage the herdchief needed. Lunging forwards, Ghroth brought his axe cleaving down into the man's chest. It was a killing blow. He was dead even before the axe was ripped free and his body crashed to the muddy street.

Ghroth licked the blood and bone splinters from the edge of his axe. He turned back to finish the screaming wretch the knife fighter had tried to save.

Fear always provided an extra savour to manflesh.

Ghroth sated his bloodlust. His axe had become dull from the number of humans it had killed. His mouth was filled with the taste of butchered foes.

All across the settlement he heard the triumphant howls of his warriors. A triumph such as the beastkin had not known before. Always they had raided the humans, stealing away with a few cattle or a few hapless settlers. Never before had they been able to accomplish such a conquest. Never before had they brought so large a town to ruin. The beastkin would remember this, and they would remember it was Ghroth who had won this great victory.

Ghroth strode through the devastation. Bodies were strewn about the streets – the carcasses of those who had fled from the walls and those who had never joined the defence. It did not matter to the beastkin whether the humans fought or not. They were intruders one and all, trespassers in the warherd's domain.

A domain that would grow. Word of this victory would spread when the other herds gathered at the herdstones. Ghroth's name would be known through the forests. More warriors would join him, and as they did he would expand his territory.

Flames from the burning houses continued to flicker all across the settlement. Ghroth found his gaze drawn to one of the fires. Purple shadows seemed to dance among the blaze, weaving in and out of the smoke. His hand curled around his axe and a trickle of drool fell from his mouth.

Ghroth stalked towards the fire, ready to launch an attack on whoever was moving around behind the flames. As he came nearer, however, he felt an increasing uneasiness. The shadows he was looking at were strange. They did not resemble humans or even beastkin. He stopped and stared, perplexed as increasingly distinct images manifested within the flames.

Ghroth saw a mountain appear amid the flames. Immense and imposing, with gnarled forests dotting its slopes and craggy cliffs stretching across its face, there was something about the mountain that filled his heart with dread. It was like gazing upon some slumbering monster, impossibly vast and terrible. He could feel a brooding malignance becoming aware of him, stirring from its ancient sleep to focus upon him.

Ghroth tried to look away, but as he turned his head he was drawn back to the image in the flames. His perspective was changing, speeding closer to the mountain. The forests resolved themselves into individual trees, the cliffs into piles of boulders. He felt himself being dragged against his will towards the black maw of a cave. He was delving down into the darkness, flying along subterranean passages with horrifying swiftness. His surroundings became a blur, alternating flashes of light and dark. He caught blurred glimpses of underground chasms and cavern pools. He saw the glow of volcanic vents and the rubble of forgotten ruins.

Deeper and deeper Ghroth was drawn, plummeting through the tunnels down into the bowels of the mountain. With a sickening abruptness he came to a stop, and all sense of motion was gone. He found himself in a gargantuan cavern lit by a weird orange light. The stony teeth of stalactites and stalagmites filled the vastness. Scattered among the natural formations were cyclopean blocks, immense beyond belief, hoary with age.

Ghroth's attention turned from the ruins, drawn to something he could sense but not see lying in the darkness. The moment his focus was diverted, the herdchief's perspective flashed across the cavern. Now he was standing upon some indistinct bulk. He felt it stir beneath him, could smell its musky odour as it filled his lungs. Compulsion seized him and Ghroth lunged at the giant hulk on which he stood. Sharpened horns and his gleaming axe ripped into the huge body, carving down through flesh and bone. His arms closed around a pulsing mass of tissue and with a howl he tore it free. Ghroth stared at the dripping trophy, a still-beating heart almost as large as his entire body. He pressed his face against the gory organ, his fangs savaging it as he began to feed.

The vision in the flames changed. No longer was Ghroth deep beneath the mountain. Instead he was standing atop a strange herdstone. All around the dolmen were piled the mangled corpses of humans and the splintered husks of tree-fiends. Weapons of steel and iron were heaped around the corpses – offerings not to the herdstone's watchers but to the leader who stood above it.

Ghroth gazed deeper into the flames and saw the multitude that surrounded the herdstone. It was a gathering of beastkin beyond reckoning, an army greater than any warherd from legend. He heard the savage voices rise, chanting his name, hailing Ghroth as beastlord. And beyond the masses of his followers, beyond the dark boughs of the forest, he saw lights shining in a human city.

Primordial power pulsed through his being. Ghroth felt his pitiless hatred of men swell inside him. He would lead the numberless hosts of his army against that city. He would pull down its walls and raze its towers. He would crush man's vile civilisation beneath his hooves and initiate a slaughter that would inspire the gods themselves.

He, Ghroth, would be the mightiest beastlord to walk the domains of Ghur. He would be the one who would drown the rule of men in a tide of blood.

Ghroth could not say how long he was gripped by the vision in the flames. He might never have broken away had some instinct not snapped him back to reality. He sprang aside just as a huge orruk blade came slashing down at him.

Kruksh snarled in rage as the herdchief dodged the murderous blow. He swiftly charged after Ghroth and sent the cumbersome blade flashing for his head.

The blow clipped the tip off one of Ghroth's horns as he ducked beneath the sweeping attack. Growling, he dived at Kruksh and brought his axe slamming into the bestigor. The weapon banged into his foe with bone-rattling force but its edge had been dulled in the fight against the humans. It didn't cleave through the armour Kruksh wore. The brutal impact made him stagger, but he did not fall.

'Ghroth die. Kruksh lead,' the bestigor spat.

The herdchief glared back at his rival. He did not answer Kruksh's boasting with words. He hurled the dull axe full into the bestigor's face. Kruksh stumbled as his nose was mashed by the flung weapon. Ghroth lunged, raking the sharpened horns down the challenger's arm. They bit deep, slashing through the heavy hide and into the meat beneath. Kruksh bleated in pain as his arm was shredded from elbow to wrist. His injured hand fell away from the heavy orruk blade. Ghroth swung around and wrenched the cleaver from the weakened grip of the remaining hand.

'Ghroth lead. Kruksh die.' The herdchief threw the words back at the bestigor. He brought the orruk cleaver chopping down with both hands. The brutal blade crunched into Kruksh's skull, splitting the mail coif he wore and embedding itself in his head. A blood-flecked gasp rose from the stricken rival. One hand reached for the cleaver as though to tug it free. A fierce shudder coursed through Kruksh's body. The bestigor pitched forwards into the mud, his hooves digging into the earth as life ebbed away.

Ghroth kicked the carcass and set his hoof down upon the bestigor's neck. Slapping his chest, the herdchief roared his victory to the smoke-filled night. If there were others of his warherd who knew Kruksh was going to challenge him, they would know something else. They would know that Ghroth had overcome his challenger. They would know that he was still herdchief.

He swung around. There was someone near. Ghroth bared his fangs in a snarl. Another rival, waiting to see if Kruksh succeeded, or to attack the weakened herdchief after the bestigor failed? It was the sort of underhanded tactic that would suit another of the warherd's bestigors, the sly Chagrak. 'Come,' Ghroth shouted and slapped his chest. 'Come to Ghroth and die!'

Out from the blackened ruin of a demolished hut someone stepped into view. Not the brutal Chagrak. It was the cloaked figure of Sorgaas. The shaman held his crooked bray-staff, the arcane glyphs carved down its length glowing with occult power. He glanced at Kruksh's corpse then fixed Ghroth with his serpentine gaze.

Ghroth met that cold stare, lips curled back from his fangs as he stepped towards Sorgaas. 'You,' he snarled. 'You tell Kruksh challenge Ghroth.'

The shaman tapped one talon against the sharpened tip of the bray-staff. 'I told Kruksh nothing. I only watched. I wanted to see what would happen.'

'Kruksh die,' Ghroth snapped. 'Ghroth stay herdchief.'

'Then you are worthy,' Sorgaas said, unconcerned with the fury in Ghroth's eyes. 'If you were not, Kruksh would be herdchief.'

The shaman's superior tone provoked Ghroth. Sorgaas might have thought his magic was enough to protect him from the herd-chief's anger, but he had underestimated the rage that thundered inside Ghroth's chest.

Ghroth rushed the shaman. A few running steps and he leapt at the wolf-faced mystic. Sorgaas raised the bray-staff to fend off the enraged attack, but a sweep of the trophy-horns tied to Ghroth's arm sent it flying across the street. He slammed into the shaman and bore him down into the mud. One hand pressed down on Sorgaas' chest, pinning him there. The other closed around his muzzle, silencing any curse he might cast upon the chieftain.

Ghroth tightened his hold on the lupine snout. The talismans dangling from the horn clattered together as the shaman winced in pain. 'Ghroth mighty,' he growled at the mystic. 'Ghroth strong. Not herdchief. Not warchief. Ghroth beastlord of great gorherd.'

He saw the disbelief in Sorgaas' eyes. Somehow, more than any curse or spell, it was the shaman's incredulity that gouged Ghroth's spirit. Angrily, he rose from the prone mystic and dragged him back onto his feet. 'Sorgaas see,' the chieftain bellowed. 'Sorgaas know Ghroth mighty.'

Still with one hand clamped tight about the shaman's mouth, Ghroth dragged him to the burning building and the fire where he had seen the purple shadows. He dumped Sorgaas on the ground and pointed at the flames. 'Look in fire. See. See Ghroth strong.'

Sorgaas did as Ghroth demanded and peered into the crackling flames. The herdchief started forwards when he saw the shaman's gloved hand make a gesture. The faint whisper of a strange word hissed from the lupine mouth. Sorgaas did not finish his conjuration, but instead leaned even closer to the fire. He raised his nose, sniffing as he tried to draw some scent from the air. Again he leaned to the flames, thrusting his face into the dancing blaze. Ghroth expected to smell the tang of singed fur and burning flesh wafting off the shaman, but there was only a musky reek. A cold and clammy smell such as he had encountered in his vision.

The shaman drew away from the fire, his face unharmed by its heat.

'Sorgaas see?' Ghroth asked, pointing at the flames.

'I saw nothing,' Sorgaas said. He raised his clawed hand, motioning for Ghroth to wait. 'I felt the magic that was here. Old and very powerful. What did you see?'

It took Ghroth some time to describe to Sorgaas the vision he had experienced in the flickering flames. The shaman interrupted him several times, asking him to elaborate on the details or to expand upon some feature he had observed. It taxed the herdchief's patience to answer all of the questions, but he was smart enough to curb his impulses. Magic was the work of a shaman. If anyone could tell him the meaning of what he had seen, it would be Sorgaas.

'What Ghroth see?' Ghroth demanded when he had related the whole of his vision.

Sorgaas crouched down beside the burning house. The flames had subsided, leaving only embers and ash. Somehow the shaman had regained his bray-staff without Ghroth noticing. He jabbed its sharpened tip into the embers, stirring them as though some secret might be unveiled.

'The mountain you saw is called Beastgrave,' Sorgaas declared.

'All who know of it hold it in awe and dread. The godbeasts of old are said to be buried under the mountain.' He gave Ghroth an appraising look. 'They say to eat the heart of a god is to take its power.'

Ghroth shook his head in wonder. 'Ghroth see. Ghroth be strong. Ghroth be mighty.'

'Beastlord,' Sorgaas said. 'Perhaps even greater than a beastlord if you eat the godbeast's heart.'

'Great! Mighty!' Ghroth stamped his hooves in the mud. 'Crush all manflesh. Rule all wood-places.'

Sorgaas tapped his claws against his bray-staff. 'Even more,' he suggested. 'More power than you ever knew. Stronger than a hundred bullgors. Taller than a gargant.'

Drool fell from Ghroth's fangs as his mind raced with the shaman's words. He would do more than just smash the places of men with such power. He would go and destroy the tree-fiends. He would take their forests as his own. All the warherds would bow to him.

Ghroth listened to the bellows and howls of his warriors as they feasted amid the ruins of the human settlement. He would summon the warherd from their revels and goad them to this mountain Sorgaas called Beastgrave. They would scour its depths and find the resting place of the godbeast.

'Sorgaas lead warherd to mountain,' Ghroth ordered. He did not question that the shaman knew the way.

The shaman shook his head. 'That would be unwise,' he said. Sorgaas pointed at Kruksh's body. 'The treasure you seek could be stolen by a rival. You should only take a few followers with you. Those you can trust.' His claws tapped against the glowing bray-staff. 'It is not enough to be strong. You must be cunning as well if you would triumph.'

Ghroth digested the shaman's caution. He wrenched the huge

orruk cleaver from Kruksh's skull. 'Sorgaas cunning. Ghroth strong. Together find mountain.'

The herdchief raised the huge weapon over his head. 'Sorgaas find godbeast. Ghroth kill godbeast. Ghroth be strong. Ghroth be mighty!'

CHAPTER TWO

The earth was thick and cool, rich with nutrients. There was a crispness to the breeze that wafted through the trees, gently plucking at their branches and tickling their leaves. The sun, warm and vibrant, sent brilliant beams through the gaps in the forest canopy and bathed the ground in life-giving energy.

Kyra exulted in it all. This part of the vast Thornwyld was ever her favourite, drawing her back to it again and again. The black soil was the finest in the entire forest, the breeze was rarely violent and never did it bear upon it the polluted smells of humans, duardin and orruks.

Birds flocked to this secret place, hopping about the open ground to pick at the seeds blown there by the breeze or to hunt the worms that wriggled through the dirt. Their songs rang out in a hundred melodies as they flitted from tree to tree, declaring their territories or crying out for their companions. Great silvery squirrels danced about the trunks, climbing and descending with jerky flicks of their bushy tails. An old black fox, its ears adorned with crimson tufts, studied the other animals from a hole it had dug under a thick root. It seemed lazy and idle, but Kyra knew if it saw a chance at a quick meal it would fly from its den in a blur of motion.

This place had no name. Even if it had, it would not change the way Kyra thought of it. This was her refuge, her place of repose. Here she came to restore herself, to regather her energies and to reclaim her mental focus. It was so easy to relinquish both, to have them ebb away. The Thornwyld would do that if one was not careful. It would disperse one's energy among its vastness. It would drain away the mind itself and leave only a little seed of awareness behind.

Kyra had too much pride to submit herself so completely, even to something she venerated as dearly as the Thornwyld. She had not grown here. Her earliest days had been spent in another forest, but that had been far away and long ago. Nothing remained of it, only the memories Kyra carried with her – a remembrance she feared would be lost if she did not cherish it with all her being.

She felt the grip of tiny feet on her arm. Kyra slowly shifted her head to observe the dun-coloured shrike that was preening itself. The bird noticed her motion, holding still as it tried to make sense of the face it was gazing at. It cocked its head one way and the other, making a careful study of the wooden countenance. Kyra kept still, but her lack of movement did not allay the shrike's qualms. With an alarmed cry, it took wing and darted off into the deeper forest.

Kyra curled her long fingers back to her branch-like arm and brushed the marks left by the shrike from her bark. She turned her gnarled head again, little green shoots falling about her face like leafy strands of hair. Cavities in the wood served as her eye sockets and from within them twin motes of emerald light shone. Their brilliance grew as Kyra focused on the shrike, feeling the beats of its wings in the breeze, hearing the sound of its throbbing heart. The gash across her head that served as a mouth curled back in a rough approximation of a smile.

It was a curious thing, Kyra mused, how the simpler the creature the more aware they were to the presence of the sylvaneth. Human trespassers had been unable to tell her apart from the trees. Not until she chose to reveal herself to them. Not until they did something to offend the Thornwyld.

A ripple of regret flickered through her neural capillaries. Humans rarely entered the forest without provoking a response. They would try to claim the timber for their own, or gather the berries and seeds. They would hunt the animals without consideration for the careful balance the Thornwyld maintained. So the trespassers would be driven forth, their violations returned in degree to their severity. It was not done out of maliciousness, but necessity. Fear had ever been the quickest way to lessen the ambitions of humans. Still, it was something that had to be repeated often. Unlike the sylvaneth, the quick-blooded humans had short memories. After only a few of their brief generations they would need to be reminded again why they did not journey into the Thornwyld.

Humans were an enigma to her. Kyra could not understand the quick-blooded races, but of them all it was humans who were the most unpredictable. The animals of the forest had their ways and habits, dependable reactions to the conditions in which they were cast. Even the orruk and duardin were not so difficult to anticipate when compared with the actions of men. Kyra had seen humans fight and struggle beyond all chance of escape. She had seen them do so for petty, selfish reasons and she had seen them do so for noble, impersonal causes. There had been armies of men who had striven to preserve the old forests long ago, when the hordes of Chaos descended upon Ghur. Hordes that had been largely composed of men who swore themselves to the Dark Gods.

For Kyra, it was the unpredictability of mankind that made it doubly imperative to punish any person who transgressed and entered the Thornwyld. Let them eke out their swift, brief lives elsewhere. The forest had no place for them. It simply could not.

Kyra felt the tremor that rustled through the trees. It vibrated through the blood-sap in her bark. An alarm, silent except to the sylvaneth, swept through the Thornwyld. There were trespassers in the forest. Her gash of a mouth drew into a deep scowl. So this was why her thoughts had turned to humans and their erratic ways. Her aetheric attunement sometimes caused her to have nebulous forewarnings. She would perceive things without understanding their import until later, when the events unfolded. This was such an instance.

Kyra drew her toe-roots up from the rich dark soil. The leafy stalks about her head swept back into a sharp mane of sticks. Her fingers narrowed, the bark at their tips thickening into thorns.

There were intruders in the Thornwyld. The time of peaceful solitude was over. Now there would be pain and fear.

Blood and death.

It was never a question of finding the intruders. The soundless harmonies of the Thornwyld conveyed their presence to Kyra continuously. The vibrations that shivered through her were stronger the nearer she was to the trespassers. If the quick-blood suspected they were being hunted, they might try to run, but as long as they were in the forest they could not hide.

She felt other presences, shapes that moved through the forest as soundless as the morning mist. Kyra was not the only sylvaneth who had come in answer to the alarm. She drew out a seed from one of the knotholes in her trunk. As she concentrated upon it, she could focus her magic and reach out with her mind. Her awareness brushed against those of the other sylvaneth within the great Spirit Song, seeking their acceptance. One and all they opened themselves to her, letting the branchwraith know who and where they were.

'There are only six humans.' This intelligence was conveyed to Kyra by the dryad Yanir. There was a bitter flavour to her thoughts that was impressed upon Kyra as forcefully as the words. The branchwraith could envision Yanir stalking through the forest, her bark white and scarred with age and her fingers long and sharp with wrath. Yanir was one of the eldest dryads in the Thornwyld and she had many reasons to despise the quick-blood.

'I would see.' Kyra sent the request slipping through Yanir's mind. The elder dryad gave her consent and the branchwraith narrowed the focus of her magic. The presence of the other sylvaneth in the area faded, until only her own spirit and that of Yanir were clear to her. She divided her awareness between them, pouring some of her own essence into Yanir's body that she might experience the dryad's perspective.

'They have violated the Thornwyld.' Yanir's thoughts bore upon Kyra's mind as she looked through the dryad's eyes.

Kyra saw them now. Half a dozen humans picked their way through the forest. Within Yanir's body, Kyra did not simply sense the elder dryad's loathing for the quick-blood, she felt it as well. It took effort for her to subdue the impression and study the invaders with a less distorted view.

'There is something wrong here.' Kyra had seen many humans over the course of her long life. She had seen hunters and lumberjacks, foragers and char-burners. She had seen those who came to steal and those who came to conquer. The ones she looked upon bore as little similarity to those invaders as a pine resembled an oak. Their coverings were ragged and torn, stained with soot.

Their skin was blackened by smoke, cut and bruised by some recent ordeal. Their eyes were wide with fright, their breath hissing from their bodies in exhausted gasps. They entered the Thornwyld unburdened with supplies and between them they had only a single spear for a weapon.

'They did not come here to defile the forest,' Kyra decided. She observed the humans as they glanced all around with panicked eyes. They did not see the sylvaneth among the trees. Kyra felt it was something else they were frightened of. 'They came here to hide.'

'Others are in the Thornwyld.' The observation came from the dryad Nyiss with such intensity of thought that it reached Kyra even with her consciousness split between bodies.

Kyra's spirit withdrew from Yanir and ensconced itself completely in her own body. She could still sense the vibrations of the trees, but it was a limitation of both their ability and their perception that they could only convey so much through the crude communication. They had reported the human intruders, but that was all. The trees had not warned the sylvaneth that there were more trespassers.

'What do you see?' Kyra asked. She did not want to exert her magic again by flowing directly into Nyiss. It might be that she would need all the aetheric power she could draw upon if some greater menace had pursued the humans into the Thornwyld.

'I see twist-flesh,' Nyiss replied. She did not have the ancient experience of Kyra or Yanir, but in one respect she had no equal among the forest's dryads. Nyiss could blend herself into any surrounding with such expertise that she would be unseen by even other sylvaneth. Kyra could imagine her stalking through the forest, her bark shifting in hue to match that of the foliage around her. Nyiss would watch and lurk, sneaking up on the invaders, who would be unaware.

'Twist-flesh.' The name reverberated through all the sylvaneth. The twist-flesh were despised more than any other quick-blood. They were creatures of Chaos, hideous admixtures of human and animal. Unlike the other quick-bloods, they did not invade the forests to steal and conquer. They came to defile and corrupt, to inflict upon their surroundings the foul taint of Chaos. Many sylvaneth had been driven from their glades by the beastkin, their homes profaned by the filth of the warherds. Where the twist-flesh raised their abominable braystones, nothing clean could remain.

Kyra pushed her thoughts through those of the other sylvaneth. 'How many are they? Do they hunt the humans?'

'I see ten... no, there are fifteen,' Nyiss replied. 'They are very near to me. One prowls ahead of the others like a wolf, sniffing at the earth. Yes, they hunt the other quick-blood.'

Kyra made a quick decision. 'Leave the humans,' she stated. She felt Yanir's annoyance at the order. 'The twist-flesh are the graver threat. They must be dealt with first.'

Certain that the tracking beasthound would lead its fellows to the humans, Kyra gave the other sylvaneth instructions. They would lie in wait for the twist-flesh, placing themselves between the hunters and their prey. There was a slight danger that the primal instincts of the beastkin might alert them to the ambush, but Kyra felt it was a minimal risk. With the herd fixated upon tracking their prey, they might not think they were being hunted in turn.

The wait was not a long one. The snuffling of the beasthound was the first sound that reached Kyra. The creature soon loped into view. It had the lithe yet powerful build of a panther, prowling forwards on six clawed feet. A thick tail with a club-like nodule of bone at its end swung from side to side, betraying the brute's eagerness. Its head, broad and boar-like, sported a pair of long, sharp horns. The swinish face was pock-marked with bulbous growths and it took Kyra a moment to recognise that each of these was an eye. There was no glimmer of intelligence in any of the scattered orbs, only a vicious intensity.

Behind the tracking beasthound came more humanoid members of its herd. These stalked through the forest on cloven hooves and carried an assortment of clubs and spears in their clawed hands. A few of the bigger ones even brandished axes, a weapon that made them Kyra's first priority. She did not want to chance any of her companions coming within reach of those chopping blades.

The beasthound snuffled its way closer. For Kyra and the dryads it was clear where the humans had stumbled through the forest but she wondered if the twist-flesh had the same discernment. Perhaps, if forced to by losing the scent, they would draw upon some manner of crude woodcraft. Now, however, they were content to follow where their tracker led them.

A bit further and the twist-flesh would be within the cordon the dryads had quietly formed. When they were, the corrupt brutes would be swiftly dealt with.

The beasthound stopped. It jerked its head back and snorted at the air. A goat-headed hunter stalked up and kicked the creature, trying to goad it onwards. The beasthound ignored him and just swayed its head from side to side and kept sniffing. It whipped around, its multitudinous eyes glaring straight at Kyra. Its lips pulled back in a snarl.

The goat-headed hunter stared towards the cause of the beasthound's growl. With the tracker drawing his attention to where she was, Kyra realised the intruder could see her.

'Tree-fiends,' the hunter howled in his guttural language. 'Frang has spotted tree-fiends.'

The hunter had no chance to shout further alarm to his herd. Kyra focused on the brute and from her outstretched hand a ripple of power was channelled into its flesh. The creature shrieked as the arcane energies seared through him. Sprouts burst forth from his flesh, green tendrils that erupted from the organs beneath. The hunter collapsed as thin branches stabbed up from his throat.

'Daughters of the Thornwyld,' Kyra cried out in a voice that was like the rumble of a storm-wracked fir. 'Now is the season of wrath.'

The beastkin were still reeling from the grotesque death of the hunter. Before they could recover from their surprise, the dryads came lunging at them from all quarters. Where a moment before they had seen only the forest, now they were confronted by a dozen charging enemies. Each of the dryads was taller and heavier than the invaders, their bodies shaped from wood and bark rather than delicate flesh and fur. They bore no weapons, for they had no need of any. They had taken on the aspect of battle and their spindly fingers had thickened into dagger-like thorns capable of rending the hide of any quick-blood.

Kyra harnessed her powers, sending a pulse of magic through the dryads, invigorating them with a terrible rage. They sprang forwards at incredible speed, falling upon the beastkin in the blink of an eye.

The dryads brought their talons ripping into the brutish invaders. Several of the smaller, semi-human beastkin were torn apart in the first heartbeats of the fray. Yanir impaled two of the stunned brutes before they could even start to raise their weapons, lifting the mangled wretches off the forest floor and casting them aside like dead leaves.

Nyiss, alone among the dryads, attacked the invaders from behind. She raked her claws across an elk-headed hunter, rending his face a gory ruin. The stricken beast clutched at his face and fled back towards the other dryads and through the rest of his warherd. Kyra appreciated the strategy Nyiss was employing. Lurking nearer to the beastkin than any of the sylvaneth, she was trying to throw them into still greater panic by making them believe themselves surrounded.

Panic did indeed grip the twist-flesh, but they reacted with viciousness instead of fright. Nyiss had plotted too well. The invaders did think they were surrounded. Like animals cornered in their burrows, the beastkin reacted with frenzied desperation. They stabbed at the dryads with their spears, struck at them with their clubs. A big bruiser wielding an axe turned to chop at Yanir while she was finishing a smaller beastman. Before he could bring the blade cracking against her trunk, Kyra sent a shiver of violent magic sizzling through him. The ox-headed brute fell limp against Yanir's side, an array of green shoots bursting from his chest. The dying invader pawed at the dryad's bark as he slid to the ground.

'Calm the twist-flesh,' Kyra ordered.

The next moment, a soft, placating melody whispered through the fray. Rising from each dryad, the song was as gentle as the breeze, teasing its way into the ears of the beastkin and down into their savage brains. One by one, the brutes staggered back, their eyes dull with confusion. Weapons sagged down to their sides as the urge for conflict was smothered in their minds. Still singing, the dryads towered over the invaders who could only regard them with a bleary fascination.

'Kyra! Beware!' The cry drew the branchwraith's attention away from the enraptured beastkin. Ahead of her she saw the swine-faced beasthound rushing in her direction. Even as she started to conjure another magical bolt, the creature was leaping for her, its array of eyes glaring with rabid fury.

Before the beasthound could lock its jaws around Kyra's neck, a dark figure sprang into view. Kyra recognised the lunging shape as that of Eshia, a dryad she had watched over since her first blooming. Quickly she banished the spell she had started to conjure, lest its violence afflict the young dryad as well as the corrupt beast.

Eshia crashed against the beasthound, throwing it away from its intended victim. The creature struck the ground hard, but with a flash of motion it was back on its feet and snapping at the dryad. Eshia's talons raked the beast's side, popping one of its many eyes. It replied by sinking its fangs into her leg and worrying at the limb with its brutal strength. Bits of bark and spurts of blood-sap flew in every direction.

Kyra flew to Eshia's aid. She stabbed her hand at the beasthound, her thorn-like fingers piercing its thick hide. The creature released the dryad's leg. It growled at the branchwraith, but when she struck at it again, the thing scurried away. It dashed around the melee, skirting the other dryads as they felled the rest of the beastkin.

'Do not let it escape,' Kyra urged the other sylvaneth.

Only Nyiss was in position to intercept the beasthound. Even Kyra could not see the dryad as she shifted her colouring to blend into the trees. The horribly mutated invader detected the lurking sylvaneth. It darted around Nyiss, easily distancing her on its six legs as she hurried after it.

'Pursuit is useless.' Kyra sent the thought to Nyiss. 'It will be gone from the Thornwyld before you can catch it and there might be more of its herd waiting outside the forest.' Kyra felt Nyiss' disappointment but knew she would obey. Yanir and the others had quickly dispatched the enraptured twist-flesh, killing them before they could break free of the dryads' song.

Kyra turned towards Eshia. The young dryad was peeling bits of broken bark from where the beasthound bit her. Syrupy blood-sap oozed from the exposed wood beneath. It was an ugly wound but Kyra considered it could have been worse. Sometimes the very bite of a creature of Chaos was enough to spread its corruption. She had seen quick-blood rapidly degenerate from such bites, befouled by the touch of Chaos. Sylvaneth would suffer a more gradual decay, sometimes taking many seasons to display any trace of blight.

'I do not sense any contamination,' Kyra told Eshia after letting her essence briefly share the dryad's body. 'You were fortunate.'

'I could not allow that mongrel to...' Eshia did not finish her statement. Kyra would not let her.

'Your intention was admirable,' Kyra said, 'but you must use better judgement before you act. Had the beast's bite spread its corruption, what could have been done for you? I am a priestess of the wyld. I have protections against such blight, defences you do not.' She gestured to where the beasthound had fled. She considered explaining that without Eshia's intercession she might have prevented the creature from escaping, but Kyra thought better of it. The young dryad was already humbled enough. It would serve no good to prune her confidence further.

Nyiss beckoned to Kyra. She stood over one of the twist-flesh she had killed in the melee. As the branchwraith came near, the carcass was turned towards her. There was a crude scar across the brute's shoulder, a mark that had been carved there when it was young. 'I recognise the brand,' Nyiss said.

Kyra stared at the ugly scar, a primitive resemblance to a horned skull. 'As do I,' she replied after a moment. 'See if the others have the same brand.' It was possible that this brute was a stray from another warherd. Or maybe it was an old brand. If there were younger twist-flesh among those who had been killed, it might be that the worry she felt was unfounded. *He* might be dead and some less fearsome chieftain ruling in his stead.

'The marks are the same,' Yanir reported as she inspected the beastkin she had killed. Her head creaked around, staring off into the dark of the forest. 'The other quick-blood fled while we were fighting. We must find them.'

Kyra waved aside Yanir's eagerness. The humans were no immediate threat. They had intruded upon the forest to escape the beastkin. Fear, not malice, moved them to such action. They could neither hide nor run while they remained in the Thornwyld. The trees themselves would warn the sylvaneth where the trespassers were.

The threat Kyra saw was the meaning behind the ritual scars the twist-flesh bore. They were the dominant brand of the herd-chief Ghroth the Rootcutter. The beastman had proven himself a cunning and tenacious enemy of the Thornwyld. Repulsed by the sylvaneth in summer and spring, he had brought his loathsome kind back in the dead of winter, when the wyldwood slept and the blood-sap flowed slow in the dryads. Unlike many of his savage breed, Ghroth did not shun fire and made free use of it in his efforts against the Thornwyld. What the herdchief could not conquer and corrupt, he would destroy.

It had been many winters since the warherd of Ghroth had moved against the Thornwyld. Kyra knew the herdchief had not fallen in that last battle, but she had let herself hope he was dead. The season of rulership among the twist-flesh was usually brief and they were known to eat their disgraced leaders. Somehow Ghroth had endured and his hunters again trespassed in the Thornwyld.

Kyra thought of Ghroth's old attacks on the Thornwyld, but as she stared at the scarred corpse her memories fled. The light of her eyes faded to a mere ember, the tremor within her wooden body slowing to a dull shiver. Her bark grew pale and wintry, and her feet dug their roots into the soil. She stood transfixed, as rigid as the most somnolent of the ancient tree-lords at the heart of the forest. Only dimly could she sense the dryads rushing to her, alarmed by the change that swept over the branchwraith.

Far clearer to Kyra were the images that spiralled through her consciousness. She saw the herdchief Ghroth, more cruel and vicious than before. He led a vast host of the twist-flesh against the Thornwyld, a warherd such as Kyra had seen when the great armies of Chaos raged across the whole of Ghur. The beastkin marched against the forest, pulling down the trees with their brute strength, cutting down the groves with their axes, burning down the wyld-wood with their fires. Sylvaneth hunters were pulled down by packs of baying beasthounds. Venerable treemen were crushed in the paws of horn-headed ghorgons. Companies of tree-revenants were chopped to splinters by a tide of howling warriors. Dryads perished under the blades of goat-faced killers, their blood-sap spattered across the land. She saw Ghroth standing triumphant at the heart of the forest, the Sylvan Conclave broken at his feet. The invader raised a megalithic herdstone where the heart of the Thornwyld had been. Her spirit railed against the profane glyphs that marched across the crude monolith's face – symbols etched in adoration of Chaos. She cried out in defiance as the beastlord planted this evil seed, forever corrupting the forest, twisting and defiling all that would ever grow there.

The vision drew back, speeding away from Ghroth's savage victory. Kyra saw the events unfold in reverse, filing back from the herdchief's rise to beastlord. The twist-flesh flocked to join Ghroth, swelling the numbers of his warherd to a mighty horde. She saw the great power that pulsed through the goat-headed monster, could almost hear the magical energies that coursed through his body. Even the mightiest, most colossal of the twist-flesh creatures balked at the slightest glance from Ghroth and abased themselves before him.

Further the vision retreated, showing a dark cavern deep beneath the earth. Piles of worked stone were scattered about the cave, their immense age evident by the stalactites and stalagmites that sprouted from their fallen shapes. Kyra felt the clammy chill of the air, heard the deep and thunderous breathing of some vast creature. A titanic body lay hidden in the darkness, but she could distinctly see Ghroth standing upon that body. He was ripping into a colossal heart with his fangs. With every bite, Kyra sensed the power swelling inside the chieftain, magnifying him from mere herdchief to mighty beastlord. In the weird reversal of her vision, Ghroth set the heart back into the chest of the fallen titan. Posed atop the body, he swung his axe against the breast while flesh flowed back into each cut.

Still farther into the past the images withdrew. Kyra saw the dank tunnels that burrowed their way deep into the earth, strange etchings in the walls, weird relics scattered about the floors. There were pools of molten fire and rivers of icy water, bubbling and flowing far from the light of the sun. Eerie things crept through the darkness, falling on one another in bursts of desperate savagery. Ghroth led a small pack of his bestial followers through the tunnels, drawn ever downwards by the gory prize he sought to claim.

Again the images receded and Kyra saw a towering mountain. Its slopes were rocky, bare cliffs standing exposed in many places. Other parts were covered by gnarled trees, a forest of dark and grim aspect that struck her with a sense of foreboding. Not the taint of Chaos, but an enmity that was older and more primal than anything she had ever conceived of.

Across the slopes of this gargantuan mountain, Ghroth and his pack were making their way. They emerged from the black opening of a cavern and started to descend the rocks into the dark forests of the mountain. At last Ghroth was at the base and staring up towards the heights, eyes alight with nightmarish ambitions.

Kyra reeled as the visions left, deserting her as abruptly as they had set upon her. A ragged moan rose from within as the blood-sap resumed its flow and the roots recoiled into her feet. The glow of her eyes flared back into life and her bark darkened to its more usual brown. She looked across the visages of the dryads, feeling their concern.

'I am well,' Kyra said. 'There is no need to fear for me.'

Eshia stood at Kyra's side, the leaves on her head trembling with anxiety. 'What happened to you?' she asked.

Kyra did not answer directly. How could she explain something that was beyond her understanding? 'I am uncertain what beset me,' she answered at last. She kept the fear buried deep inside her heartwood. It could do no good to reveal the particulars of that dire vision. At least, not to the dryads. There were others who had the wisdom to help her.

'I must go and speak with the Sylvan Conclave,' Kyra decided. She looked over the other dryads. She would explain just enough to excuse her haste. 'These twist-flesh bear the brand of Ghroth the Rootcutter. The Conclave must be told he has returned.'

The dryads reacted as Kyra expected, with a mixture of fear and anger at their old enemy's name. They did not look forward to fighting against the warherds again, but neither would they shun such eventuality. The sylvaneth would not cede a single blade of grass to the twist-flesh.

'Kyra, the other quick-blood cannot be forgotten,' Yanir said. Unlike the other dryads, her fingers retained their clawed aspect.

Eshia turned to the branchwraith. 'They only came here to hide from the twist-flesh.'

Yanir stepped towards the young dryad, her gnarled face peeling back in a pitiless glower. 'The quick-blood have violated this forest too many times with torch and axe. None of their breed can be allowed to trespass here.'

'If we force these to leave, they will not come back,' Eshia protested.

Kyra rested a sympathetic hand on Eshia's shoulder. 'Mercy is a luxury those who guard the Thornwyld cannot indulge. Perhaps the humans would not return, or their story would bring others to the forest. We would betray the Thornwyld if we took that risk.'

She turned towards Yanir. 'I must seek the Conclave. This duty I entrust to you. The quick-blood cannot leave the forest.' Yanir had no mixed feelings towards humans. Of all the dryads, she was the best one to put in command. She would ensure the intruders were dealt with.

Kyra felt a pang of guilt when she met Eshia's gaze, but there was nothing else to be done. Humans were too uncertain in their ways to be depended upon. The only way to predict what they might do in the future was to take that future from them.

Ancient trees of every description grew from the black earth of the Sylvan Conclave. Pines hoary with centuries stabbed high into the air, their tops drooping from the weight of their needles. Silver-barked oaks with serpent-like ground roots stretched away for hundreds of yards, their thick branches reaching out to form complex tangles of stems and leaves. It was a display of every manner of tree in the Thornwyld, the oldest and stoutest of their kind, called from wherever they had grown in the forest to sink their roots.

The trees were impressive to Kyra. They always had been. The vibrations that sounded from them were more complex than those of younger trees. There was wisdom and meaning there, if one but had the patience to listen. Everything the ancient trees had experienced was recorded in their rings and drawn into their thrumming melody.

Among the ancient trees were equally elder sylvaneth. Some were so old that their spirits were but the merest flicker, their eyes naught but a distant twinkle of light. Their years were beyond easy reckoning, even for Kyra. Many of them were as stolid and unmoving as the trees around them, only the faint suggestion of an animate shape betraying their true nature.

The voice of the Conclave impressed itself on Kyra's mind, rolling slowly through her consciousness. They were ponderous in their deliberation, cautious about reaching judgement in all things. A day had passed since she brought to them the dire vision that had come to her. The sun had risen and set with no decision from the ancient sylvaneth.

Now that decision was reached.

'You are a branchwraith, a priestess of the wyld,' the Conclave stated. 'The very fact of your being places importance upon the vision you have witnessed. However, there is no precedent for what you have undergone. Not the oldest among us can declare the provenance of this vision. Because of this, there is no certainty of its truth, or its timeliness. How much of what you have seen is already past and how much of it is yet to unfold? Are the things yet to come immutable, or may they never come to season? These are questions of grave import for which there is no absolute answer.'

Kyra bowed her head to the assembled elders. 'In uncertainty there may also be found opportunity. A chance to change what I have seen.' Her hand wove through the air, leaving behind it a glowing after-image that described the brand of Ghroth. 'This mark was upon the twist-flesh who intruded into the Thornwyld. There is no mistake here. Ghroth the Rootcutter is back. If that much of my warning is true, can we reject the rest?'

'We can neither accept nor reject what you have seen.' The Conclave's words thrummed through Kyra's spirit. 'We cannot say whether your vision was intended as warning or deceit.'

One of the sylvaneth stirred, a wooden giant four times as tall as Kyra, its bark pitted by the wear of wind and rain. An owl perched in the hulking treeman's branches and regarded her with a steely gaze. The hollows in the timber giant's face were dark and empty, devoid of the fey light that shone from the visages of other sylvaneth. As it strode forwards, the trees shifted their roots from the blind treeman's path.

'I was old even before you sought refuge in the Thornwyld,' the treeman told Kyra, his voice cracking like branches under heavy snow. 'There was much I saw before my essence grew tired and I withdrew into somnolence. There is something I can tell you of the mountain in your vision. It is a place the quick-blood call Beastgrave, a place of immense power and immense danger. An eldritch force holds dominion there, something as ancient as the land itself. It is capricious in its ways and none can say for certain how the mountain will suffer their intrusion. Some find swift destruction, others depart with wondrous treasure. Many are simply never heard from again, vanished from the knowing of even the wisest.'

'This Beastgrave is where Ghroth seeks power,' Kyra said.

'Unless the enemy has already claimed it,' the Conclave reminded her. 'As stewards of the Thornwyld we cannot say that this is not a possibility. If Ghroth is already beastlord and bringing his armies against the forest, we must use everything in our power to defy him.'

Kyra swept her gaze across the trees and the elder sylvaneth among them. 'What if the vision is true? What if Ghroth can still be stopped?'

The huge treeman bent its head towards Kyra. The owl hopped down to a lower branch and peered into her eyes. 'We will not dismiss that is possible. It is a risk we have evaluated carefully. Each sylvaneth we do not retain to defend the Thornwyld reduces the chances of saving the forest. But if Ghroth can be stopped before he can even summon the warherds to him, that chance must be taken. In your vision, the Rootcutter had but a few twist-flesh with him when he delved into the mountain.'

'This is true,' Kyra admitted.

'The compromise must be this: you will seek Beastgrave and try to stop Ghroth from ever reaching his goal.' The treeman waved one of his long arms in a chopping motion. 'Strike him down, keep him from his dark dream of atrocity. Take what resources you need to accomplish this, but know that every sylvaneth who follows you to the mountain is one less defender to guard the Thornwyld if these things have already come to pass – if you are wrong and there is no chance to keep the warherds from coming.'

A shudder passed through Kyra as she felt the weight of the responsibility she had been given pressing down on her. If even the Conclave had doubt, why was she so certain Ghroth had not already done the things she had seen in her vision?

'There is more.' The voice of the Conclave echoed through Kyra's essence. 'It is not enough to just keep Ghroth from this evil arte-fact. Simply killing Ghroth would leave this seed of evil there to wait for the next enemy who would make use of it. You must find this black treasure. You must learn where the artefact is and destroy it. That duty is even more vital than stopping Ghroth. Kill the beastlord and you save the Thornwyld for today. Destroy this evil seed and you save the Thornwyld from tomorrow.'

Kyra bowed her head to the Conclave. 'What can be done, I will do,' she vowed. 'To the last drop of my blood-sap, I swear the Thornwyld will be saved.'

CHAPTER THREE

Ghroth could still see the smoke rising from the ransacked human settlement, a greasy smear that curled up into the dawn sky. If he took a deep breath he could catch the scent of blood and meat on the wind. He could imagine the contented brays and bleats of the beastkin as they supped upon the remains of the massacre. They would be satiated for days on the men and animals they had taken in the raid. A satiated warherd was a placid warherd. They would not wonder where their chieftain had gone. Not until they grew hungry again.

Ghroth turned to the woods and the jagged hills beyond. These were still familiar lands. The mountain Sorgaas promised to lead him to was far beyond these regions. Far beyond any territory Ghroth had prowled. There was no chance the herdchief would be back before his followers questioned his absence. Some aspiring champion would rise up to claim the leadership. Perhaps several of them would fight to see who would be the new chieftain.

It was of small consequence to Ghroth which of his old

underlings claimed the title of herdchief while he was gone. The usurper would not hold it long. When he returned from the Beastgrave he would reclaim the warherd as his own. He would seek others and build such a horde as Ghur had never seen.

No, the reason for stealing away from the warherd while they were fat on the spoils of victory was calculated for a different reason. Ghroth did not want any of those ambitious rivals following him, dogging his tracks along the way. Trying to steal the power that waited for him in the depths of Beastgrave.

The beastkin who followed Ghroth were the most loyal of his warherd, carefully chosen by him for the trek to the mountain. Twenty warriors to challenge the unknown dangers of the journey. The herdchief would have taken more, but he was wary of making his absence more notable by drawing too great an entourage. A few missing beastmen might be out hunting stray manflesh like Tharg had. Ghroth was annoyed at the hunter for leaving, for he'd taken the animalistic Frang with him. The beasthound's sharp nose would have been an asset on this journey. And of course the creature was too savage to have any notions of treachery. Frang simply did as it was told.

Ghroth's eyes narrowed as he focused on the cloaked shape of Sorgaas. He wished he was able to say the same for the wolf-faced shaman. Sorgaas was a turnskin – he had been born to human parents and slowly developed his bestial aspect. As Ghroth understood it, the parents had hidden him for many years until at last the turnskin was discovered. The entire family was mobbed and thrown out of their village, left to perish in the wild.

Only Sorgaas did not perish. Ghroth suspected he had eaten his parents that first winter. For a time he existed as a hermit deep in the forest, preying on whatever and whoever he could catch. Human, beastkin, grot... it made no difference to Sorgaas. Some of his victims ended up in his larder. Others were offerings to the Three-Eyed Raven, the god of magic and cunning. One day, without warning or explanation, Sorgaas appeared at the Blackfold herdstone and proclaimed himself a messenger from the gods. There were some who challenged his claims, but his magic was such that neither champion or shaman was able to overcome him. Grudgingly, Sorgaas had been accepted into the warherd.

Ghroth scowled as he remembered what happened next. Sorgaas had encouraged him in his challenge against the old herdchief, offering to lend his magic to support him in that struggle. Ghroth had been too cagey to accept that assistance, biding his time and waiting for an opportunity that would favour him without the shaman's meddling. He was certain that Sorgaas resented Ghroth's success, won by strategy rather than sorcery. Sorgaas wanted a herdchief he could control and Ghroth refused to be controlled.

It would have been better to simply kill Sorgaas, but Ghroth saw too much use for the shaman's spells. He was not content to be a simple chieftain. Even before the vision in the flames, he had ambition. He would see the foul domains of man brought down, the delvings of the beard-jaws turned to ruin, the witch-woods of the tree-fiends destroyed. The wild places belonged to the beast-kin, and to the beastkin alone.

Sorgaas promised that Ghroth could make that vision a reality. Ghroth was too tempted by that promise to reject it out of hand. He was also too wary to trust the conniving shaman completely. Sorgaas did nothing unless it was to his own benefit.

As though he felt Ghroth's eyes upon him, Sorgaas turned back towards the herdchief. He leaned on his bray-staff, using it to help support him as he descended a small knoll and joined Ghroth.

'We are leaving the warherd's territory,' Sorgaas said.

'Ghroth know this.' The herdchief glanced at the beastmen who had followed him from the settlement. 'All know this.'

Sorgaas' fur bristled at the scornful tone. 'I tell you this because we do not know what lies ahead of us.'

'Use magic,' Ghroth snapped. 'Call spirits. They tell Sorgaas. Sorgaas tell Ghroth.'

'There is a limit to all power. Just as there are only so many warriors in your tribe, so there is only so much magic I can draw upon. If I employ my spells for petty things, I will not be able to help when my magic is needed most.'

Ghroth scratched his ear and turned over the shaman's words. It was unlike Sorgaas to so freely admit any weakness. Either it was the truth or it was part of some ploy. Or it was both at once.

'Sorgaas show way.' Ghroth waved the orruk cleaver at the shaman.

'The way ahead is perilous. If you lose me, who will lead you to the mountain?' Sorgaas shook his head. 'You might never find your way and while you were looking, some other might steal the power you seek.'

There was a hint of mockery in the shaman's words. Ghroth loathed the glib way Sorgaas spoke, the slyness of his tongue that always made him think of humans and their trickery.

'Send scouts ahead of us,' Sorgaas advised, stopping short of making the suggestion sound like an order. 'They can spy out the lay of the land and warn us what dangers may be ahead of us.'

Ghroth glanced back at his followers. Sorgaas was baiting him. He'd even said that while magic was the shaman's strength, warriors were the strength of a herdchief. It was a test to see how far Ghroth could be pushed. If he sent some of his followers ahead as scouts he would be weakening his strength. If he refused he would be showing weakness.

'Zhaa, Khuug,' Ghroth growled as he turned and faced his warriors. He waved a shaggy arm at the jagged hills. 'Be scout. Seek trail.'

The two ungors Ghroth called came loping forwards. Their faces were not quite so manlike as most of their short-horned kind. One had a bovine cast to its features while the other resembled an equine. It was common wisdom among the beastkin that the further from the human shape, the sharper a warrior's senses. If he was going to risk warriors, Ghroth wanted them to at least be capable of passing a warning to the rest of his warband.

'Great warchief.' The equine-headed Zhaa began to protest the command Ghroth had given him. The herdchief kicked the ungor and knocked him to the ground. Ghroth glanced at Sorgaas and his lips peeled back from his fangs. He would show the shaman how strong he was. Ghroth would show him that he did not need to be afraid to spend his strength.

Zhaa lifted his spear in an attempt to fend off the massive cleaver as Ghroth brought it chopping down. The crude blade snapped the wooden shaft like a twig and did the same to the arm that held it before it crunched down into the ungor's chest. Zhaa was killed instantly.

Ghroth looked up from his gory work and glowered at Khuug. There was no question that she would obey him. He turned his gaze on the rest of his warriors. Any spark of dissent there had been quelled by Zhaa's blood. His eyes roved across the horned beastkin until he spotted a bray with the curled horns of a ram jutting from his skull. 'Tograh be scout,' he snarled. The named beastman darted forwards. Together with Khuug he was soon hurrying through the woods and towards the distant hills.

The herdchief faced Sorgaas, searching for some sign of trepidation on that lupine face. He was disappointed to find the serpentine eyes showed no trace of intimidation. Ghroth's brutality had failed to impress the shaman. Annoyed that the murderous show of authority might have somehow been exactly what Sorgaas wanted, Ghroth made a sweeping motion to his warriors. Excited growls rose from the gors and brays as they rushed forwards and fell upon Zhaa's corpse. Knives and claws went to work, swiftly butchering the body.

It was the savage law of the wild. Meat was never wasted.

The ground felt strange under Ghroth's hooves. They were several days away from their territory, far beyond the ken of even the furthest of his hunters. Forests and hills had given way to sparse, scraggly woods and strange trees with thin trunks and thorny leaves. The earth was parched, the soil like sand. Ugly outcroppings of rocks littered the horizon, their sides mottled with a bewildering array of coloured clay. Enormous hairy bees used holes in that clay for their burrows. Their wings struggled to keep them aloft as they prowled through the air. The dog-sized insects were wary of the beastkin, but were not so shy about the creatures they were accustomed to seeing. Buffalo grazing on the needle-leafed trees were felled by the barbed stingers, always struck from behind by their flying killers. The bees did not feed on the animals they killed, at least not immediately. Ghroth saw them several times hovering about some old carcass. It seemed they waited for their prey to rot before setting upon it. They would use their mandibles to chew the softened meat into a kind of jellied paste that they rolled into balls and stuck to their back legs.

'Vulture-stings.' Ghroth named the hideous bees. He gazed across the dreary woods at the clay mounds the insects called home. 'Not near nests.' He swung around to Sorgaas to make it clear to him that the words were a statement, not a question. 'Many stings in rocks. Kill too much.'

The shaman pointed his bray-staff towards the horizon. 'The mountain is that way,' he said.

Khuug and Tograh glanced warily from Ghroth to Sorgaas.

The two scouts were less than eager to move any closer to the vulture-sting hives. The herdchief considered ordering them to do so anyway, simply as a display of dominance over them, but he resisted the impulse. The scouts would achieve nothing except to provoke the giant insects. Their loss would not get Ghroth closer to Beastgrave.

Ghroth peered into Sorgaas' cold eyes. 'Around,' he grunted. 'Take trail around vulture-stings.' He looked over at his scouts. 'Find trail.'

'If there is another trail,' Sorgaas said. He gestured again with his staff. 'The swiftest course is the direct one. Even if there is a way around, we will lose time taking it.'

The herdchief shook his head. He was not going to let Sorgaas lead him by the nose. Just like the scouts, the shaman needed to know who was leader. 'No vulture-stings,' he said. 'Around. Take trail around.'

The talons of Sorgaas' hand clicked against the side of the bray-staff, a habit the mystic developed whenever he was irritated. Ghroth felt a sense of petty triumph to have provoked the shaman.

'You may find the way around to be more dangerous,' Sorgaas warned. 'And there may be others looking for your prize.'

Ghroth stamped his hoof and glared at Sorgaas. 'Ghroth take power. Power belong Ghroth. Sorgaas say.' His hands tightened around the big cleaver as an infuriating thought occurred to him. 'Sorgaas say only Ghroth?'

The shaman nodded his head, a human gesture that only angered Ghroth further. 'I told no one! It was you who was in the vision. Only you are meant to claim the power you saw.'

'That good,' Ghroth decided. 'Sorgaas remember. Power only for Ghroth. Ghroth only beastlord.' He turned back to the scouts. 'Find new trail,' he said. Khuug and Tograh slipped away, each in opposite directions. They would find a way around the hives.

'We will lose time,' Sorgaas warned again.

Ghroth looked at the rest of his warriors. He saw the uneasiness in their eyes, the subtle twitches that passed beneath their fur, the way they fidgeted with their weapons. The hundred different ways they betrayed their anxiety. They were as loathe to run into the bees as the scouts were.

'Sorgaas worry,' Ghroth told the shaman. 'Worry prize gone. Worry Ghroth eat Sorgaas instead.'

The wolf-faced mystic bristled at the threat. Good. It was something to bother him. Ghroth was not so proud to ignore that Sorgaas was smarter than him. The only thing he could do to match the shaman's cunning was to be unpredictable. The less Sorgaas could depend on how Ghroth would react, the more dangerous it would be for him to plot something.

The shaman cast an apprehensive eye back the way they had come. For a moment he looked as though he would say something. He turned and stalked off, his talismans jangling against his horns. Ghroth grunted in amusement. Let him sulk. As a turnskin, he could never have rule over the warherds. He needed someone like Ghroth to be dominant, to take the power in the mountain. That made the herdchief essential to his designs.

No, Sorgaas could not do without Ghroth. But there would come a time when Ghroth would no longer need Sorgaas.

Khuug found the trail Ghroth needed to avoid the vulture-stings. Once Tograh returned, he sent both scouts ahead of the warherd to lead the way.

Khuug picked her way down a rocky defile. Tograh was a bit behind the other scout, his bow at the ready. The two ungors were wary as they climbed from the plain into the narrow defile. The bottom was sand, a dull red in colouring. Weird whorls and lines marked the surface, erratic patterns that swept across the ground from side to side. They reminded Sorgaas of ripples across a pond, flowing away to opposite shores.

A sense of threat nagged at the shaman. He could tell the other beastkin felt it too. Even Ghroth prowled the rocks with agitation. The herdchief growled and snapped at any of his warriors who came too close, perhaps out of worry that they would notice his uneasiness. The offending beastmen would cringe away in deference to their leader, the bigger ones venting their anger against the smaller brays and ungors.

With the visible menace of the vulture-stings to unite them, the beastkin had drawn together, seeking security in numbers. Whatever threat was hanging over them was not so easily quantified. So they shunned the closeness of the herd, instinctively hoping that the danger would strike in some other when it finally descended on them. It was animalistic in its simplicity, the peril of one acting as the alert for the others. Yet the weaker still had enough sense to crowd towards the stronger for protection, until that strength lashed out at them.

Sorgaas felt contempt for these brutes as he watched them climbing into the fissure. They were not joined by any sense of purpose, only a mutual hatred for everything else. Humans, duardin, orruks, grots – it did not matter to the beastkin. All were despised. Enemies to be brought down and devoured. The only reason the gors and their ilk banded together was to expand the scope of their attacks. There was no planning, no strategy. Only attack and attack and attack. So long as there was the strength to prevail.

The shaman noticed that Khuug was creeping out onto the sand. She moved with uncertainty, her ears flicking with anxiety. The ungor glanced all around as she started down the bed of the defile. Sorgaas sensed that the menace was about to reveal itself. With his attention focused on Khuug, he missed the first faint shiver that passed through the rocks. He spotted the movement only when a great slab of stone reared up from the slope and plunged down at the scout. Tipping on its end, the stone smashed down on her before she could react. The ungor was crushed under its weight, blood seeping away from the pulverised body across the sand.

The beastkin looked on in shock as more rocks slid down onto the sand, gathering wherever Khuug's blood flowed. Tograh, slinking in the wake of Khuug, was almost caught by a second slab that slid after him from the side of the defile. The scout turned and leapt onto the slab that had smashed the other ungor. From his perch he watched as the block that had tried to smash him fragmented into smaller rocks, each piece slithering across the sand to the nearest slope. The curious patterns in the sand were explained. They were the trails left by these animate stones.

'Tograh! Back!' Ghroth shouted at the scout. The herdchief started to charge down towards the sand.

Sorgaas held his bray-staff out and blocked the chieftain. 'Tograh, stay where you are,' he warned the scout. If he did not need the herdchief, he would have let him keep going. He tried to explain to Ghroth why he should stay on the slope. 'These stones,' the shaman said, stamping his foot against the rocks, 'prey on whatever steps on the sand. They come together in amalgamations to feed on blood.' He gestured with his staff at the sand. 'They must use the sand to let them absorb...'

'Tograh not eaten,' Ghroth objected.

'The stones need both blood and sand to feed,' Sorgaas repeated. 'Tograh is safe where he is. At least until the amalgamation is finished feeding and returns to the slopes.'

Ghroth stared at the far side of the defile. The scouts had found this route past the vulture-stings, but to make use of it, the warherd needed to be on the opposite slope. 'We cross,' Ghroth decided. 'Tograh cross,' he bellowed at the scout.

The ungor dipped his head in deference to his chieftain and stalked out to the edge of the slab. Tograh hesitated, then flung himself out over the sands. His hooves scrambled on the inert rocks on the far side.

'We cross,' Ghroth snarled at the rest of his warriors.

'Tograh was lucky,' Sorgaas said. He pointed to the gap between the edge of the slab and the other slope. 'Do you think you can make such a leap?'

Ghroth thought about that. Surprisingly, he had a solution to the problem. Before any of his warriors knew what was happening, the herdchief grabbed the closest bray. The creature had only a moment to bleat in distress before Ghroth's fangs were worrying at his throat. The chieftain hefted the bleeding beastman onto one shoulder and strode down to the bottom of the slope. Displaying his vicious strength, he lifted the body with one hand and shook it over the sand.

Amalgamations of stone, smaller than the slabs that had smashed Khuug and tried to crush Tograh, tumbled down into the sand. They slithered to wherever the bray's blood fell. Ghroth stamped his hooves on the closest of them and stepped out from the slope. He shook the body again and sent more blood onto the sand. Again, small amalgamations of stone were drawn to the gore.

Ghroth looked back at Sorgaas, blood dripping from his fangs. 'We cross,' the herdchief said, this time with a note of victory. Still shaking the dying bray, he drew more rocks down from the slopes. Bit by bit and drop by drop, Ghroth was creating a pathway, a bridge across the sand.

Some of Ghroth's warriors did not wait for their chieftain to reach the other side before following him across the bridge. Sorgaas kept his eyes on the slab that had caught Khuug. He wanted to evaluate how slowly the stones fed before venturing out over the sand.

Ghroth snorted at the shaman's hesitance. 'Spell-sayer afraid.' He laughed. Several of his warriors added their own howls to his humour. He lifted the now dead bray above his head and threw the body into the middle of the sand. The beastkin shifted aside as dozens of smaller stones clattered together and melded into a big slab that tipped and tumbled after the body. 'Sorgaas cross now.'

The shaman stepped out onto the stones. Sorgaas reminded himself that he still needed the herdchief. He had proven to be the strongest in the warherd many times. He was the only one who might be strong enough to withstand the trials that awaited within Beastgrave.

Sorgaas indulged in a slight smile as he walked across the newly amalgamated slab. If there was one constant that characterised Chaos, it was change.

The fissure of the hungry rocks was many days behind Ghroth's warriors. The warherd had trudged through icy marshes, climbed over desolate hills, fought past the grazing grounds of shaggy mammoths and crossed eel-infested streams. The score of followers that had been chosen by the herdchief at the beginning of the trek had dwindled down to a dozen.

Yet as Ghroth emerged from the green hell of a slimy jungle, he felt a flush of triumph surge through him. The sacrifices and hazards had all been worth it. Ahead of the beastkin stretched a wasteland of windswept spires of rock and jagged canyons, but beyond that terrain loomed a landmark that was burned into his memory. It was the towering mass of Beastgrave, the mountain that had appeared to him in his fiery vision, so immense it vanished into the clouds. The mountain held within its depths the power to make him beastlord and to crush the human kingdoms beneath his hooves.

'There it is, just as I promised,' Sorgaas said as he stepped from the jungle and approached Ghroth. His ophidian eyes glittered in the last daylight as night encroached upon the land. 'There is where your destiny awaits you.'

Ghroth studied the mystic carefully. With the mountain before them, Sorgaas was no longer an indispensable guide. In that aspect, his utility was at an end. He could be disposed of and Ghroth would still be able to find his way.

An eventuality that Sorgaas must have prepared for. On the journey, the shaman had only reluctantly employed his magic. Ghroth suspected he had been husbanding his spells, saving his arcane energies for... this moment?

Cunning as much as brutality had made Ghroth chieftain. It was not a question of choosing one over the other, but rather knowing how to blend the two qualities together. If Sorgaas was ready for some kind of confrontation now, then it was not the time to face him. When Ghroth brought him to account, it would be on his own terms, not the shaman's.

'Ghroth soon beastlord,' the herdchief stated, drool spilling from his mouth. 'Sorgaas soon great shaman. Gods reward Sorgaas.' Ghroth searched for any hint he was mollified by the flattery.

'I do what will serve the Dark Gods,' Sorgaas said, his claws caressing the talismans hanging from his horns. 'It is enough reward to do their bidding.'

'Gods say Ghroth soon beastlord.' He reminded Sorgaas of this key aspect of the vision. The promise that burned in his heart like a flame.

'Of course,' Sorgaas said. 'That is what you saw in the fire.' There was uncertainty in the shaman's eyes. It passed too quickly for Ghroth to be sure he had seen it at all.

Ghroth turned and watched his warriors creep out from the jungle. 'Dark now. Make camp.' He waved the huge cleaver towards a barren patch of ground where a natural wall provided some measure of shelter. The beastkin stalked over to the place and started dropping the provisions they carried.

'It has been a hard march,' Sorgaas said. 'We could all use a rest.'

A cold smile spread on Ghroth's face. 'Stop,' he bellowed at his warriors. 'We go. March in dark.' The herdchief looked over at Sorgaas. 'Sleep later. March now.' He grunted in amusement when he saw the shaman's shoulders sag in disappointment. Whatever Sorgaas expected him to do, Ghroth was determined to confound him.

'Tograh take scouts,' Ghroth snarled at the ungor. 'Hunt food. Find path.'

At their chieftain's command, Tograh and three of the smaller beastmen loped away into the gathering darkness. Though they were more manlike than the larger gors, their senses were far sharper than those of a man. They would be able to find their way in the dark.

Ghroth strode through the ranks of his frustrated warriors. He knew they wanted to rest as eagerly as Sorgaas. They did not have the fire of ambition egging them on, goading them to greater and greater effort. But, like the shaman, they were careful not to express their displeasure. The herdchief's word was law. To question his orders was to invite a quick and savage death.

'Follow Ghroth,' the chieftain growled. He raised the orruk cleaver to remind his warriors of his strength. He grinned at Sorgaas to remind him of his cunning. There was a word the shaman had used that had pleased Ghroth. He used it as he barked encouragement to his gors. 'Follow Ghroth to destiny.'

Sorgaas gnashed his fangs as his foot stamped down on another thorn. He leaned against his bray-staff and pinched the offending bur from his skin. This night march Ghroth insisted on was vexing. Just another of the multitude of annoyances the herdchief had inflicted upon Sorgaas since he had become leader.

The shaman drew on his magic to let his gaze penetrate the darkness sufficiently that he could see Ghroth up ahead. The herdchief did not seem concerned that Sorgaas was falling behind. In his arrogance, he probably thought it amusing that the turnskin was not able to keep up. The decision to march all night was another of those petty reversals that Ghroth thought was so clever.

Sorgaas let his enhanced vision sweep over their surroundings. Some spiky palm trees and a sort of sticky fern were the only real foliage, sprouting from the dirt in small clumps here and there. Big heaps of boulders were everywhere, though most numerous at the bases of the wind-ravaged rock formations. Those features had an almost tortured quality, twisted into strange arches and spires by the caprices of the elements. In some ways they struck Sorgaas as weird echoes of Beastgrave itself. Stunted siblings or the deformed spawn of the colossal mountain.

Beastgrave. Sorgaas did not focus enough enchantment into his eyes to pierce the night so that he could actually see the mountain, but he sensed it all the same. Monstrous and imposing, a black titan sprawled across the horizon.

There were other things to be seen in the dark of night and Sorgaas felt a deep satisfaction when he saw them creeping among the rocks. Ghroth thought himself quite clever, pushing ahead instead of letting his followers rest. They would have had a defensible position with the wall at their backs. The warriors were spread out and with their scouts so far ahead that even the shaman couldn't see them. Ghroth was so intent on what was before him that he didn't waste much thought on what might be chasing after him.

Ghroth's absence had been noticed. A second group of beastkin had taken up the herdchief's trail. The shaman saw the atavistic Frang crawling on the rocks and it was certain the beasthound's unrivalled sense of smell let them follow the track. All the beastkin were from Ghroth's herd. Among them Sorgaas spotted the hulking Chagrak. The ram-headed bestigor was just the sort to seize an opportunity to depose Ghroth while he was away from the rest of the warherd. Chagrak was not exactly brilliant, but he did have the sort of conniving streak in him that detested a fair challenge.

Sorgaas quickly evaluated the positioning of Chagrak's followers. There were almost thirty of them, more than double Ghroth's warriors. They were spreading out like the legs of a spider, intent on catching the herdchief's retinue between them. If Ghroth had not pushed his beastmen so hard, if they were not so fatigued, they might have noticed the ambush that was about to catch them.

It was possible to warn Ghroth. A display of magic would throw the beastkin into confusion and spoil the ambush. Sorgaas could manage it easily, but he was not going to. He had fallen far enough behind that he was outside the attention of Chagrak's pack. When the trap was sprung, he would not be caught in it.

The ways of Chaos were intricate and subject to the whims of the gods. The destiny Ghroth had seen for himself was not immutable, however much the herdchief wanted to believe it was. Sorgaas wondered if another champion might be just as useful as Ghroth. Maybe even more so, since Chagrak could prove less unpredictable and therefore more malleable to the shaman's purposes.

Sorgaas clasped his hands together and hissed an incantation. The spell he evoked drew the shadows tighter around him, hiding him from sight. Other conjurations obscured his scent and muffled the sound of his heart. He felt confident he was concealed from even the keen senses of Frang. Safe from detection, he watched as Chagrak's warriors closed in on those loyal to Ghroth.

Chagrak started the attack. The bestigor reared up atop one of the rocks and gave voice to a bellowing war-cry. As he did, the ram-headed champion hurled a barbed spear down at Ghroth's warriors. The shaft crunched into the chest of a gor who was marching a small distance from the herdchief. The stricken beast-man crashed down on his side, a groan of agony rasping from him as he feebly pawed at the spear.

From all sides, the rest of Chagrak's pack leapt into action. Howling and shrieking, they charged into Ghroth's followers. One bray was pulled down by Frang, the beasthound's jaws snapping tight about the screaming warrior's neck. An elk-headed gor was slashed by the axes of three ungors and brained by the club of a fourth when he slumped to his knees. Another fighter was almost decapitated by the Chagrak's glaive when the bestigor threw himself into the fray.

Ghroth's followers, though taken by surprise, were not overwhelmed. With the savagery of cornered wolves, they fought back. One of Chagrak's gors collapsed in a welter of blood and brains when an axe split her skull. A treacherous ungor was spitted on a spear by a loyal warrior. Ghroth himself split an attacker in half with a hard swing of the orruk cleaver.

'Chagrak traitor,' Ghroth roared as he decapitated one of the bestigor's fighters. He kicked the severed head away and stomped on the quivering corpse. 'All follow Chagrak die now.'

The bestigor slashed his glaive through the body of a club-wielding bray, a splash of blood spurting across his brutal visage. 'Ghroth weak. Ghroth coward. Chagrak eat Ghroth-flesh.'

Despite his bold boast, Sorgaas saw that Chagrak was not going to tackle Ghroth alone. While the bestigor circled the herdchief, three of his warriors were also moving to surround their former leader. Before the circle could close, an arrow whistled out of the night and embedded itself in the throat of a pig-faced gor. Tograh and the other scouts came rushing back, hurling themselves into the fight. Sorgaas was puzzled as to why the scouts would risk themselves in such a manner when they could have slipped away in the confusion. Then he saw that the beastkin were not alone.

Sorgaas drew more power into his spell, binding the shadows still more tightly around him. He sensed others moving in the darkness. Their scent was not that of beastkin, nor was it entirely like that of any human he had ever encountered. When they drew near enough that he could make out their shapes, the shaman saw them to be squat and broadly built, moving with a hunched and ambling gait.

Cries of alarm rose from the feuding beastkin as the scent of the lurkers reached them. Those already locked in combat exerted themselves in a frenzy to bring down their opponents quickly. The beastkin not engaged in battle turned and stared at the darkness, challenging the new enemies they sensed closing in on them.

For Ghroth and Chagrak, there could be neither truce nor mercy. With his supporting warriors either brought down by Tograh or else turning to face the lurkers, Chagrak found himself alone in his challenge with the chieftain. The realisation sent the bestigor running amok. Stamping his hooves, waving his horned head from side to side, he rushed at Ghroth, seeking to impale the herdchief upon the tip of his glaive.

Sorgaas let his attention shift away from the hunters that were closing on the beastkin. He fixated on the fight between herdchief and challenger. A minor spell could have been enough to tip the balance either way, but the shaman was not going to interfere. Whichever of them was strongest would prevail. That would be the one to take into the mountain.

Ghroth swung away from Chagrak's charge. While he saved himself from being impaled on the glaive, he was not so agile that he escaped the bestigor's raking horns. His face was split open from cheek to jaw by the challenger. Chagrak brought himself around in time to fend off the orruk cleaver with his glaive, circling it around so that its momentum was lost.

'Weak,' Chagrak hissed through the froth bubbling from his mouth. 'Ghroth-meat fill Chagrak belly.'

Ghroth snarled at his challenger and lunged for him with the cleaver. This time when the heavy blade crashed against the glaive, the axe-head was warped by the impact and it was all Chagrak could do to maintain his grip. Ghroth pressed the attack, forcing the bestigor back.

'Chagrak fool,' Ghroth snarled. 'Believe Chagrak strong.' He brought the cleaver down again. This time, instead of denting the glaive, he gouged a sliver from its blade. 'Believe Chagrak mighty.' The cleaver smashed down into the bestigor's weapon, causing it to curl backwards at its tip. 'Believe Chagrak better.' Ghroth swung his blade once more, this time with such force that Chagrak could not maintain his hold. The glaive went flying from his grasp and clattered across the ground.

Sorgaas expected Ghroth to run in and slaughter the disarmed bestigor. A heartbeat earlier and it certainly would have happened. But as the herdchief started to move, crazed shouts sounded from the darkness all around the beastkin. Crude spears with stone tips came flying out from the night. One of them plunged into Ghroth's leg and turned his charge into a stumble.

The lurking enemies the shaman's magically heightened senses had detected were converging upon the beastkin. Just as Chagrak's followers had ambushed Ghroth and his warriors, so too were they caught in a trap. Scores of short, powerfully built hunters charged out from the night to attack the beastmen. Sorgaas was surprised to find that these new foes were some strange breed of human the likes of which he had never seen before. They flung themselves on the warherd with a vicious savagery that was nearly the equal to that of the beastkin. In a matter of moments, many of the gors and ungors had been smashed down by bone clubs and stone axes.

Sorgaas looked back to the feuding leaders. The fate of their followers made little impact on their bitter struggle. Growling their hate, Ghroth and Chagrak fought with tooth and claw, raking each other with their horns, snapping at one another with their fangs. So intent were they on the destruction of their rival that neither reacted when the squat humans swarmed around them and cast nets over them. Bone clubs cracked down against the fallen beastmen, raining blows upon their horned skulls until both of them were still.

The shaman could only watch as both of the champions were captured by the strange hunters. Tied to long poles, they were lifted onto the shoulders of the humans. Along with the bodies of the other beastkin, both living and dead, the herdchief and his rival were borne away into the night.

CHAPTER FOUR

The trees were tall, their branches lush with leaves, their trunks thick and strong. Birds sang their melodies from the heavy forest shadows. Squirrels darted in and out of holes in the bark. The ground was carpeted in greenery – ferns and vines and grasses that sprang from the leaf litter in wild vibrancy. The breeze that sighed through the boughs was crisp and clean, just the faintest touch of cold in its soft caress.

For all the beauty of the forest, Kyra noticed what was absent the most. These woods had no voice, no presence that reached inside her, that connected her to the land. With every step she took, she was reminded that this was not the Thornwyld. This was not a domain of the sylvaneth, however pleasant its appearance. This was a part of the outside world, the realm of the quick-blooded races and all their petty greed, senseless hate and savage war.

If anywhere in the realm of Ghur could be said to have been cleansed of the blight of Chaos it would be the sylvaneth refuges. The world outside bore the stains of the ancient battle against the ever-hungry Dark Gods. Kyra sensed the contamination all around her, even in a place as physically unmarred as this forest. However dormant or residual, the branchwraith felt it there. At any time the taint might manifest, twisting the essence of whatever it infected. That was the true curse of Chaos, that it could never be completely burned away. Something always remained, sleeping until a spark brought it blazing back in all its horror.

Ghroth the Rootcutter would be such a spark unless Kyra could stop him. If it wasn't already too late to stop him.

Kyra felt the delicate touch of Eshia's hand on her shoulder. 'What troubles you?' the young dryad asked.

Kyra wanted to laugh at the question. By bringing herself into contact with the branchwraith, Eshia had connected their essences. Kyra felt the magnitude of the anxiety that coursed through her. This was the first time Eshia had ever left Thornwyld, ever been detached from that spiritual connection with the land around her. It was all a strange and frightening new world to her, an experience for which she had no perspective to understand.

Yet Eshia still had it in her to fret over Kyra's worries. Not because they could affect the small band of sylvaneth she led, but because of the burden they presented to the branchwraith herself.

'We are far from home,' Kyra said. 'It is strange to be away from the Thornwyld's song.' She felt the approbation in Eshia that she and the branchwraith should feel the same. It was not a falsehood, even if it was a small thing beside Kyra's bigger concerns.

'There are some songs it is better not to hear,' Yanir said, overhearing the exchange. She reached down with her long hand and brushed aside the branches of a small bramble bush. Beneath the bush was a decaying tree stump. 'The forest here would sing of its fear. The threat of the axe and the hunger of the quick-blood.'

Kyra winced at Yanir's words. Even the grey-barked dryad was not old enough to recall a time when the Thornwyld was beset by such fears and its trees murmured with terror. Such a song was vivid in Kyra's memory. It was something she never intended to hear again. Something she would give everything she had to keep from the sylvaneth of her adopted home.

Everything. It was Kyra's great worry that she had not done enough. The Sylvan Conclave had entrusted the task of reaching Beastgrave and stopping the Rootcutter to her, but with the caution that the Thornwyld's defence would be diminished with every sylvaneth she took away with her. If it was already too late to stop Ghroth, she would be weakening them for no purpose. So it came that she decided to take only three dryads with her. Yanir, Eshia and Nyiss would have to be enough to prevail against the twist-flesh.

'The quick-blood must sustain themselves like everything else,' Eshia told Yanir. 'The beetle eats into the bark, the strangler fig burrows down through the heartwood, beggarweed binds itself around the trunk and feeds on the sap, broomrape feeds from the roots...'

The branches on Yanir's head quivered with irritation. 'All of those take only what they need to survive. They do not set out to kill and destroy, only for themselves to live.' The fingers at the end of her hands sharpened into thorns. 'But the quick-blood take more than they need. They are never content. Their hunger is never appeased. They give no thought to what they do, only to how it will sate their greed. Except their greed can never be sated. They will fell a tree and take the entire copse. If they are able, the whole forest will be consumed. They will reshape the land, remake the earth itself to suit them. Where the quick-blood stands, there is no place for anything else. They must dominate all, and if they cannot dominate they will destroy.'

Eshia seemed to wilt before Yanir's tirade. 'Why are they so thoughtless? Why don't they understand?'

'Because they care only for themselves,' Yanir said.

'No, Yanir,' Kyra interrupted. 'That is not the reason. It is because they are quick-blooded. Their lives are so short they do not see the impact of their actions with their own eyes. They cannot appreciate the things they change when they build their towns and plant their fields. They are not in the world long enough to know what they are doing.' The light in her eyes dimmed as she cast her memories back to distant times, to old stories and whispered tales. 'Even the aelves the tree-revenants enshrine did not understand, and they were the longest-enduring of the quick-blood. They could appreciate the necessity of harmony, but even the wisest of them could not really understand. In each quick-blood there is the germ of independence, a blight that makes them reject their place.'

'Are they truly so terrible?' Eshia wondered, regret underlying her words.

Kyra knew what Yanir would say, but her own perspective was different. 'They have moved away from order, but in doing so have given themselves their own purpose and role. The quick-blood do not thrive as long as the sylvaneth, but they have made that into their strength. They are swift to see and swift to act. They are immersed in immediacy and because they are, they will strike out when they find the seed. They do not wait for the first shoot to grow.'

'It is because they are destroyers,' Yanir said. 'What is worse than a destroyer?'

'The corrupter. The destroyer can only destroy. What has been is torn down, but something else may grow in its place. Corruption defiles what is already there, twisting it into something it was never meant to be. The only things that sprout from corruption are those that share in its foulness.' Kyra glanced about the woods. No, it was not the Thornwyld, but it still had its beauty. 'The season of destruction is fleeting, and a time of growth may come again. Corruption endures and once its blight has crept into the land its purity is lost. Whatever is done to cleanse it, the germ of Chaos will remain.'

Kyra heard the crackle of underbrush behind her. She turned to find Nyiss moving towards the other sylvaneth from the outskirts of the forest. The dryad's bark was chipped in a few places and there was a raw spot that looked like it had been cut by a blade. Dark stains on her hands told their own part of the story.

'I have spied upon the twist-flesh,' Nyiss reported. 'They are Ghroth's warherd.'

When they left the Thornwyld, Kyra had decided to retrace the steps of the invaders they had eliminated and try to find Ghroth's camp. It was important to know what the situation was there. How near the monsters might be to attacking the sylvaneth.

Kyra drew close to Nyiss and evoked her magic. Pressing her hand against the dryad, she let her energies flow into her. The scarred bark began to regenerate and the fires in her eyes grew more vibrant as Kyra dissolved her fatigue. The wood on Nyiss' hands flaked away, exposing a fresh and unsoiled surface.

Nyiss, the stealthiest among the sylvaneth, had been sent alone to observe the twist-flesh. 'I was compelled to seek a captive,' she explained, and waved a hand at her fading scars. 'It did not come easily, but I learned what needed to be learned before it died.'

'What have you discovered?' Kyra asked.

'The Rootcutter left here three dawns past,' Nyiss said. 'He took about twenty of his warriors with him. Another group left the next day with about twice as many twist-flesh.'

Eshia gasped at the numbers Nyiss described. Yanir simply shook her head. Kyra felt a chill sweep through her. So many enemies and so few of them. She looked down at the ground, at the hoofmarks that they had discovered. It was the trail of a pack of twist-flesh. She was confident it was that of Ghroth and his followers, or else the second pack that had followed after them.

That news made her think hard about the Rootcutter and her vision. Kyra felt that if Ghroth were already so powerful that he could threaten Thornwyld, he would not need to sneak away with only a few followers. No, he had yet to go to Beastgrave and draw that power into himself. The second group of twist-flesh was even more intriguing.

'We may be fortunate,' Kyra told the dryads. 'The slaves of Chaos are fractious, dominating one another with fear and brutality. Given the chance, they will turn against each other.'

'You think the second pack is hunting the first?' Nyiss asked.

'I do,' Kyra answered. 'If they are, sooner or later the two will meet. Should that happen, we will find the task ahead of us made much easier.'

The dryads were heartened by Kyra's words. She did not tell them her other worry. If Ghroth was killed before he reached the mountain, how would the sylvaneth find the obscene relic buried within Beastgrave?

How would they end the menace not just of Ghroth, but of all the others who might seek the same power he sought?

Kyra felt the uneasiness of her companions as they crested the hills and stared down at the desolate scrubland. This was farther from the Thornwyld than any of the dryads had gone before, even Nyiss, who would frequently leave the forest to spy on the nearby quick-blood settlements. The scraggly trees with their contorted boles and needle-like leaves were strange to the dryads, alien to anything in their experience.

'What kind of place is this?' Eshia asked, the branches on her head drooping as she gazed at the unfamiliar terrain.

'A place far different from the Thornwyld,' Kyra replied. She considered each of the dryads before she explained the nature of the land they would have to traverse. 'When I left my home, I saw many things and wandered many lands.' She pointed to the scraggly trees. 'There is little nourishment in the soil, for all but the very dregs of vitality are left in the sun-baked ground. Seldom does rain fall in such places, and when it comes it descends in a violent deluge. Of one thing alone is there abundance.' She jabbed a finger upwards at the clear sky and the blazing sun.

Nyiss descended the slope and caressed a rubbery cactus. 'How do these strange blooms endure?'

'They survive because they cast aside anything that is not necessary to them,' Kyra said. 'The life here does not strive to flourish in excess, only to maintain the flush of life.' She climbed down to join Nyiss. Her finger brushed across the thorny arm of the cactus. 'This one hoards the water of many seasons, saving it from drought. It does not expend itself by sinking deep roots to hunt the meagre sustenance in the soil. It does not waste itself with delicate leaves to catch the sunlight when there is such excess.'

The branchwraith waited while Yanir and Eshia descended from the hill. 'We must follow the example of the life here if we would cross the desert,' she stated. 'Conserve your energies. Do not over-exert yourselves. Know that there is little nourishment to be drawn from this land. If there is trouble, my magic can sustain us for a time, but we must be wary of depending on spells too greatly.'

Yanir set her foot beside the hoofmarks visible in the dirt – the trail the sylvaneth had been pursuing for days. 'If we should catch the twist-flesh here, we will be at even more of a disadvantage.'

Nyiss was in agreement. 'This parched land will suit the beast-kin better than it will us,' she said.

'There has yet been no sign of Beastgrave.' Kyra waved to the distant spires of rock that sprang from the desolation. 'So long as the Rootcutter is not near the mountain, we can avoid conflict with him. It will be our task to watch and to follow. To wait until *they* are the ones at a disadvantage.'

Kyra felt the grim vibrations emanating from the dryads. They were as fiercely resolved to see Ghroth stopped as she was. When the time for action came, they would not falter. To save the Thornwyld they would all gladly sacrifice themselves. No, her concern was not timidity but aggression. She gave Yanir careful scrutiny. 'Until I give the command, we must all be restrained in our actions. It will be of little consequence if all the Rootcutter's herd are killed if he is left free to draw more twist-flesh to his banner.'

'I will remember,' Yanir vowed. 'It is not to my liking, but I will remember.'

The dryad's promise would have to be enough, little as it was. Kyra was not concerned that Yanir would wilfully disobey. She was fearful that hate of the quick-blood had become so instinctive with her that the dryad might fall upon the twist-flesh before she was even aware of what she was doing. The branchwraith hoped there would be enough warning before they came upon Ghroth's pack so that she might weave a spell to join the essences of herself and Yanir. Melded together, there would be two minds to restrain the dryad's instincts.

Kyra waved at Nyiss to take up the trail again. Accustomed to ranging ahead of the other sylvaneth, she headed out across the barren ground. There was little here for her to blend into, so Nyiss let her bark lighten until it was ashen in hue, so that her body would draw less heat and the blood-sap inside would not dry out. Kyra and the other dryads maintained a steady pace, keeping the warning against excess activity in mind. They quickened their march only when they saw Nyiss stop and beckon to them with her branches.

Nyiss stood over a mangled carcass. Flies buzzed around it and there were signs it had been picked at by scavengers. There was enough of it left to recognise it as beastkin.

'I could not find the Rootcutter's brand,' Nyiss apologised to

Kyra. She turned the corpse over with her toe-roots. 'The haunch has been chewed away completely. Ghroth's mark could have been there.'

'Even without the brand, we know this is still the trail,' Eshia said.

The branches on Yanir's head swayed as she studied the ground. 'Little one,' she told Eshia, 'this may still be the trail, but it is important to know that no other twist-flesh has joined with the Rootcutter.' Her claw poked the mangled body. 'He might have killed this one to take over its pack and add more warriors to his herd.'

'Is there any sign that more twist-flesh have joined those we have followed?' Kyra asked. She dreaded to hear the answer.

Nyiss circled around the body. 'I do not see where more have joined the trail,' she finally decided. 'This may be one of Ghroth's minions that disobeyed.'

'With the twist-flesh, it could also be that they simply grew hungry,' Yanir suggested. She seemed to enjoy the shudder that passed through Eshia.

'Whatever happened, the condition of the carcass tells us we are only a day behind the twist-flesh,' Nyiss said. 'If it had been longer the meat–'

Kyra interrupted her. 'It is enough that you know what details to look for. Is it your opinion we run the risk of catching them too soon?'

Nyiss looked around, her gaze sweeping the terrain. 'There is little here to hide our presence. They could see us from far away, if their other senses did not detect us first.'

The branchwraith pondered that possibility. The quick-blood lacked the sylvaneth ability to feel the vibrations that grew from all living things, but she knew they had other senses that were incomprehensible to her. She was familiar with terms like taste and smell, but precisely how such capabilities functioned she had only the dimmest appreciation. She only knew that creatures like the twist-flesh had them.

'We must be careful and watch for any divergence from the trail,' Kyra said. 'Leaving or joining, we have to be vigilant for any change.'

'At the least there is nowhere they could hide,' Eshia stated. 'Except for those spires of rock, there is nowhere they could be concealed.'

'They may have dug themselves into the ground,' Nyiss cautioned. 'Many animals find burrows to hide from the sun, and the twist-flesh are a corruption of beasts. It could be they have found holes for themselves and are waiting for dark before setting out again.'

'Perhaps,' Kyra mused, 'but if our worry is unfounded, we allow the Rootcutter to draw farther away.' She let a sigh moan through her trunk. 'No, we will press on. Seek signs that the twist-flesh have gone to ground, if that is their strategy.'

Nyiss bowed to the branchwraith. 'I will be vigilant. The first evidence, and I will warn you at once.'

The lights dimmed in Kyra's eyes as she drew on her magic. She tried to draw upon the essences of the desert trees. Though they were not so vibrant as the wyldwood, there was a residual energy in them. Difficult to tap into, and with resistance to rapport. It was strenuous to try to draw information from them. As she had told the dryads, the desert plants focused solely on their own survival. They could reveal what birds might have landed in their branches, but as to anything that had passed even a few feet from their roots, they could reveal nothing. Kyra soon abandoned the effort. They would have to depend on what Nyiss could learn from the tracks.

The day grew hotter as the sylvaneth pressed on. Kyra judged it wise to keep moving through the day. The quick-blood became lethargic once temperatures reached a certain point. If the twist-flesh had found burrows to hide in, there was a good chance they were too oppressed by the heat to keep a steady watch.

The spires of rock drew nearer. Kyra saw the bands of col-oured clay that were layered across their faces. Shaped somewhat like mushrooms, the vibrant streaks set off the dull stone of the formations to remarkable effect. Dark spots peppered the clay, suggesting to her knots on the trunk of a tree.

Motion stirred within the spots and Kyra saw that they were holes, not mere discolourations, when huge hairy insects crawled into the light. They were bees, astounding in their size. They climbed out onto the clay and opened their translucent wings to dry them in the sun.

'It must take a great deal of pollen to feed such bees,' Eshia said, amazed by the huge insects.

Yanir's opinion was more cautious. 'I have seen no flowers here,' she warned.

The bees took flight. First one and then another, their bulky bodies seemingly too massive to be carried by the wings on their backs. They spread out across the desert, keeping high above the land. It was clear to Kyra that they were searching for food. The nature of that food was revealed a few moments later when one of them dropped down and landed atop the carcass Nyiss had found. The branchwraith watched in astonishment as the bee chewed the decaying meat into little balls and stuffed the carrion into pouches on its legs.

'Oh,' Eshia muttered, disappointment in her voice.

'I said there were no flowers.' Yanir relaxed and her claws thinned back to twig-like fingers. 'If they only scavenge flesh they will not bother us.'

'But they may show us where the Rootcutter has gone,' Kyra

said. 'If the twist-flesh have left more of their own butchered along the trail, the bees will be drawn to them. If we can't follow the tracks, watching the bees could tell us where they have gone.'

Nyiss pointed at the feeding insect. 'I will watch for tracks. If the rest would observe the scavengers we might regain the trail if I lose it.'

The sylvaneth followed the plan. While Nyiss watched the ground, the others kept their attention on the sky. There were many of the huge bees flying to and from the nests. The insects lighted upon dark bodies lying on the sand – the remains of antelope and buffalo. Kyra was worried about how many animals had died in the desert. It was far different from the forests she had known, where death was not so ravenous and the evidence of its coming was quickly cleaned away.

The giant bees took on a more sinister quality when Kyra saw why there was so much carrion. A big hog was resting in the shade of a thorn tree. It did not see the threat that hovered over it. Wheeling about the tree was one of the bees. It had an attitude of searching, looking for some way to drop past the thorny branches and get at the hog. After several circuits, the bee found the opening it wanted. Diving down at a steep angle, it hit the pig from behind, stabbing its long stinger into the animal's back. The hog squealed and struggled onto its feet, but an instant later it slumped back down. Its legs kicked for a few moments as the bee's venom did its deadly work. The insect crawled away from the carcass. Once it was out from under the tree's shadow, it flew away.

'They make their own carrion,' Yanir said. 'Leave the kill to rot and come back for it later.'

'An awful land.' Eshia's bark was thickening, taking on a defensive aspect, bracing her for danger.

Kyra eased the young dryad's anxiety. 'They do what they must to survive. No different from the wolf and the bear.' Her mouth thinned down to a smile. 'Yanir is right, these creatures seek flesh. We do not need to worry about them. We have nothing they want.'

Only a short time passed before Kyra doubted her reassuring words. As they continued along the trail, one of the bees circled them overhead. She thought the insect's interest was more ominous than mere curiosity. A second appeared, soon to be joined by a third and finally a fourth. *One for each of us*, Kyra thought. The observation did not lessen her uneasiness.

The four giant bees circled for a time, as though debating what to do. If they could smell, surely that sense must tell them that the sylvaneth were not flesh and therefore not their prey. Kyra had seen panthers claw trees to mark territory, but never had she seen the cats try to eat one.

'Stop moving,' Kyra told the others as the bees tightened their circle. She hoped it was only their motion that had drawn the interest of the bees.

One of the insects dived down at Yanir. The old dryad struck at the creature with her claws, tearing its abdomen away from its thorax. The bulbous abdomen rolled on the ground, the barbed stinger on its end dripping venom into the dirt. The remainder of the bee clung to Yanir's back, its segmented mouth chewing at her bark. She tried to rip the thing free, but it resisted her efforts. Only when Nyiss ran over and tore the bee off were the dryads able to see why the creature had attacked. It had bitten down past Yanir's bark to tear into the wood within. The blood-sap dripping from its jaws told the rest. The bee had been trying to get at the syrupy substance inside the sylvaneth.

A second of the bees dropped down to attack Eshia. Again the creature struck from behind. She fell as the stinger crunched into her body and pumped its venom into her. Eshia pressed her hand against the bee's head, forcing it back so the mandibles couldn't reach her. The dryad's fingers elongated into claws and punched through one of the segmented eyes. A scum of pulpy liquid gushed from the wound, but the insect was oblivious to its injury.

Kyra moved to help Eshia. In doing so, she exposed herself to the bee that had been hovering above. The insect darted down for her back, a low drone sounding from its whirring wings. She pivoted to face her attacker. Kyra stretched her hand towards the flying enemy. A spell whispered from her mouth and in response a burst of brambles erupted from her palm. The mesh of ropey thorns covered the bee, binding it tight. The insect crashed to the ground and writhed against the living net that held it.

Nyiss and Yanir were beset by the last of the bees. With mindless determination, it kept circling the dryads, seeking to come at Nyiss from behind while keeping out of the reach of their claws. The insect readied its stinger, wheeling away again when Yanir slashed at it with her hand. The deadly dance finally ended when Nyiss deliberately turned her back on the creature, giving it the opportunity it had been searching for. Before it could sink its stinger into her, Yanir intercepted it. Seizing the bee in both hands, she smashed it against the ground, not relenting until it was still.

The bee atop Eshia continued to pump venom into her. The young dryad's grip on the thing's head began to weaken and its mandibles dropped closer to her body. Kyra reached the scene before the insect could bite its victim. Her fingers folded into a sickle-like claw and she swept its sharp edge across the join between the bee's head and thorax. Eshia threw the severed head away while Kyra worked to pry the decapitated body from her back. There was a grotesque sucking sound as the stinger was extracted from the dryad's wood. A foamy green froth bubbled up from the wound.

Kyra flung the insect's body away. Their own attackers dealt with, Yanir and Nyiss stood over Eshia. The branchwraith deadened her arcane awareness and shut out the grave concern she felt emanating from them. She focused all her energies on Eshia and the venom that had been pumped into her. The bee's sting was causing a disruption inside her, evaporating the dryad's connection to her own body. Left to spread, it would leave her an inert bulk unable to twitch so much as a twig.

'Is there anything you can do to help her?' Nyiss asked.

Kyra let more of her own essence flow into Eshia. 'I can, but it will take time and much energy.' She looked away from Eshia and stared at the sky. 'While I work on her, I need you both to stand guard. Do not let more of the bees attack.'

Pouring more of herself into Eshia, the branchwraith forced the dryad's body to repulse the bee's venom. Drop by drop, she compelled the poison out through her bark in a toxic sweat. A gruelling, arduous process. The sun was beginning to set before Kyra was able to withdraw fully into her own form. A shudder swept through her as the fatigue of her ordeal struck her heartwood. Her skin cracked and split, sloughing away in crumbling patches.

By contrast, with the venom expelled from her, Eshia suffered no lingering effects from her wound. The young dryad almost looked refreshed by the experience. Her vigour evoked a feeling of guilt and she averted her eyes when she thanked Kyra for helping her. 'I regret being such a burden,' Eshia finished.

Kyra felt like sagging to the ground, but she knew doing so would only upset Eshia further. She tried to turn the discussion to other avenues. 'We made a mistake and underestimated those creatures. It is reckless to make presumptions.'

'Why did they attack us?' Nyiss wondered. 'And why only four of them when they could have brought an entire swarm against us?'

The branchwraith pointed to Yanir's wound. 'They must have smelled our blood-sap and found it enticing. It could be that the bees marked us in some way, claiming us for their own. Some special scent that would keep others away.'

'How long do you think the rest will ignore us?' Eshia asked.

Kyra could not give an answer to that. She turned to Nyiss and posed her own question. 'Did they return to their nests when the sun went down?'

'Somewhat before then,' Nyiss replied. 'I should think they went back to the rocks when it started to cool down.'

'Our safest course is to keep going,' Kyra said. She felt the hesitance of her companions and knew they were worried about her fitness for such a march. 'We cannot depend upon the bees to ignore us tomorrow. Our best chance is to be away from their nests when it gets hot enough to draw them out.'

Nyiss waved her hand at the parched earth. 'When it was clear the bees were going back to the rocks, I checked the tracks. They steer away from the spires and down into a sandy fissure. I found a few of their bodies down there. They were crushed, and without a drop of blood. Whatever happened to them it did not interfere with me. I was able to find their tracks again on the other side.'

'That will be our plan,' Kyra decided. 'We cross the fissure and continue following the Rootcutter.' She glanced at the dark shapes of the spires. 'It would seem the twist-flesh were as eager to avoid those nests as we are.'

'That is to be regretted,' Yanir said. She brushed her fingers across the raw wood where the bee had bitten her. 'I would not mind being bitten by them if they had saved us a lot of trouble and finished our enemies for us.'

The desert was far behind them, but still the sylvaneth seemed no closer to their quarry. Kyra knew the limitations of flesh, the weariness that so swiftly set into the muscles of the quick-blood. Ghroth must be driving his warriors mercilessly to keep them moving at such speed. Whatever brute led the second pack of twist-flesh was no kinder to them, for they were keeping pace with Ghroth's group.

Any question that the two bands of twist-flesh had joined was banished after they left the desert. The second group had diverged from Ghroth's, adopting a parallel path to the one taken by the Rootcutter. Nyiss was able to differentiate the more recent trail from the older one by the freshness of the plants crushed under their hooves. She quickly realised that the tracks of the beasthound which had escaped from the Thornwyld belonged to the second warherd. Sometimes its footprints would drift back to Ghroth's trail, then shift away to rejoin the other one. The creature's senses were letting the Rootcutter's rival keep tabs on him.

The trail led into a foggy marshland. The mists that rose up from the stagnant pools were dense and had a slimy feel to them as the sylvaneth moved through them. Kyra and the dryads extended their toe-roots, splaying them out to create broad foot-pads and disperse their weight as they navigated the mire. Small animals slithered through the water. Kyra had to keep shifting her bark to dislodge the little black salamanders that kept crawling onto her. The croaks of frogs and crows echoed from deep within the fog. Twice the sylvaneth stopped when they heard something big splashing through the marsh in the distance.

'We have not lost the trail,' Nyiss told Kyra. She pointed to a stand of weeds where a big green snake was coiled atop the body of a goat-headed warrior. The swollen state of the corpse and its purple colour suggested the serpent was responsible for the creature's end.

'Forgive me for doubting your skill,' Kyra said. 'This kind of terrain makes it difficult to believe anyone could find tracks to follow.'

Nyiss found humour in that statement. 'There are no tracks to follow here, but there are other traces of their passing. The stink of the mire probably confounded the nose of their beasthound, so the other twist-flesh have had to look for other ways to follow the Rootcutter. They were not subtle in their efforts.' She pointed out places where the moss dangling from the trees had been disturbed, patches of reeds that had been crushed down, floating worts that had been broken by something pressing against them.

'Still there is no evidence the two have found one another,' Yanir said. She jabbed a claw at the dead beastman. 'We found one or two of them, struck down by some animal or hazard, if not by their own kind, but we have not seen any trace of a fight. Perhaps they are not in conflict after all.'

Kyra thought that to be unlikely. 'No, if they were united in purpose they would be together, not stealing through dangerous lands–'

A cry from Eshia broke into the branchwraith's speech. She shook her arm at the dense fog. 'Did you see?' she asked. 'Did you see the mist turning black?'

The other dryads looked out across the marsh but they saw nothing and told Eshia as much. Kyra was not so certain. There was nothing visible, but she sensed a chill worming through her – a cold that had nothing to do with the absence of heat. It was the icy finger of black magic and old evil.

'Eshia is right,' Kyra said. 'Something is here.' She tried to draw a greater sense of what it might be or at least where it was, but to no avail. All she could tell was that some malignant magic was at work and it was all around them.

'Can you describe what you saw?' Kyra asked Eshia.

'It was just a kind of darkness,' she said. 'Like the fog itself was turning black.'

Nyiss swung around and pointed to a distant stand of reeds. 'There,' she said. 'I saw something. Something that cast a black shadow over the reeds.'

'I saw it too.' Yanir stepped forwards, putting herself between the others and the suspicious reeds. 'It was darker than any shadow. Like the reeds themselves turned black and just as quickly returned to normal.'

Kyra evoked her arcane senses, opening herself to the aethyr. The nature of whatever was out there remained nebulous. All she could tell was that it was a kind of hostile magic... and that it was hungry.

'We must be away from this place,' Kyra told the others. 'Whatever is here, it is nothing we want any part of.'

'Some kind of monster?' Eshia asked.

'I am not sure if it even has that much identity,' Kyra speculated. 'It may simply be the residue of some powerful spell, lingering on far past its time. Nothing more than force and energy.' The idea sparked an old memory of a quick-blood witch who had once preyed upon the sylvaneth long ago. She had harvested the living wood of their bodies, drawing out the fey energies to feed her own enchantments. This could be a similar kind of magic, aroused by the mere presence of her and the dryads.

'It is over here now.' Yanir drew their attention to a weed-strewn hummock a few hundred yards from the sylvaneth. Kyra was able to see the last flicker of blackness before normalcy resumed. The brief glance was not enough to confirm her speculation. All that was apparent was that the phenomenon was getting closer.

The branchwraith focused her magic into her fingers, their tips aglow with arcane power. The thing, the force, whatever it might be, manifested as a crawling shadow, an oily scum that rippled through the water. Kyra sent the eldritch light surging into the creeping malignance.

If the shadow on the water had truly been oil there could have been no less violent a reaction. The instant the blackness was struck by the light, it surged up, a geyser of boiling night. The dark cataract billowed outwards, launching itself upon Kyra, all of its slinking coyness forgotten. It fell upon her in a roiling shroud, swathing her from top to root.

Kyra felt herself being smothered in that blackness. Every speck of her being felt as though sharp nettles were piercing into her. She felt her essence drying out, withering away with each flicker of motion. Dimly she could perceive Yanir charging towards her, the dryad's hands transformed into great raking claws. Kyra tried to shout, tried to warn her away, but no sound would come.

Yanir struck, and when she did the black mantle shifted away from Kyra and descended upon the dryad. The branchwraith tried to focus her essence, bind her ravaged being back to her wooden body. She saw the hideous force swirling around Yanir. The glow in the dryad's eyes flickered and flashed, ebbing away as the thing tried to draw her out and consume her being.

'Nyiss, don't.' Kyra tried to stop the dryad from rushing to Yanir's aid. Nyiss had her own claws ready to tear at the shadow. Doing so would simply transfer it from Yanir to her. Kyra could not let that happen. She wove a compelling imperative through Nyiss, preventing her from touching the darkness.

Fixated on stopping Nyiss, Kyra could not restrain Eshia. The young dryad's right arm was fused into a great scything claw. The fingers of her left were elongated into probing talons. Kyra could only watch in despair as Eshia struck at the shadow and tried to rescue Yanir.

Strangely, Eshia did not lash out with her right hand, but jabbed at the shadow with her left. When the darkness came swirling away from Yanir, that was the moment she struck with her claw.

Eshia brought it scything down through her own left arm.

Kyra ran to Eshia, helping her away even as Nyiss supported the reeling Yanir. The sylvaneth staggered deeper into the marsh. Behind them they left Eshia's severed arm floating on the water, a scum of shadow swirling around it.

'Your arm…' Kyra did not know what to say to Eshia. It would take her centuries to grow another limb and it would never be as strong as the one she had sacrificed. To draw out the shadow she had left some of her own essence in the arm before cutting it from her body.

'I had to save Yanir,' Eshia said. 'This seemed the only way. There was not time to think of anything else.'

Despite the strain it put on her energies, Kyra cast a spell upon Eshia, sealing her wound and preventing any more blood-sap from leaking out of her body.

CHAPTER FIVE

Consciousness returned slowly to Ghroth. The first thing he was aware of was pain pulsing through his head, throbbing from the gash in his face, flaring from the dozens of places where he had been cut, bitten, gored and bludgeoned. The herdchief took a grim solace from his many hurts. They meant he was still alive.

Ghroth drew a deep breath and forced himself to fight through his pain to make sense of the many scents that filled his nose. There was the sharp smell of burning meat – the meat of beast-kin. There was the odour of blood, both dried and fresh. The musky scent of other beastmen still living. He could pick out his rival Chagrak, the scout Tograh, the beasthound Frang and several others. The smell of turnskin was absent and Ghroth wondered what had become of Sorgaas. Did he die in the fight or had the shaman escaped the attackers?

The scent of those attackers was strange to Ghroth. He had seen them when they clubbed him and Chagrak down. They seemed human to him then, but their scent was much different. Stronger and more distinct with a rotten quality to it. He heard them laughing like men, but the grunts and whistles they strung together into some sort of language were strange to him.

Ghroth did not know if these enemies thought him dead, so he opened his eyes to the merest slits. He kept his head still and stared at the limited view his position afforded him. He saw a ring of stones and a big fire blazing. Bits of meat impaled on sticks were leaning against the stones, angled so that they could cook in the flames. He saw a few bones scattered about the ground and what was certainly the severed hand of an ungor.

Ghroth's jaw tightened. He was not going to end up as a feast for these scavengers. Carefully he tried to move, testing to see how serious his injuries were. Trying to move his hands, he met with resistance. Through his pained awareness, it dawned on him that he was bound. Flexing the muscles in his legs and arms told him that they too were tied tightly together.

Even a primitive did not waste time tying up someone he thought was dead. There was no purpose in trying to deceive his captors. Ghroth opened his eyes and shifted his position so he could have a better view of his surroundings.

He found that he was in some kind of village, albeit far cruder than any manflesh settlement Ghroth had encountered. The simple huts were fashioned from uncured hides pinned together with sharpened bones. Upright logs stood between the huts, skulls tied to their branches with strips of sinew. Racks woven from sticks held thin strips of dried meat and charred insects. The fire he had seen was just one of many, each with its own array of cooking meat. A central fire, larger than the rest, had a long stake laid across it. Spitted on the stake was the skinned corpse of a gor warrior.

The humans who had captured the beastkin were there too, crouched around the fires and tearing at the butchered flesh of

on his back, able to manipulate only his hands, he was dragging himself away from the others and trying to reach one of the nearby huts. It looked to be both arduous and painful, but it was not Ghroth's discomfort that concerned Sorgaas – it was whether the herdchief could make good on his escape. If he reached the hut, he might find something with which to cut his bonds.

Was that what Sorgaas wanted? Ghroth was already a difficult chieftain to manipulate. With the power waiting inside Beastgrave, he would be even harder to control. The ways of Chaos were always capricious. It might be that Ghroth's vision was intended as a warning. A warning to Sorgaas. A warning of the threat he posed.

Sorgaas lifted his eyes from the village to the mountain that loomed above it. The forests and crags still beckoned him. He was certain it was more than his imagining. As his gaze swept across it, he was drawn to a dark opening in the side, midway down its slopes. A cave. Just such a cave as Ghroth had described. An entrance to the chambers within Beastgrave. A passage to the slumbering titan and the prize that could make someone beastlord.

Why Ghroth? Why even Chagrak? Why not Sorgaas himself? If the vision was meant as a warning to him, then the power was still there to be claimed.

Sorgaas returned his gaze to Ghroth. The chieftain was making steady progress towards the hut. None of the tribesmen had noticed his sluggish crawl. The shaman decided to change that. He was uncertain of many things, but on one point he had come to a decision. Ghroth was not going to seize the power he craved.

The shaman's sight narrowed, focusing on the bear-garbed witch doctor. He siphoned some of his magic to interfere with the man's divinations. Manipulating the painted teeth being tossed on the ground, Sorgaas alerted the witch doctor to what was happening only a dozen yards away.

The witch doctor rushed out from his hut. He turned to where the captives were lying. He spotted Ghroth crawling away. The man rushed to the fires and waved his arms in alarm. A mob of tribesman dashed away from their meals and converged on the herdchief. They battered Ghroth with clubs and fists, relenting only when he stopped moving. They dragged him back to the others and dumped him beside Chagrak.

Sorgaas let the spell enhancing his senses fade away. He was disappointed that the tribesmen had allowed Ghroth to survive, but at least they had kept him from escaping. The herdchief would be watched more closely. He would not get another chance. Before too long he would be turned over to the women and their knives. That would be the end of Ghroth.

Sorgaas looked back to Beastgrave. The location of the cave was fixed in his mind. He would go there while the tribesmen feasted. While Ghroth was being devoured, he would find the power hidden inside the mountain.

Ghroth drifted in and out of consciousness for the rest of the day. The beating he had been given by the tribesmen left his head feeling as though a mammoth had stepped on it. Every time he took a breath he found another chip from a broken tooth to spit out of his mouth. His nose was so choked by dried blood that it was impossible to draw air through it. One eye was sealed shut by the blood that had dripped across it while the other felt like it wanted to pop from its socket. His left ear was still ringing after a hunter had used it to stop his club.

For all of that though, the herdchief was still alive. The witch doctor had prevented the men from going too far when they attacked him outside the hut. Bearcloak had even inspected Ghroth afterwards, checking to make certain he was still alive. Even when the warchief came looking for more meat to feed his tribe, the leader was warned away. The witch doctor wanted the rest of the beastkin alive.

Ghroth was certain the human's reasons were far from pleasant.

It was late afternoon when the witch doctor came for the captives. He was accompanied by dozens of tribesmen who were caked in white mud and had simple pictoglyphs painted on their chests. Even the axe-carrying warchief adopted the mud mantle, though he remained detached when the other mud-shirts gathered up their captives and carried them through the village. Ghroth saw humans at the entrance of every hut, young and old, male and female, watching with ghoulish interest as the strange procession marched past.

Bearcloak took a place at the front of the group as they left the village and started towards the base of the mountain. The axeman and the mud-shirts not carrying prisoners went to the back of the procession. Each of them had a weapon of some kind. Ghroth noted that some of the hunters carried weapons they had stolen from the beastkin. One of them had Tograh's bow while another had the orruk cleaver Ghroth had wielded.

The tribesmen carried their prisoners through a narrow gorge, the walls so close together that they were forced to proceed in single file. Ghroth saw that they were marked with many pictoglyphs that depicted everything from men hunting animals to winged dragons hunting men. There was a certain vividness to the simple pictures and the herdchief was struck by the variety of figures painted on the sides of the gorge. There were humans of far different aspect than the tribesmen, arrayed in heavy armour of varying types. He saw the bearded duardin with their weird devices and strange sticks that dealt death from a distance. There were fanged orruks and sneaky grots, the greenskins depicted in battle with the tribesmen. Verminous raiders with long tails were shown being chased from the canyon village. Hulking ogors surrounded by hunters casting spears into them. Monstrous troggoths smashing through the tribesmen who tried to stop them. Ghroth even saw tree-fiends, the branches atop their heads splayed out like great antlers.

What most arrested the herdchief's interest was the one common feature of all the images. Whether the tribesmen were shown chopping away at a tree-fiend or being struck down by a gold-armoured knight, rising over them was the same shape, setting the scene for their battle. It was the distinct outline of the mountain that Ghroth had travelled so far to find: Beastgrave.

The savage procession at last reached a part of the gorge where a subsidence had brought part of the wall crumbling down. The fallen earth and rock created a ramp, up which the tribesmen carried the beastkin. They had been moving closer to the mountain and were now at the base of Beastgrave.

Bearcloak called out to the humans, whistling and grunting as he waved his hands over them and spat a dark liquid into the air. The ritual was short and soon the procession was moving again. The warchief and the armed tribesmen marching at the back of the column spread out to flank the hunters carrying the beastkin. The human warriors watched the boulders and trees, alert for danger.

The tribesmen drew nearer to the slopes of Beastgrave. The raw cliffs of the mountain towered over them. Ghroth felt a sense of awe despite his situation. The place had a presence that surpassed anything he had felt before. He could not define the sensation, but only liken it to when he was a cub and had hidden in the brush from an amok tuskgor. It was like that – feeling small and helpless before an immeasurably more powerful creature.

The witch doctor cried out again and stopped the procession. They stood before an open area at the foot of the mountain. No trees grew here, no rocks lay strewn about the ground. The earth was barren, devoid of any feature that might distinguish it. Its emptiness was what made it remarkable… and sinister.

After a last show of ceremony from Bearcloak, the tribesmen walked out onto the barren ground. They drew help from the guards as they lifted the posts on which the beastkin were bound. One by one, they lifted the logs so they stood at a sharp angle, and with stone hammers drove them into the ground. Each stake was spread several yards from the others and positioned so the captives bound to them would face the mountain.

Ghroth's stake was raised last of all and the tribal warchief himself swung the hammer that drove it into the ground. The squat human's dark eyes stared into the beastman's in a silent expression of hate. The warchief fingered the strap of his axe and looked as though he might strike Ghroth down and cheat the witch doctor out of whatever fate he had chosen for the captives. An ugly leer worked itself onto the man's face. He glanced from Ghroth to the mountain and laughed. He turned away and joined the other tribesmen as they retreated back towards the trees.

The captives around Ghroth were silent. They had abandoned whatever hope they had that the chieftain could rescue them when he was caught crawling towards the hut. It was impressive enough that he had survived the beating. Chagrak, however, still found the breath to mock the herdchief. 'Still wait?' he snarled. 'Ghroth not break bonds. Wait for bonds to rot, then break?'

Ghroth spat at the bestigor, the spittle hitting his challenger in the eye. The outraged howl that rose from Chagrak was a petty comfort, but he found it satisfying.

Chagrak's howls fell silent when the tribesmen chanted. The harsh, guttural voices sounded in a deep-throated cadence that surged through the air. Ghroth felt the post he was tied to vibrating. It shivered with increasing violence, sending a shudder through his bones. Other beastkin cried out in fright and confusion. The very ground under their hooves quaked. A powerful tremor rolled through the earth, increasing in intensity with each heartbeat.

A thunderous groan roared across the scene. The cries of the bound beastkin turned to wails of horror as they beheld what was happening at the bottom of the mountain. The cliff cracked apart, extending long fingers of rock out over the barren ground. To Ghroth they looked like colossal worms made of stone burrowing out from the side of Beastgrave.

The gigantic protrusions stretched further and further out from the cliff, pawing blindly at the ground. The sweep of those tremendous fingers explained why the terrain was so empty, and why the hunters had placed the stakes where they had. The captives were there for the reaching mountain to find – sacrificial offerings to Beastgrave.

One of the gargantuan fingers fell upon a bison-faced gor. The beastman shrieked as his body was pulverised under the tremendous mass. The protrusion stopped moving for a moment, as though registering the fact it had crushed someone under its bulk. It slid backwards and withdrew into the cliff, grinding the captive against the ground and leaving a hideous smear of blood and flesh in its wake.

A fierce shout of delight boomed from the watching tribesmen as the mountain claimed its first sacrifice. Ghroth cursed the humans and wished he could get free so that he might have a chance to repay their viciousness in kind.

Though one of the rock fingers had withdrawn, the others continued to advance and grope blindly at the ground. Soon one of them found a second beastkin, crushing him in the same way as the first. Ghroth saw there were enough of the protrusions to claim each of them. The witch doctor had planned it this way. An offering for each claw in the hand of Beastgrave.

Beastgrave. The mountain was every bit as ominous as in Kyra's premonitions. As she looked upon its slopes from the broken, boulder-strewn land that bordered its western face, it occurred to her that nothing about it was natural. From the cut of the cliffs to the depths of the forests that grew upon it, everything had an uncanny quality. The branchwraith was familiar enough with the ways of magic to feel when a site had been exposed to some powerful sorcery. Typically it was an area no bigger in circumference than the trunk of a pine midway through its second century. The residue from the conjuration was localised, restricted to a confined area, and could only be felt when a sensitive was right at the edge of the afflicted region.

This was different. Kyra could feel the magical aura of Beastgrave from miles away. She could even catch something of its flavour. It was old, so old it might have been contemporary with the gods themselves in the Age of Myth. It was sinister, rife with a macabre essence that betokened its grim beginnings and dire intentions. It was hungry. That last property was the one to make the branchwraith the most uneasy. The former betokened the mountain's background, its power and nature. The latter was a warning of its motivations.

'A horrible place,' Yanir declared as she walked from the last vestiges of the jungle. Eshia was with her, her body held at an awkward angle as she moved. The loss of her arm in the marsh had thrown off the dryad's balance and she was still figuring out the best way to compensate.

'Anywhere that could harbour the kind of power the Rootcutter craves was bound to be unpleasant,' Kyra said. She tried to mitigate exactly how unpleasant her impression of the place was. There was no sense alarming the dryads. Troubled or at ease, they still had to go to the mountain.

'How far ahead do you think the twist-flesh are?' Eshia asked. 'We seemed to be gaining on them when we reached the jungle.'

It was true. For all their woodcraft, the beastkin were still clumsy amateurs beside the sylvaneth. Kyra judged that a gap which might have been days in Ghroth's favour had narrowed down to only a few hours when the trail delved into the jungle. Nyiss had continually warned them against moving too fast lest they stumble on stragglers and thereby alert the rest of the twist-flesh.

'We will know better when Nyiss comes back,' Kyra said. As usual, the sylvaneth tracker had ranged ahead of the rest of them. None of them had seen her since she drifted back to advise them that the jungle was going to end and they would be entering a desolate land of rock and dirt.

'Do you think she is in trouble?' Yanir's voice had an edge to it. After skulking about the marsh and jungle, she was eager for an enemy against which she could fight back.

'She has been gone a long time,' Eshia added. Her tone was not eager but worried.

Kyra folded her hands before her, letting the fingers grow out and twine together. Shoots from the tips branched out, forming arcane symbols. Through her mouth, a name was whispered. 'Nyiss. Nyiss.'

The spell was simple when Kyra wished to merge her essence with a sylvaneth who was close. She had no idea how far away Nyiss had gone. That made the enchantment far more difficult. Most branch-wraiths would not even attempt it. Had the fate of the Thornwyld, and possibly all the sylvaneth refuges in Ghur, not been in jeopardy, Kyra would not have attempted it either. A single mistake, some unforeseen counter-magic, and the astral projection would be disrupted, that part of her essence scattered beyond recall. She would be diminished, left with only what she retained in her own body. At best her magical powers would wither. There was also the possibility she would be so reduced as to render her an imbecile.

Kyra could not think about those hazards. Any distraction would cause her to lose focus and she needed her entire concentration for the spell. As she felt her essence streaming away from her wooden body she felt it trying to dissipate and scatter in every direction. Only by force of will was she able to bind her spirit and keep herself whole.

The landscape flew below her as Kyra's essence soared through the air. She could not pick out features or distinguish particulars. There was only the sense of motion and the knowledge that she was flying across the land beyond the jungle.

No. There was something more. Something that remained sharp and distinct despite the haze of her disembodied senses. The mountain. Beastgrave itself was as clear and sharp as when she'd seen it with her corporeal form. That fact sent a shudder through Kyra's spirit. The enormity of the mountain's power would have to be tremendous for it to retain such clarity to her as she was now.

The branchwraith's concentration faltered as panic gripped her. She felt her essence starting to fray. Her fear intensified as she fought to bind the strands back together, making the task even more difficult. A vicious circle that intensified her agitation and made her efforts even harder.

Kyra was at the edge of despair, her spirit threatening to lose all cohesion, when all the frayed strands snapped back together. She felt herself being funnelled into a new vessel. At the very moment of disaster, her projected essence reached Nyiss and poured into the dryad's wooden body.

Nyiss swayed in shock at the abrupt transposition of Kyra's essence. In normal circumstances the spell would have been smooth, soothing. Now it was violent, a psychic invasion that had the branchwraith's presence flooding through Nyiss, coiling around her own spirit like a python. Even divided between bodies, Kyra's spirit dwarfed that of Nyiss. Her essence was capable of smothering the dryad's. She struggled to restrain the flood, condensing her awareness in the recesses of Nyiss' being.

Kyra felt the surge of pain crackle through Nyiss as her body adjusted to the shock of the sudden translocation. Bark flaked away from her trunk. Some of the branches on her head crumbled away entirely. The light in her eyes flickered and struggled to retain its glow. Her legs creaked as they struggled to keep her upright.

'Forgive me,' Kyra's essence begged Nyiss.

'There is no need for pardon,' Nyiss replied. 'The abruptness… it has made me know… Parts of your essence have bled into mine. I know the desperate need that made you take such risk.'

'The mountain is here,' Kyra said. 'I have seen the terrible power of Beastgrave. If it is but the smallest part of that power Ghroth intends to steal, he will destroy the Thornwyld.'

'I know,' Nyiss said, a tremor in her mind. 'When you joined to me, I saw Beastgrave as you have seen it.'

'The Rootcutter must be stopped. If it means all our lives, we have to prevent him from reaching the mountain.' Kyra directed her attention to the dryad's eyes. She could see what Nyiss was looking at. More, she could interpret what she saw as Nyiss would – a benefit of their melded essence.

The ground was rocky with only limited vegetation. It was not the best terrain for showing footprints, but Nyiss had found them all the same. She had detected the trail of Ghroth's warherd as well as that of the rivals already following them. With the Rootcutter as their primary concern, his was the path Nyiss followed. Before too far, it transpired that either trail would have lent itself to the same purpose. They converged. Ghroth's rivals had decided they were tired of following.

'Ambushed.' Kyra interpreted the signs in the dirt. Splashes of blood were everywhere, as were a few discarded weapons. Broken arrows and spears, the odd knife or club. For the most part they were the rough weapons favoured by the twist-flesh, but there were a few stone-tipped spears that looked crude even by their primitive standards.

'It may be that Ghroth was attacked by his own kind,' Nyiss said. She drew Kyra's attention to other tracks. They were not the hooves and clawed feet of beastkin. These prints were those of human feet. 'Other quick-bloods attacked the twist-flesh.' She pointed in the direction of Beastgrave. 'They came from the direction of the mountain. And they were the victors.'

Kyra looked at the signs left by the battle. 'No corpses,' she said. 'The victors took away the dead. Their own and those of the twist-flesh.'

Nyiss gestured to the tracks that led away from the fight. 'See how deep the human prints are? They were carrying heavy burdens when they left here. It is possible they will eat the dead.' Kyra felt the hope flare inside Nyiss as she added, 'Maybe Ghroth is already dead.'

'We must know he is,' Kyra said. 'We must verify his threat is ended.' She turned Nyiss' head back to the mountain. 'And we will still need to go inside Beastgrave and destroy the thing that would have given the Rootcutter such power. Only then will the threat to the Thornwyld really be over.'

Kyra sensed the disturbance in Nyiss' mind. 'If Ghroth is dead there will be no one to follow. No one to lead us to the relic.'

'It will make our duty much harder, but not impossible,' Kyra said.

'You do not believe that,' Nyiss corrected her. 'Without the Rootcutter, we may never find it.'

'We will try,' Kyra declared. 'My body will guide Yanir and Eshia to us. Once we are all here, we will follow this new trail. We will see for ourselves if Ghroth is dead.'

CHAPTER SIX

The sylvaneth followed the trail left by the quick-blood. The force
that had prevailed against the beastkin was joined at several points
by smaller bands of hunters. Always they marched closer to the
mountain. It was clear to Kyra that whoever these humans were,
their habitation was somewhere near Beastgrave, if not on or in
the mountain itself.

With increasing frequency, the sylvaneth encountered steep
drops into winding canyons. The trail they were following skirted
these, at least until they came to one where an incline offered
easy passage into the fissure. Nyiss went down the gorge a short
distance and confirmed that the quick-blood had gone through
it and that they were still carrying their burdens.

Kyra looked across the plateau. Off in the area of the mountain she could make out several plumes of smoke. 'We do not
need to follow them into the gorge,' she told Nyiss, and pointed
to the rising smoke. 'That is where we will find their village. That
is where they are going.'

Yanir was pleased by the news. 'It is fortunate we can avoid the fissure. The walls are narrow there, with less room to move. Good for the quick-blood, maybe, but not so good for us.'

'If these people have killed the Rootcutter, why should we have cause to fight them?' Eshia shook her head in regret.

'The quick-blood are always ready to fight,' Yanir told her. 'With or without cause, their first thought is violence. If you expect different from them you may not be able to learn from the mistake.'

Kyra dampened some of Yanir's rhetoric. 'Quick-blood are not so vicious. Some at least.' She waved her hand at the tracks. 'Even though these have fought the twist-flesh, we cannot assume they are friendly to us. How they might regard us is unknown. It is always prudent to be careful about the unknown.'

The sylvaneth continued across the plateau, moving towards the distant smoke. Except for a few buzzards soaring overhead and some scraggly hares that kept close to the shelter of their burrows, Kyra saw no signs of activity. Nyiss kept close to the gorge, but apart from a few lizards nothing was moving down there either. The humans and the twist-flesh were not abroad, it appeared. As the evidence that they were gone increased, Kyra urged the dryads to make haste.

'It seems certain they have gone to their village,' Kyra said. 'If we can still find the twist-flesh, that is where they must be.'

'We can let the quick-blood attend to them,' Yanir reminded Kyra.

The branchwraith was not sure that they could afford to take such a strategy. But what would be the alternative? Their chances against the twist-flesh warbands had been poor enough. They would be far worse trying to fight an entire village of humans, especially to capture someone the sylvaneth wanted dead anyway.

'It may come to that,' Kyra told the dryads. 'We will know when we reach their village.'

The plumes of smoke grew larger and more distinct as the sylvaneth marched onwards. So too did the imposing bulk of Beastgrave. The ominous presence of the mountain became a permanent chill inside Kyra's being, an icy finger that poked into her mind. It was goading her, pulling at her with an allure that was at once fascinating and repulsive. Even if Ghroth was destroyed, she would have to go to Beastgrave. The knowledge was as enticing as it was terrifying.

From the lip of a wide canyon, Kyra looked down on the village. She had seen many human settlements over her long life and especially on her journey to find Thornwyld, but this was unique in her experience. It was so raw and primitive it would have suited the simplest of orruk tribes or an ogor hunting camp. The huts were made from hide and bone, carved femurs from large animals serving as their supports. They were spread out along the tiered basin of the canyon. From what Kyra could tell, lone tribesmen lived in the huts scattered on the higher levels while family groups occupied the dwellings clustered towards the centre.

At that centre, the sylvaneth saw many cookfires over which chunks of meat were laid. Kyra's first good view of the tribesmen came from those gathered around the fires. They were short but powerful in build, their bodies almost entirely covered in wiry hair. They had heavy features and low foreheads. They wore only scraps of clothing fashioned from animal hides.

'Look.' Nyiss directed everyone's attention to a big stone slab where several tribeswomen were skinning a carcass. When they were finished, a couple of hunters lifted the body and carried it down to the fires. There was no mistaking the flayed corpse. It was that of a twist-flesh.

'They are eating them.' Eshia shuddered.

'No less than what the twist-flesh would have done had the positions been reversed,' Kyra stated. Her eyes scoured the village, dreading and hoping to see some proof that Ghroth had been butchered by these people. As her gaze roved across the settlement, she spotted a line of tribesmen caked in mud marching away towards a nearby fissure. Some of the hunters were carrying long poles between them. Bound to each of the poles was a captive beastkin.

'They are carrying away the rest of the twist-flesh,' Kyra said. She drew the notice of the dryads to the file of hunters moving into the fissure.

'Where are they going?' Yanir asked.

'The direction they are moving in, unless the fissure doubles back on itself, will take them closer to Beastgrave,' Nyiss observed.

'Or to the mountain itself,' Kyra said. 'Or inside the mountain,' she added with a shiver. It was possible that the tribesmen would take Ghroth right to where the sleeping godbeast was entombed. 'Whatever their intention, we have to follow them.'

Eshia waved her remaining hand at the fires. 'Maybe they have already eaten the Rootcutter.'

'We have to be sure of that,' Kyra told her. 'We have to make sure.'

Nyiss expressed the grim thought that was nagging at all of them. 'It would be easier for us if he is alive. The Rootcutter may know where this relic is hidden. If we could follow him, we could destroy both him and it.'

'That would end the threat hanging over Thornwyld,' Kyra agreed. 'But we will learn nothing if we stay here. We must follow the quick-blood and find out if Ghroth is alive. We must see what they intend to do with him. Once we know that, we will know better what we can do.'

The sylvaneth drew back from the canyon and started across the plateau. They would follow the tribesmen, discover who their captives were and see where they were being taken. Despite the more obvious dangers of their task, it was a different aspect of it that dominated Kyra's mind and made her blood-sap cold.

Soon they would not merely be gazing upon Beastgrave. They would be on the very mountain itself.

The forest that clothed the slopes of Beastgrave was sick. Kyra felt its vileness vibrating from the trees. There was an awareness here, but it was a depraved sort of intelligence, malformed into something monstrous. It was not the taint of Chaos, but a contamination far older and more complete. The gnarled trees had not been perverted out of all semblance to what they should be. It was more like they had been completely taken apart and rebuilt, shaped into a new and terrible aspect.

Kyra knew the dryads sensed the wrongness of the trees. They had been hesitant to follow her into the forest to flank the procession of tribesmen. The branchwraith had expended some of her magic to block the vibrations from her companions, allowing them to press on without feeling the worst of the sickness all around them.

For Kyra there was no such respite. She was open to the full perversion of the forest, the ghastly impulses that whispered through the malformed trees. The urge to destroy for the sake of destruction. The compulsion to kill for the sake of death. The lust for carrion decaying and being drawn up into the roots. The hideous desire to have the sylvaneth join the forest's eternal misery. A beckoning whisper asked Kyra to forget about fear and duty, to discard all of her obligations and become part of the mountain.

'Will they never stop?' Kyra moaned. She was unaware she had spoken until Nyiss turned towards her.

'The quick-blood took no provisions with them,' the dryad said. 'Even if they intend to eat their prisoners, they would have brought water with them. 'I do not think even they would trust water drawn from the mountain.'

Kyra was thankful Nyiss believed it was the tribesmen she was speaking about. At least she could spare the dryads the loathsome whispering. 'When they stop, we must be ready.' She looked at her companions and impressed on them a further point. 'We may need to act fast, so everyone be ready to do what I say.'

The dryads bowed in acknowledgement of her authority.

The journey through the forest continued. Nyiss hugged the edge of the treeline, slipping through the profane timber, her bark shifting to adopt the colour and contour of her diseased surroundings. Kyra was hard-pressed to spot the dryad. She knew the tribesmen would have no chance at all.

They heard the procession marching along the edge of the forest, grunting and whistling in their crude language. Soon the sylvaneth saw the humans and their prisoners. Kyra gave a start when she saw the goat-headed Ghroth among the captives. The fiend from her premonition was still alive. Battered and bloodied, but still alive. Doubt gnawed at her. Alive he remained a threat to the Thornwyld. Alive he could still lead her to the sleeping godbeast. Or she could simply remain in this horrible forest and become one with the mountain.

Kyra railed against the beckoning whispers. She would not forget who she was. She would not forsake the Thornwyld.

The tribesmen moved away from the forest and carried their prisoners to a barren stretch of ground. The sylvaneth watched as their bearskin-wearing priest performed some sort of ritual. A flicker of power rose from the man and dispersed towards the mountain. Some of the hunters broke away and carried the captives closer to the raw cliffs of Beastgrave. They drove the posts into the ground at sharp angles and quickly retreated.

The sylvaneth were forced to move around the tribesmen as the quick-blood withdrew into the shelter of the trees. Before, the men had been wary of the forest, but now they sought to hide themselves within it. Kyra pondered the purpose of their priest's spell and what the human had sought to conjure with his magic. What they could fear enough that they would seek safety in a forest they shunned.

Kyra's answer came with a quaking rumble. She watched in amazement as the face of the cliff split open and fragmented into long tendrils of rock.

'The mountain is moving,' Eshia gasped.

The branchwraith shared Eshia's amazement. The ominous presence, the fearful impression of malignant intelligence that surrounded Beastgrave – none of these had suggested to Kyra that the mountain was animate in any way. She was no less transfixed with horrified fascination as the stony tendrils groped across the barren earth. But when one of those tendrils came smashing down on a tied beastman, she saw the energy that went slithering back into the mountain. In some way, it was feeding on the life force of its victims.

Kyra shifted her gaze to where Ghroth was tied. In a matter of moments, the Rootcutter could be crushed. Was that something she could allow to happen? With a new appreciation for the malevolence of Beastgrave, she did not think she could. In her vision, Ghroth found his way to the grave of the godbeast. It was a gamble, but she had to trust that part of the vision was true, and that she could act to prevent the rest of it from unfolding.

'Watch over me,' Kyra told the dryads. 'I must fix all my attention on my magic.'

Yanir gripped the branchwraith's shoulder. 'What are you going to do?'

'What has to be done,' Kyra said. 'We need to destroy the relic. To do that we need the Rootcutter to guide us to it.'

There was no time for further explanation. Kyra focused on her conjuring, sealing off her mind from all other concerns. She envisioned a root burrowing through the earth, speeding away to free Ghroth from his bonds. Disgusted, she channelled that purpose into one of the trees and compelled its roots to accomplish what she demanded of them.

The tree responded, but as it did, all of its vileness came pouring into her. The rest of the forest exulted in the lowering of her defences and all the filth of their debased essence came slithering into her mind. She fought to partition their influence, to keep part of herself clean and maintain the clarity to work her magic.

Her efforts were only a partial success. Kyra's spell expanded beyond her intentions. Other trees responded to her call and sent their own roots burrowing to the sacrifices. Instead of freeing only Ghroth, there were roots erupting from the ground beside each of the stakes. Sharp thorns projected from them as they slithered upwards to cut away the bindings.

Kyra struggled to maintain her focus even as she felt the forest trying to consume her. Some of the twist-flesh were free and broke away, fleeing towards the trees. The tribesmen howled in outrage and charged off in pursuit. Dimly, she heard Yanir and Nyiss shouting at her, trying to warn her that the quick-blood were coming.

She refused to break the spell. Ghroth was still tied. She had to keep working her magic until he was free, otherwise it was all for nothing. Something slammed into her and she felt blood-sap trickling down her trunk, but still she refused to relent. The angry howls of the tribesmen joined the shouts of the dryads, but Kyra kept her mind upon her conjuring.

As the rock protrusions drew still closer, Ghroth felt something crawling around his legs. Twisting his head, he was able to look down and see a green vine with long thorns rising up from the earth. Snake-like, it slithered up his body. Around him, other beastkin cried out in surprise.

'Silence,' Ghroth snapped at the others, worried their cries might draw the attention of the tribesmen. The sudden appearance of the vines was unnatural and smacked of magic. The witch doctor had no need to work spells against the captives now that the stone fingers were crushing them. This had to come from somewhere else. It could even be the work of Sorgaas.

Ghroth was more certain than ever that the shaman's spells were in play when the vines reached his legs and the thorns bit into his bonds. In a short time, the cords were cut through. 'Still,' Ghroth barked to the beastkin. 'Wait for all be free.' It was a risk shouting to his followers, but thus far their captors had shown no sign of understanding their speech. He judged the risk was less than it would be if his warriors tried to flee while others were still tied to the stakes.

The vines were crawling higher. Ghroth felt them sawing around his hands. As the thorns did their work, another beastman was crushed by the protrusions and his body dragged back to the mountain. This reminder of looming death was too much for some of the beastkin. Three ungors, already free from their bonds, scrambled away from their stakes and made a frantic dash towards the forest.

At once there were enraged cries from the watching tribesmen. Many of them set off in pursuit of the escaped sacrifices. The warchief shouted at some of the hunters to come with him and check the captives who remained.

Ghroth knew whatever chance he had would be gone once the warchief reached the stakes. He looked over at the beastkin who remained. Two of them were ungors – Tograh and a long-horned raider from Chagrak's group. 'If you free, cut me loose,' he growled at the two beastmen.

'No,' Chagrak snarled. He thrashed against his own bindings. 'Help Chagrak, leave Ghroth.'

The two ungors did not hesitate. When they dropped clear of the stakes, they scrambled to where Ghroth was tied and tore at the last cords that held him. The herdchief just had time to gain his footing before the tribesmen were on them.

'Now you fight Ghroth,' he growled at the human warchief. The man snapped something at the four mud-shirts with him. Showing more mettle than Chagrak, he sent them after the two ungors. The man intended to finish Ghroth alone.

Ghroth was taller and heavier than the warchief, but he was still weak from his ordeal. The first slashes of the warchief's axe bit into the beastman's hide, carving ugly furrows in his flesh. The sight of blood caused the human to smile and laugh. His next blow raked a gash across Ghroth's chest. A clump of fur dangled from the bloodied axe.

Rage swelled inside Ghroth. He fought down the pain from the axe and charged at his foe. He caught the warchief's arm as the human took another swing at him. 'Fight Ghroth. Manflesh die.' Exerting his fury, he bent the tribesman's limb back upon itself and broke the bone. The enemy screamed in agony and smashed his fist into Ghroth's face. He was still numb from the beating he had received, so the punch barely made any impression on the herdchief. He brought his hand raking down across the mud-caked chest and slashed deep cuts in the flesh beneath.

The warchief reeled under the sudden, vicious assault. Ghroth gave him no opportunity for escape. He pressed his advantage and seized the man by the shoulders. A red frenzy gripped Ghroth, clouding his vision in a haze of madness. He lifted the struggling hunter off the ground. He glared into the man's dark eyes and slammed him into the same stake the herdchief had been tied to. The force of the blow impaled the human on the sharpened log and drove it through his chest in a welter of gore. Ghroth snarled at the dying hunter and seized the axe hanging from his broken arm. With a brutal wrench, he broke the tether and held the axe high. For an instant he was tempted to bring it down, but then a cold smile formed on his face. Ghroth quickly backed away. The warchief stared at him in bewilderment until a dark shadow fell across him. The next instant the human was obliterated as a finger of stone smashed down on the stake.

Tograh and the other ungor had managed to hold off the other hunters long enough for the duel between Ghroth and the warchief to reach its savage finish. The other tribesmen saw the destruction of their leader and moaned in despair. Throwing down their weapons, the humans fled back towards the forest. The two ungors, their anger roused, made to chase after them.

'Stay. No chase,' Ghroth ordered. 'We go mountain. Let manflesh run.' He pointed the two beastkin towards the woods that dotted the slopes of Beastgrave. There was no measure for argument. With the rock protrusions still reaching out to claim victims, there also was not the time to disagree. The ungors simply nodded and took up the fallen weapons before dashing from the slope.

Ghroth started to follow them, but he stopped and turned back. He intended to deal with Chagrak and make certain the bestigor would never challenge him again, but when he looked, he found only an empty stake. His rival had broken free during the fight with the warchief and slipped away. Had one of the mountain's hungry fingers taken him, the stake would have been pulverised.

A low whine had Ghroth turning again. There was one stake that still held a captive. Tied to the post lengthways, the beasthound Frang had yet to be freed by the vines. One of the stone protrusions reached towards the trapped creature. Before it could come smashing down, the herdchief ran to the stake and with a swing of the axe he cut the last of the ties. Frang fell to the ground and loped away, scurrying off towards the woods.

As the protrusion came crashing down and splinters from the

stake pelted his body, Ghroth decided to follow Frang's example and strike out for the mountain. He circled around the area the first ungors had fled towards, aware that the witch doctor and many of the hunters had gone off in pursuit of the beastkin. He headed after the tracks left by Tograh and his companion. They would prove useful if he caught up to them, having already exhibited their readiness to take his commands.

Now that they were finally outside Beastgrave, Ghroth felt half the quest was over. What was left was to find a way down inside the mountain, to probe its caverns for the grave of the godbeast and the power that pulsed within its heart. The prize that would make Ghroth the mightiest beastlord to prowl the wilds of Ghur in an age.

Ghroth would soon claim his destiny.

A shock rippled through Kyra when she felt Ghroth break free. She tried to break clear of her spell, to close herself again to the noxious vibrations of the forest. But as she did, she felt an awful resistance to her efforts. The trees had been quick to answer her magic, but they were not so eager to withdraw from her. They were trying to pour more of themselves into her, to profane that part of her essence she had denied them.

Kyra struggled to free herself from the forest's possession, but her efforts only made their attack stronger. The barriers were fraying and little weeds of filth were crawling into her essence. She was being consumed, transformed into something as abominable as the foul forest itself.

With an abruptness that nearly shattered her mind, the forest's presence fled from her. At the very threshold of destruction, the branchwraith was reprieved. She sank her toe-roots into the ground to keep from falling as her essence flowed back through her body.

The cause for the sudden retreat of the forest's influence was quickly evident. Orange fingers of flame were licking around the nearby trees.

Kyra's mind snapped back to full awareness. She saw the stone-tipped spear embedded in her side and wrenched it free. The dryads were around her, their hands transformed into long claws as they slashed at mud-painted tribesmen. Several of the humans had been struck down, but many more remained. They flung themselves against the sylvaneth with the wild abandon of fanatics, indifferent to the death of their comrades so long as they might get closer to their foes.

A ball of searing flame flashed past Kyra, striking one of the gnarled trees. The grey trunk instantly caught fire, crackling and splitting as the incendiary ate into it. No natural flame could have spread so quickly. Kyra knew it was magical. She turned to confront the conjurer.

The bearcloaked priest met the branchwraith's gaze. He flinched when he felt her glowing eyes on him, but his moment of fright only redoubled his hostility. Clasping both hands together, he focused on Kyra. He drew a deep breath, but when he exhaled it was not air but fire that left his mouth. A mote of flame grew larger and more violent as it sped away from the witch doctor.

Kyra worked her own hasty magic, issuing a pulse of arcane energy that unravelled the witch doctor's spell. The ball of flame fizzled away, little drops of liquid fire flashing along the ground as it dissipated. The witch doctor stamped his feet and shouted in fury. He bit down on his tongue, drawing a trickle of blood, then clasped his hands together again.

Kyra started to weave her own spell to attack the man, but as she did a surge of fear held her back. After her near escape from this forest she was reluctant to give shape to her magic.

The witch doctor seized upon Kyra's hesitation. Again he took a deep breath, but the magical fire he conjured was tinged a bright red and swelled to far greater size than it had before. Kyra tried to dissipate the attack, but all her counter-spell did was crackle ineffectually around the oncoming attack.

Before the blob of fire could strike Kyra, Yanir stepped in front of her. The old dryad held two tribesmen in her claws. One after the other, she threw the screaming men into the oncoming flame. The first was consumed utterly, his head and chest evaporating into a puff of smoke while the rest of his body went tumbling across the ground. The ball of fire continued on and seared into the second man, but with far less effect. His body was a scorched mass when it crashed to the earth, charred but complete. The spell's strength all but spent, it swept on through Yanir as little more than a haze of heat.

'We cannot fight that man here,' Kyra told Yanir. 'We have to get him away from the forest.'

The sylvaneth disengaged from their foes and fled through the trees. The tribesmen were after them in an instant, crying and growling like a pack of hounds.

'They came after us when you freed the twist-flesh,' Yanir said. It made sense to Kyra. The tribal priest was not without arcane abilities. He would have sensed where Kyra's spell came from.

They raced through the trees. In any other forest, the sylvaneth would have easily lost their pursuers, but here it was different. The terrain conspired against them, obstructing their flight while rendering aid to the hunters. Kyra slammed against trunks of trees she was certain had shifted their positions. Even the stealthy Nyiss stumbled over some ground roots that got under her feet.

'You must leave me,' Kyra told the dryads. 'The forest resents my escape from its possession. It wants to see me destroyed.'

'We are not leaving you,' Nyiss snapped at her. 'We set out together and we will finish this thing together.' She twisted around as a stone spear thunked into the ground beside her. 'The quick-blood will tire of the chase before we do.'

'You have to get away,' Eshia said. 'Without you how can we follow the Rootcutter?'

Kyra knew Eshia was right, and the enormity of that knowledge sent a fire of determination racing through her. She had been the one to release Ghroth. It was her obligation to see him destroyed.

The branchwraith looked at the gnarled, ugly trees. There was a way she could still use her magic. Something she would dare only in a place as profane and debased as the forest of Beastgrave.

'Upend those trees,' Kyra ordered Yanir and Nyiss, directing them to two wizened pines. She knew how gravely her command must disgust the dryads, yet they did not hesitate to obey. Seizing the two trees, they wrenched them from the earth and threw them to the ground.

The exhibition of strength was something the pursuing tribesmen had not expected. Their pursuit faltered and they fell back, grunting uncertainly to one another. They did not flee, and Kyra knew they were simply waiting for their witch doctor to catch up with them.

Kyra acted before that could happen. She opened her essence once more, letting the force of her magic spread outwards. This time her object was the two trees the dryads had knocked over. Pulled from the ground, they had only a fragmentary connection to the forest, enough that Kyra could harness them for her spells without immediately exposing herself.

The tribesmen started to advance once more. Several cast spears at the dryads, the weapons stabbing down into the earth only inches away from their targets.

Kyra replied to the spear-throwers with her own missiles. Expending some of her magic, focusing it into the fallen trees, she exploded sections of their trunks. A spray of splinters slashed into the hunters. Blazing with the arcane energies of Kyra's spell, they gashed the tribesmen, cutting their flesh and skewering their organs. Several were killed outright, collapsing as they were struck in vital spots. Others crawled away, bloodied and moaning in agony. Only a handful were left unharmed, and these backed away, their eyes wide with fright.

There should have been a complete rout in that moment, had the witch doctor not arrived. The bearskin-clad priest glowered at the carnage wrought on his people. His intense gaze swept across the dryads to focus on Kyra. The man's face pulled back in a snarl of hate.

Kyra focused her magic into the ruptured tree trunks. A second explosion of splinters went scything into the tribesmen. Several were wounded in the blast, but the one she intended to kill was still on his feet, apparently oblivious to his cuts and the blood streaming from his body.

The witch doctor stretched both his arms outwards. Kyra felt the aetheric energies swelling around him. The blood streaming from his body no longer dripped towards the ground but was pulled up, drawn outwards. It pooled together, binding itself into the semblance of a body. Flames crackled around the shape and the witch doctor made a chopping motion with his hand.

The shape charged forwards, a boiling mass of blood and fire that resembled an enraged bull. The apparition smashed through the fallen trees, shattering their trunks as it swept through them.

Kyra did not try to intercept the witch doctor's spell. She focused on the man who had conjured it into being. As the fiery bull charged through the trees, she exerted her energies into wrenching one of the branches away from the trunks. Like a javelin, the branch shot back along the path of the human's spell, hurtling along the arcane residue to impale the caster's breast.

The fiery bull evaporated, winking out of sight the instant the branch struck the witch doctor. The man clutched at the spear, his face a mix of shock and confusion. He struggled to speak, but only a blob of blood left his mouth. Strength left his legs and he crashed to the earth.

The death of their priest brought screams of horror from the tribesmen. Wounded or whole, they fled back through the forest, scrambling over each other in their haste.

'Do we pursue them?' Yanir wanted to know. She flexed her claws, letting them click against each other.

'No,' Kyra said. 'They will not bother us again. It was their priest who was a threat to us. Without him they will not come back.' She staggered as a wave of weakness swept through her. With the witch doctor's fire quenched, the forest was groping at the edges of her mind, trying to find its way back into her spirit. Nyiss caught at her and helped steady the branchwraith.

'We cannot rest,' Kyra told the dryads. 'We have to find the Rootcutter.'

'This forest will not help us,' Eshia warned. 'The trees will not speak to us.'

Kyra found bitter humour in the dryad's concern. If she lifted her protection from them, they would all find the trees only too eager to speak with them. 'We will have to find Ghroth's trail,' she said. 'We know where he entered the forest. If we start from there, Nyiss can follow his tracks.'

Nyiss gave Kyra a dubious look. 'I can follow his tracks,' she said, 'but only if they are left alone.' Unlike Eshia, she had some inkling of why this forest was so silent. She suspected the overt hostility of the forest. If the trees could block their path, they could certainly interfere with the herdchief's trail.

'We have to try,' Kyra decided. Her eyes took on a subdued glow. 'If we cannot find tracks to follow, there are ways to force the forest to tell me what we need to know.'

Kyra hoped her words sounded reassuring. Because she knew what that kind of magic would entail. She would learn where Ghroth had gone through her spells, but it would be a last resort.

If she opened herself again to Beastgrave's hideous forest, Kyra did not think she could keep it from consuming her.

CHAPTER SEVEN

Ghroth plunged into the sinister forest, finding it preferable to the crushing fingers of stone. He followed Tograh's scent in preference to that of the other escaped beastkin. He needed followers to add to his strength, not traitors he would be compelled to fight. In his weakened condition, even a hornless bray might be able to overcome him. The surge of strength that enabled him to overcome the warchief had left him utterly drained. Stubbornness alone kept him upright and moving through the trees.

There were other scents in the air beyond those of the surviving beastkin. The smell of the tribesmen was prominent and Ghroth knew there were many of them hunting through the forest, trying to find their escaped sacrifices. Other scents were those of the animals that dared dwell in this eerie forest. Some were familiar to Ghroth. Most beasts took the odour of their fodder into their scent. He could pick out the smells of deer and caribou, the fug of something similar to a boar. There were carnivorous smells as well, those of wolf and bear. The musky reek of lizard, strong enough that Ghroth was left wondering how large the reptile was that had left the odour behind.

As Ghroth trudged onwards, higher up the mountain slope, another scent reached his nose. A familiar scent, one that brought him to a halt when he smelled it. 'Sorgaas,' he muttered. So the shaman was around, slinking through the trees. He had likely been driven off when the tribesmen rushed into the forest. Ghroth could not completely begrudge the turnskin for trying to save his own hide. Though had Sorgaas fought when the humans ambushed them, perhaps there would have been no need to rescue the beastkin from the stakes.

Ghroth fingered the axe he'd claimed from the warchief. The human had chosen a good weapon for himself. It had a fine balance and Ghroth knew from experience how keenly it could cut. Still, it felt odd in his hands after the brutal orruk weapon he had carried since killing Kruksh. In his weakened state he would not have been able to swing the cleaver anyway.

Cries rang out through the forest. Ghroth listened to the shouts of tribesmen off in the distance. He could tell there were many of them. Too many to fight. Fortunately they were away to his left and somewhat below, while the scent he was following strayed up and to the right. The other ungor was still with Tograh. It was only natural that they would band together and double their chances to survive. There was no hint that any of the other beastkin had joined up with them. Then again, the noses of ungors were not as keen as those of gors. They might have failed to pick up the trail of Sorgaas and the others.

That thought gave Ghroth a troubling idea. Chagrak was free in the forest. If the bestigor should pick up his scent and follow it, there would be no better opportunity for his challenger to confront him. Already weak from his beating and still further by his fight with the warchief, Ghroth wondered if he could fight even an unarmed Chagrak.

The chieftain growled at his own fears. Worry was a luxury he could not indulge. There was nothing he could do to keep Chagrak off his trail. Either his rival would find him, or he wouldn't. If he did, all Ghroth could do was ensure he made the bestigor earn his victory.

The distant shouts of the tribesmen assumed a distinct character. Ghroth was certain the hunters had caught someone and were locked in battle. The more he listened, the more puzzled he became. Whoever the humans were fighting, it sounded like they were getting the worst of the battle. His brow knotted in bewilderment as the smell of smoke reached him. Were the tribesmen so confounded by their enemies they had resorted to burning the forest? He did not think a few stray ungors could provoke such desperation. Sorgaas might, but the shaman's scent was up here, not down with the fighting.

Whatever had confronted the hunters, Ghroth was thankful for it. If they were occupied with another enemy they would not be able to focus on him. If things went well, he might even find his way inside the mountain before they had the chance to look for his trail.

Ghroth rested beside one of the trees and closed his eyes. He clawed through the corridors of memory to see again the vision that had drawn him to Beastgrave. He fixated on one moment, trying to draw it into complete clarity. The cave he had seen himself entering. The opening that would lead him deep inside the mountain. He tried to recall little details, anything that might suggest where on the slopes the entrance might be.

The sound of a stick snapping broke Ghroth from his recollections. He sprang away from the tree an instant before a spear gouged the trunk. He spun around and brought his axe up, but before he could swing he was thrown back by the kick of a cloven hoof. Sprawling on the ground, Ghroth looked up at his attacker.

'Ghroth slow,' Chagrak snarled at him. 'Ghroth weak. Too weak stop Chagrak.' The bestigor lunged at him with the spear he had stolen from some tribesman. The stone head scraped across the herdchief's ribs as he tried to roll away from it.

Chagrak gnashed his fangs at Ghroth and stamped down on his arm, keeping him from swinging his axe or rolling away. The bestigor drew the spear up, ready to drive it down into his victim's chest. 'Ghroth die now.'

Before the spear could come stabbing downwards, a feral shape lunged at Chagrak. He was sent sprawling as a multitude of clawed feet tore at him and swinish jaws clamped tight around his throat. Dark blood spurted from the bestigor's neck as he struggled to free himself from his attacker.

Ghroth looked on, baffled by the sudden change of events. Chagrak was being mauled by Frang. Simple in its mentality, the beasthound had sought its adopted master after escaping into the forest. Chagrak had used Frang to track Ghroth, unaware that it had been the herdchief who had rescued it from the stake. The beasthound was not so mindless that it failed to remember who had helped it. When Chagrak attacked Ghroth, Frang had been forced to choose which side to take.

Chagrak pushed up against one of the trees, pressing Frang against it and using his greater weight to crush the beasthound. Its claws lost their grip as pain shot through its body. The bestigor locked his hands around the boar-like head worrying at his throat. Slowly he pried the jaws open and freed himself.

Chagrak scrambled away. He snatched up his fallen spear and made ready to impale the stunned Frang. Before he could, the cold steel of an axe chopped down into his skull. The stricken bestigor stumbled and turned. There was a dull emptiness in his eyes as he watched Ghroth raise the axe for a second blow.

Ghroth wasted no words on his rival. The axe came flashing down, crunching between the bestigor's horns. Chagrak crumpled under the blow, his body pitching backwards to land beside Frang. Ghroth looked over at the beasthound and down at Chagrak's body.

'Eat now,' he told Frang. 'Chagrak big. Meat for both Ghroth and Frang.'

Ghroth felt some measure of strength in his body after he had eaten. His last meal had been back in the jungle. The tribesmen had not bothered to feed their captives. From the way Frang gorged itself, he judged that it had been at least as long since the beasthound had been fed. By the time they had both got their fill there was not much left of Chagrak. What little was still fit to eat was tied in a little bundle slung over Ghroth's back.

Frang took up Tograh's trail when Ghroth decided it was time to move along. The sounds of combat and the smell of smoke had diminished in the interim. That could mean the tribesmen had settled their fight and were looking for the beastkin. If they were, Ghroth did not intend to give them an easy hunt.

The density of the forest grew less as they continued to follow the trail. Ghroth judged they must be angling back towards the bare rock face over the cliffs. An anxious whine from Frang reinforced that possibility. The beasthound could smell the blood of the sacrificed beastkin. It took some coaxing to get it to continue along the trail.

The beasthound stopped abruptly and pawed at the ground. Ghroth stepped forwards and brushed away the soil. He soon found himself looking at a skull and the corroded remains of armour. The armour might have been iron at one time, but the skull was too thick and bulky for a human. One of the beard-jaws? The bones were too old to have any distinct scent, so Ghroth could not be certain. Shifting the dirt around, he found a dagger that had miraculously defied the ravages of time. He studied its bright metal and tested the sharpness of its blade. With a grunt of appreciation, he tucked the weapon under his belt and waved Frang away from the grave.

As the trail snaked around the last of the trees, Frang found more remains just under the surface. Indifferent before, now Ghroth took interest in the skeletons the beasthound unearthed. The herd-chief was beginning to wonder if he was the first to come to the mountain seeking the godbeast's grave and the power there. Surely a relic of such awesome might would have others looking for it. The sheer variety of bones littered about the slope convinced him it was so. The skulls of grots and ogors, bodies of humans and rat-kin – each find made him more determined to press on.

Gradually, as the trees thinned out still further and the terrain gave way to a sparse scattering of bushes and great jumbles of stone, Ghroth felt a sense of familiarity to his surroundings. Nothing so distinct as to make him certain. It was more nebulous than that, an idea that if he could just gain the right vantage, everything would fall into place. So strong did that inclination grow that he started to backtrack and circle the area.

It was as he turned past an outcropping of stone, which had the rough semblance of a jumping fox, that Ghroth saw the place from his vision. The way the rocks lay, the trees off to one side, the scattered bushes with their scraggly branches – all of it matched the image he had beheld in the flames. There, below him, he knew he would find the cave. His way down inside the mountain.

The moment Ghroth came to this realisation, the scent he had been following shifted. No longer was the smell of Tograh coming from ahead of him. The ungor's scent came from behind.

Clenching his fist tight around his axe, Ghroth spun around. Near the base of the fox-rock he saw Tograh and the other ungor. He saw someone else as well, someone whose scent only now came to him.

Sorgaas lifted his arms and gestured with his bray-staff. 'You are on the threshold of your destiny, mighty Ghroth. Surely you will not turn back.'

Sorgaas enjoyed Ghroth's confusion. It would be too complicated to explain to the herdchief the spell he had cast over him. The shaman had never faltered in his belief that Ghroth knew more details from his vision than he was capable of relating. There were things in his memory that were obscure to his consciousness, but they were there just the same. All that was needed was the proper coaxing to make them manifest.

He had found the two ungors after their escape. They had credited Sorgaas with freeing them from the stakes, a misconception he did not intend to contradict. It worried him that someone else had used magic to save the beastkin. It meant there was another sorcerer who saw the potential in using Ghroth to guide them down inside Beastgrave. Sorgaas had been content to leave the warherd to their fate and seek the path on his own, but now that there was someone else involved in the hunt he was not willing to take that risk. He needed the quickest way to the slumbering godbeast. Ghroth's memories were that way.

Projecting the scent of the ungors Tograh and Vuluk ahead of Ghroth acted as a focus to distract his mind while drawing out the obscured memories to truly guide him. Of course, Sorgaas was nearly too clever for his own purposes. Chagrak's attack had been an unanticipated complication, fortunately one that had not ended in disaster.

'This is the goal you have come so far to find,' Sorgaas said. He kept his voice low and even, letting his tone unravel the magic he had cast upon Ghroth.

'Sorgaas find cave first?' Ghroth wanted to know. He still maintained a wary grip on his axe.

The shaman shook his head. 'This is your destiny. Only you know the way. It was our place to follow you.'

'Sorgaas use magic save Ghroth?'

'I put myself at great risk,' Sorgaas told him. 'The magic of the witch doctor was very strong, but I could not forsake my chieftain.'

The glib reply appeared to satisfy Ghroth. He lowered his axe and walked towards Sorgaas. 'Ghroth become beastlord. Make Sorgaas greatest bray-shaman.' He grunted and stamped his hoof. 'Sorgaas chief all shamans.'

Sorgaas simply bowed at the vapid promise. Ghroth had no understanding of the ways of magic or of those who communed with the Dark Gods. Greatness among such was not a matter of appointments by lords and kings, but a measure of ability, knowledge and power. True power. The kind of power that was invested in the spirit of the one who possessed it, not in the mindless masses at their command.

'I am honoured.' Sorgaas was certain the sarcasm was unnoticed by Ghroth. The herdchief simply nodded and waved towards the ungors.

'No more?' Ghroth asked.

'Tograh and Vuluk were the only ones who escaped from the hunters,' Sograas claimed. 'I found them and kept them with me while we looked for you.'

Ghroth scratched his ear as he listened to the explanation. He was already forgetting that it was the scent of the ungors that he had followed here. In a few hours even that scrap of doubt would be gone.

'Frang find Ghroth,' the herdchief said. 'Chagrak also find Ghroth.' He swung the bundle of meat off his back and let the other beastkin draw its scent into their noses. A crude but effective way of telling them the challenger had failed to kill him and a stark warning to anyone with similar ideas.

The morbid display had a note of ridiculousness about it, at least from the shaman's point of view. Ghroth was on his last legs. His struggles with Chagrak, his abuse by the tribesmen, his fight with their warchief, the flight through the forest and across the mountain – all of these had taxed Ghroth to the limit of endurance. Sorgaas could tell there was nothing left but bluster. Frang could still put up a fight, but not Ghroth. The way he was now, even one of the ungors could finish him off.

Sorgaas set the temptation aside. He was thinking of the magic that had freed the beastkin. He could not take any chances with Ghroth. It was a race, a contest between Sorgaas and whoever had rescued the herdchief. With Ghroth under his influence, the shaman held an advantage over his unknown competitor. Whatever his feelings, he had to maintain that advantage.

'You have endured much,' Sorgaas told Ghroth. 'You must allow me to bind your wounds and heal your hurts. You must be strong when you descend inside the mountain.'

With his encouragement, Ghroth sat down at the base of the fox-rock. When he was settled, Sorgaas barked orders to Tograh and Vuluk, explaining to them the roots and tubers he wanted them to find.

'I will make a salve for your cuts,' Sorgaas explained. 'Then make a broth to make you strong again.' He tapped the bundle of meat. 'I will use this. You will drink and add Chagrak's strength to your own.'

Ghroth grumbled in protest. 'Ghroth already strong. Stronger than Chagrak.'

Sorgaas detected the faintest suggestion of doubt in the herdchief's voice. He noticed Ghroth glance towards Frang. It wasn't necessary to evoke a divination spell to tell that however Chagrak was defeated, the beasthound had played some kind of role. Ghroth wasn't so confident in his unconquerable strength as he had been.

That, Sorgaas decided, was something that could prove very useful to him.

Nyiss found Ghroth's trail easily enough. 'He is not trying to hide his tracks. Either he does not think anyone will pursue him or he does not care if they do.'

Kyra pondered the dryad's report. 'I doubt the Rootcutter surrendered to the tribesmen without a fight. He may even have had to fight when he was freed.' The last impression she had when she directed the roots to free the beastkin had been some of the tribesmen charging towards the stakes.

'If he is injured he should be easy to follow,' Yanir said. 'Easy to deal with when we do find him.'

The sylvaneth were just inside the forest, near where the tendrils of stone had emerged from the cliff. Everything was quiet. The rocky projections had swept away the stakes and the bodies. Terror at the death of their witch doctor had sent the rest of the tribesmen fleeing back to their village. Even the malignance of the forest felt like it had drawn back into itself.

'He has to be left at liberty until he has led us to the godbeast's tomb,' Kyra cautioned Yanir.

The old dryad's mouth twisted into a scowl. 'It is dangerous to toy with him,' she said. 'If the quick-bloods had overcome us after you set the Rootcutter free, what would have happened?'

'What good does it do to kill the Rootcutter but leave this terrible power for another to find?' Eshia responded. 'Kyra has been given a warning this time, but what if there is no warning when another enemy–'

'We know this enemy is real,' Yanir interrupted. 'Let us settle him and have done with it. The risk is too great to do otherwise.'

Kyra appreciated Yanir's position, as far as it went. 'The Sylvan Conclave charged us with not only stopping Ghroth but ending the threat of another like him. To do that we have to find the godbeast and destroy its heart.' She gestured at Beastgrave's peak. 'The mountain is vast. Without anything to guide us, we might spend years wandering inside it seeking the godbeast's grave. And while we are looking, some other enemy, some new threat to the Thornwyld, could lay claim to it. No, we have to keep following the Rootcutter.'

'Your choice will either save Thornwyld or betray it. I hope you understand that.'

The branchwraith's branches quivered at the damning words. They expressed perfectly the awful burden Kyra carried. 'Let us do all we can to ensure we are saviours,' she told Yanir. She rested her hand on the dryad's shoulder. 'I need your help. If we have any chance at all...'

'I have said what needed to be said.' Yanir gestured at the tracks. 'You can follow only so long before the race is lost. How will you know when it is too soon to act and when it is too late?'

Kyra was saved from trying to answer Yanir when Nyiss suddenly called out from further up the slope. 'Someone has either joined the Rootcutter or else is following him,' Nyiss said. 'More twist-flesh. The beasthound that escaped the Thornwyld and one other.'

'It will be a harder fight when we find him,' Yanir stated.

'Maybe not,' Kyra said, anxiety in her tone. 'We have seen enough to know Ghroth has enemies among the twist-flesh. It could be one of his rivals following him. If the Rootcutter were to be killed, our task would be more difficult.'

'Difficult, but clear,' Yanir said. 'There would be no question of what to do, or when.'

'Only where,' Kyra told Yanir. 'And that is a question we might never find an answer to without Ghroth.'

Nyiss followed the tracks higher up the slope. She pointed out to the others where the prints of more beastkin appeared. None of them merged with Ghroth's trail, only that of the beasthound and its companion. They kept on with the Rootcutter's trail until the sylvaneth found a scene of violence – a heap of bloodied bones lay strewn about the trees. The admixture of human and animal characteristics made it clear these were the remains of a twist-flesh.

'It is not him,' Nyiss told Kyra. She indicated the tracks moving away from the carnage. 'He left here with the beasthound.' She turned back to the pile of bones. 'Whether that was a friend or an enemy, the Rootcutter decided to make a meal of it.'

'A reminder of what we are fighting,' Eshia said.

Looking at the young dryad, it was impressed on Kyra the stark difference between the sylvaneth and the beastkin. Eshia had given up her own arm to save her companions. Ghroth had devoured one of his companions to satiate his hunger.

'And why we must win,' Kyra said. She motioned for Nyiss to take up the trail again.

The tracks led steadily upwards, winding through the forest and out towards the rocks above the sacrificial cliffs. Nyiss found further signs of other beastkin, but again the creatures made no effort to join Ghroth and the beasthound. It was only when the trail started to circle around a barren, boulder-strewn part of the slope that all of the tracks finally began to converge.

'We must be especially wary,' Nyiss told the others. 'These tracks are very recent. The twist-flesh must be nearby.'

Kyra glanced about the landscape, trying to spot anything that looked familiar. Anything she might have remembered from her vision. Finally her eyes strayed to a fox-shaped outcropping. 'I have seen that before. It was part of my premonition. This is where the Rootcutter was heading.'

'The tracks are very new,' Nyiss repeated. 'I have found five distinct prints. The pattern is a bit muddled, but all of them lead towards that stone.'

The dryads looked expectantly at Kyra. It was the branchwraith's decision. Did they stay back and wait to follow the Rootcutter down inside the mountain, or did they attack now, before he had a chance to descend into Beastgrave?

Kyra pictured the twist-flesh gathered on the far side of the rock, plotting their savage evil. Maybe Yanir was right. Maybe it was too great a risk to leave Ghroth free. Maybe the best thing to do was destroy him now and take their chances finding the relic without him.

The branchwraith trembled as the enormity of her choice swept through her. The consequences she had to balance against each other. The weight of her responsibility.

The sylvaneth approached the outcropping from opposite sides. Kyra was troubled by their lack of precise knowledge about where the twist-flesh were, but Nyiss said it was impossible to find a good vantage to spy down on the fox-shaped rock. Trying to draw information from the few trees in the vicinity was something the branchwraith did not want to risk. This close to the enemy, she did not need to be fighting an internal battle against the forest's influence.

Kyra's intention was to dispose of the beastkin who had joined Ghroth. If the sylvaneth could spring a sudden and overwhelming attack, they could dispatch the Rootcutter's allies before they were able to retaliate. Such a sudden reversal, she hoped, would panic Ghroth, and where more natural for him to flee to than the place that promised him a mighty power?

Yanir and Nyiss circled the outcropping from the left, moving cautiously among the rocks. Nyiss' bark shifted colours to blend in with the rocks, but the effect was less successful than it was when she was in foliage. Yanir followed some distance behind the other dryad with the idea that if anyone was watching they would focus on her and miss Nyiss' approach.

Kyra kept Eshia with her. They came at the outcropping from the right, moving along a sheer drop. By rights it was an impossible climb, but by sinking their toe-roots into the ground they were able to create support for themselves where none should be. It was doubtful the twist-flesh would expect enemies to set upon them from this quarter. With Eshia's infirmity and her limited magic, Kyra felt surprise even more essential to their attack. They would need to strike hard and fast, allowing their foes no chance to answer their challenge.

Inch by inch, Kyra and Eshia advanced. Closing in upon the outcropping, they lost sight of Nyiss and Yanir. Kyra kept her ears sharp for the first note of battle, the merest murmur from the enemy that the dryads had been spotted. All remained silent, and she dared to hope that fortune had favoured their boldness.

Finally they were beside the outcropping. In a single effort, Kyra and Eshia drew in their toe-roots and sprang over the ledge. They wheeled around the rock, ready to set upon the twist-flesh with their thorny claws.

Instead of foes, they found only a disappointed Yanir pacing like a hungry panther and Nyiss inspecting the ground. She looked up when she heard Kyra and Eshia coming towards her.

'The Rootcutter was here,' Nyiss said. She lifted a gnawed bone off the ground. 'The bite marks on this bone are the same as those we found before.' She pointed down at the dirt and indicated a set of hoofprints. 'These are his, and I've also found clawmarks from the beasthound.'

Kyra felt a sickness worse than anything inflicted on her by Beastgrave's forest roiling up within her. They had lost Ghroth. He had slipped through their fingers even as they closed around him. Bitterly she recalled Yanir's words. That they would either be the saviours of Thornwyld, or its betrayers. She could have let the Rootcutter die. Whatever he did, it would be her fault.

'How could he get away?' Eshia asked. 'We were so close. He could not have passed us going down and we would have seen him if he tried to go up the mountain.'

Nyiss indicated the tracks scattered all around the rock. 'There were five of them here,' she said. 'The Rootcutter, the beasthound, two of the smaller beastkin and another one with broad hooves.' She studied the marks on the ground. 'One of them was lying here for some time. Wounded, judging by the traces of blood. It may have been Ghroth. The others could have been tending his injuries.'

'But where did they go?' Kyra needed to know the answer to that question. What the beastkin had been doing, how long they had lingered here – none of that mattered if the sylvaneth didn't learn where they had gone. Kyra turned to the gnarled forest. If she was careful she might be able to open herself to it, try to learn from the trees if Ghroth had in some way continued to ascend Beastgrave.

'Everything we need to know is here in the tracks,' Nyiss told Kyra, guessing what the branchwraith was planning. 'We only have to look and try to see.'

Yanir raked her claws against a nearby rock. 'You will never make sense of that muddle,' she told Nyiss. 'A drunken gargant could have made no more confusing a mess.'

Nyiss scowled at the old dryad. 'There is nothing lost by trying.'

'Only time,' Yanir retorted.

'Stop it!' Eshia yelled at the arguing dryads. 'The only hope we still have is to stick together.'

A thought came to Kyra when she heard Eshia's plea. 'No,' she said. 'The problem is they are all together. That makes them confused. Alone is what we need.'

The dryads looked at her in bewilderment. Kyra explained what she meant. 'The tracks make no sense because they are all jumbled together. By accident or design, they are confused.' She pressed her hand to her left eye. Carefully she drew out a long thread of glowing moss from the wooden depths of her face. 'Nyiss, show me which are the tracks of the Rootcutter.'

Nyiss jabbed her finger at the hoofprints left by Ghroth. Kyra leaned above them and dropped the luminous thread into the track. A low chant rose from her as she called upon her magic. She would not harness the morbid influence of the forest to cast her spell. She would use a strand of her own essence.

The moss glowed bright in the hoofprint. A similar glow pulsated up from a second track. A third became illuminated and still a fourth. The sylvaneth watched as one after another the tracks of Ghroth were picked out from the confusion on the ground. As each print blazed with light, it appeared as if a ghost were prowling around the rock. Following each light, they saw the path Ghroth had taken.

'The tracks vanish into the rocks,' Yanir marvelled. Indeed, the glowing prints, after wandering around the area, set off towards the piles of boulders facing the outcropping.

Kyra drew back from her spell and, as the magical energy returned to her, the light around the tracks vanished. It took a moment for her to recover from the conjuration and rekindle the light in her eye. When she did, she walked warily towards the boulders. She waved her hand before them and detected the aura of an enchantment.

'Something has been hidden here,' Kyra informed her companions. 'Let us find out what it is. Be ready in case something is waiting for us behind the illusion.'

Drawing upon her power once more, Kyra focused a counter-spell upon the illusion. She was surprised by the enchantment's lack of resistance. It dissipated the instant she turned her attention to it.

'That is where they went,' Eshia gasped.

What had been hidden by the illusory boulders was the black mouth of a cave. The opening was wide and deep, large enough that a troggoth could have easily lumbered inside with room to spare. A clammy, somehow oily cold wafted up from the shadowy interior, suggesting dark depths and vast caverns. Piled at the very limit of where the light reached was a heap of fleshless skulls. Kyra recognised those of humans, orruks, duardin and even aelves. Others bore no resemblance to anything in her experience. Whatever they were, the meaning of the heap was obvious. It was a warning.

A warning the sylvaneth were going to ignore. Kyra turned and motioned to Nyiss. 'This is where Ghroth has gone. He has plunged inside the mountain to find the grave of the godbeast. We will follow his trail. The Rootcutter cannot be allowed to gain the power he seeks.'

CHAPTER EIGHT

The cold dark of the cave rushed through Ghroth as he marched deeper inside the mountain. There was a dank smell to the air, of sunless lands and ancient worlds. His fur bristled with each breath, recoiling from the old evil he drew air down into his lungs. But whatever horror he felt as he plunged through the blackness, it did not reach into his mind. The only thing Ghroth could think of was the destiny that awaited him somewhere down in the bowels of Beastgrave.

'Something is wrong with these walls,' Sorgaas warned Ghroth. The shaman was following a short distance behind Ghroth, the butt of his staff tapping against the floor as he walked. He was clinging to it a bit more than was usual and there was a kind of rasping when he breathed. The herdchief knew Sorgaas had used magic to speed the healing properties of the poultices he had used to heal his injuries. Ghroth even wondered if the poultices had done anything at all except serve as a mask behind which the extent of his sorcery could be hidden.

Ghroth decided to try to test that idea. He felt strong, stronger than he had since leaving the jungle. It was time to see how strong Sorgaas was.

'Turnskin fear,' Ghroth snorted. 'Jump from shadows.' The derisive note brought amused grunts from the two ungors prowling a short distance ahead of their herdchief. Frang, scouting well ahead of the rest, came trotting back down the tunnel, drawn by the sound of Ghroth's voice.

Sorgaas glared at Ghroth, but did not say anything. The herdchief decided to push him further. 'Fear dark,' he sneered at him. 'Want run back to forest.' He tapped his hoof against the stone floor, mimicking the sound of the bray-staff. 'Want limp back to forest.'

The taunts made the shaman's lips curl back, exposing his long fangs. 'Do not provoke me,' he warned. He gestured with his staff at the walls. 'There is something not right here. Something I did not expect.'

Ghroth smelled the trace of fear in Sorgaas' scent. Whatever else the shaman might say, he *was* afraid. 'Sorgaas expect daylight in cave,' Ghroth goaded him. Tograh and Vuluk laughed. Frang simply settled down on its haunches, a wary look on its porcine face.

Sorgaas took the bait. Pulling back to his full height, the shaman stamped his bray-staff against the floor. The dim illumination provided by luminous moss clinging to the roof was washed away as a bright green glow swirled around the head of his staff.

'This is what the darkness hides,' Sorgaas snarled, and pointed his clawed hand at the wall.

The two ungors whined in fright and covered their eyes with their hands. Frang let loose a mournful howl and cringed against Ghroth's leg. The herdchief himself felt cold terror pulse through him as he looked on what the shaman's light revealed.

The wall was composed of weird angles that the light from the moss had scarcely even suggested. Parts of it seemed to be both recessed and protruding at the same time, altering their aspect the moment the eye ceased to focus on them. The stone itself – if stone it could truly be called – was an eerie deep green with veins of brightly coloured crystals slashing through it. There were markings as well, strange symbols that marched from top to bottom in waving lines. They looked like ants or termites filing away in measured ranks. Each character was painted with a dark pigment that appeared to bleed into the stone itself, visibly sinking into the wall despite the opacity of the surface.

None of this provoked a reaction from Ghroth. It was the other irregularities that met his gaze. There were larger shapes on – or in – the wall. He saw the body of a beard-jaw warrior as big and vivid as life – the long crest of hair that rose from his otherwise bare scalp, the crimson tattoos that circled his limbs, the enormous axe that was clenched in his fists, the stout chains banded around his arms. It was all there, and as he watched, the bearded warrior moved. Not outwards, away from the wall, nor forwards across the wall. There was motion, legs pumping, arms flexing, mouth open in a silent yell, but there was no movement. The axe-swinging fighter remained precisely where Ghroth had spotted him and none of his actions moved him so much as an inch from where he was. When Ghroth looked away and back again, the beard-jaw returned to its original pose and went through the same pattern of motions as before.

'There are others,' Sorgaas said. This time a sneer was in his voice. He pointed at a spot on the opposite wall where an armoured knight stood, the mask of his helm cast in a menacing scowl. The warrior was huge, a head taller than even Ghroth, but his great size did not make him any less a facet of the wall. He swung his mace in vicious arcs, trying to batter through some barrier, but only while the herd-chief was watching. As with the beard-jaw, when he looked away and back again, the knight simply repeated the same pattern.

'Magic old and horrible,' Sorgaas stated. 'Reflections of life, or life in reflections.' He nodded at a hunched, rat-faced creature a little distance further along the passage. When Ghroth looked, the ratman curled itself into a trembling ball of fur and fangs, its ears twitching back and forth.

'Do not look too long,' Sorgaas told Ghroth. 'Let your gaze linger and your image may join them.'

Ghroth felt the challenge in the shaman's tone. He refused to be cowed by Sorgaas. He also was not bold enough to accept the challenge. He stomped forwards and closed his hand around the illuminated head of the bray-staff, returning the tunnel to near darkness.

'Dark better,' Ghroth said. He locked eyes with Sorgaas. A contest of dominance. It was the shaman who blinked first.

'You are right.' Sorgaas snapped his fingers and the light vanished entirely. The weird walls with their strange script and living images returned to the shadows. 'There are times when what you don't see can't hurt you.'

Ghroth grunted and removed his hand from the bray-staff. The ungors and Frang still smelled of fear. He would show them that he was not afraid. 'Light stupid. Show everyone warherd here.'

Sorgaas bowed his head. 'Of course,' he muttered. 'How foolish of me.'

Ghroth doubted the shaman's contrition. Sorgaas was crafty. The whole scene might have been arranged by him, to show the others the strange magic of this place and convince them they needed his protection from that magic. If the herdchief was not convinced they *did* need that protection, he would end his misgivings by splitting the shaman's skull with his axe.

No, Ghroth decided, the fear was real. Sorgaas was uneasy around these walls. That meant there was good reason to be far away from them. He did not know how it was possible for the creatures they had seen to be drawn into or onto the stone, but he was happy not to know.

'We go,' Ghroth said. He kicked Frang away from his leg and motioned for the beasthound to move out ahead of the other beastkin. Tograh and Vuluk did not need any encouragement. Sorgaas was tapping his staff against the floor.

'We go,' Ghroth repeated.

Sorgaas looked up, a grin on his lupine face. 'Someone may be following us,' he said. He continued tapping the floor with his staff, inching his way across the tunnel. 'If so, I want to dissuade them from continuing such foolishness.' The staff was leaving little marks on the ground. They formed a line that stretched almost from one side to the other. Almost, because at either end there was a little gap. A space around which someone could squeeze if they pushed up against the walls.

The shaman stopped tapping and stepped across the line he had made. As he did, there was a faint flicker of green light along the floor. 'There. It is done.'

Ghroth stared at Sorgaas' handiwork and put a question to the shaman. 'Who follow?' he demanded.

'Does it matter?' Sorgaas replied. He tapped his clawed hand against the talismans hanging from his horn. 'Someone or no one, they will regret taking up our trail.'

The herdchief growled in agreement, but he did not think this was an idle precaution by Sorgaas. To Ghroth it appeared the shaman expected someone to be following them.

What was more, Ghroth suspected Sorgaas knew precisely *who* was following them.

Sorgaas took some petty pleasure in observing Ghroth as the chieftain ambled further down the tunnel. He was striving so hard to comprehend things far beyond his mental acuity. Failing, he tried to make a show of his courage and impress upon his followers that he was not afraid. That might work with the dim-witted ungors and Frang, but Sorgaas was not deceived.

The shaman tried to keep from looking at the tunnel walls. Ghroth might truly be able to dismiss from his savage brain things for which he had no understanding, but Sorgaas was not comfortable marching beside the inscrutable. That there was some manner of malevolent magic at work on or within the walls, he was in no doubt. The nature of that enchantment, how exactly it worked and how it was evoked were mysteries to him. It might be something to do with the curious angles in which the stone was shaped or the ant-line columns of symbols cut into the rock. Maybe both of them in conjunction produced the effect. Then again, they might have nothing at all to do with the spell laid on this tunnel long ago.

Whatever the facts, the trap he had left behind the beastkin would be interesting. Their pursuers would be given a good chance to discover what secrets the walls held.

Sorgaas knew they were being followed. Ghroth and the others had been freed by some kind of magic. It was useful to let the beastkin think he had engineered their escape, but he knew the spells had been the work of someone else. If he needed any further proof, it had come to him while tending Ghroth by the outcropping. He had sensed the presence of another sorcerer nearby. The witch doctor from the village or some other. Whoever they were, it was obvious to him they were following Ghroth. Fortunately, he had been able to impress on the chieftain the need for urgency without revealing any of the details. Restored by a bit more of his magic than Sorgaas was comfortable expending, Ghroth led them straight to the illusory boulders, the rocks he insisted should not be there according to his vision.

The cave was there, behind the illusion, along with a tunnel that led from the back of the cave. Sorgaas was still troubled by

the veil of enchantment that concealed the opening. On the surface, it had a simple dweomer, yet a moment of scrutiny with his
arcane sense and it took on a primal quality of age and power. He
did not like to contemplate what manner of being could cast such
a spell. It was like considering the fabric of the gods themselves.

Sorgaas shifted his attention away from the cave and the tunnel
and whoever was pursuing them. His immediate concern was
here and now, to follow Ghroth through the depths of the mountain and find the slumbering godbeast.

The shaman tapped his staff against the floor and listened to
the cadence of its echo. Quick and loud meant they were closely
bound by walls. Slow and faint would mean they were in some
larger cavern. It was a mile down into the mountain before the
echoes changed from fast to slow. Since the others did not notice
the change, Sorgaas decided to make it known to Ghroth.

'The tunnel widens here,' Sorgaas informed the herdchief.

Ghroth motioned him to be quiet and tapped the side of his
nose. Sorgaas was a turnskin and while he was able to discern the
presence of a sorcerer far more readily than the beastkin, their
facility with scents far surpassed his own. When Ghroth pointed
ahead of them and to the right, Sorgaas turned in that direction.

'Light,' the herdchief said.

Sorgaas hissed the incantation, funnelling the heavy aether
through his body and into the head of his staff. A bright light
expanded outwards. In its glow, the area ahead of the beastkin
was illuminated.

The eerie walls of the tunnel were gone, replaced by much
rougher masses of stone and earth. There were a few patches of
luminous moss on the roof which shone even brighter in the light
of Sorgaas' spell. A pool of dark water lay ahead of them, but to
the right, where Ghroth had directed his light, was a wide crack
in the wall, a cave in the side of the cavernous expanse. Sorgaas

noticed that there were bones and weapons scattered around the opening, but they barely registered with him when he looked on the hulking creature that stood at the mouth of the cave.

It was enormous. Twice as tall as the shaman and nearly as wide. It had a leathery, pale grey skin. The shoulders, top of the head and backs of the arms were covered in thicker scales that had a deep-blue colour. The creature's arms were long and powerful, hanging well past the knees of its massive legs. The head jutted outward from the sprawl of its shoulders, the merest stump of a neck supporting it. Huge ears drooped from the sides of the compressed skull, their lobes tattered. The face was dominated by a bulbous nose, to either side of which a yellow eye stared. The jaw beneath the nose jutted forwards, big tusks pressing over the upper lip. The mouth itself was a great gash that stretched from ear to ear.

The brute stared at the beastkin, gawping at them in dismay. Its sluggish wits reacted to the sting of the same light that let it see the warherd. Belatedly it brought its arm up to shield its eyes while a pain-filled groan rumbled from its cavernous mouth.

'Troggoth,' Ghroth cursed. He clenched his axe tight and snarled at the other beastkin, 'Kill! Kill while it blind.'

Uttering their feral war-whoops, the ungors rushed the scaly monster. Vuluk's stone axe fragmented as he struck the troggoth's belly. The spear Tograh carried fared a little better, punching a hole in the brute's side. When he drew the weapon away, blood flowed from the wound, but before he could stab the creature again, the flesh around the injury was stretched outwards to close the cut.

Frang sank its fangs into the troggoth's leg, worrying at its calf. The beasthound's muzzle was soon damp with the brute's blood. Ghroth brought his axe down into the monster's chest, tearing a ragged gash before he wrenched the steel blade free.

Throughout the attack, the troggoth uttered no sound, either of pain or anger. It brought its arm away from its eyes and swatted at Tograh, forcing the ungor to keep his distance. The monster turned. With Frang still gnawing at its leg, the beast started picking through the litter at the mouth of its cave.

Sorgaas did not know what the brute was looking for, but he didn't want to give it the chance to find it. He shifted his staff around, spinning it behind the creature's back, before he pointed the butt-end at the troggoth. The incantation that dripped from his lupine muzzle sent a flash of fire shooting from the staff and into the monster's scaly back. Smoke bubbled up from the blackened flesh and a trickle of burned meat dripped from the wound.

The troggoth was not slow to appreciate the hurt Sorgaas dealt to it. The brute's head swung around and it fixed him with an angry stare. There was no dull vacancy there now – there was violent purpose. Its gash-like mouth opened with a booming roar. The hand still fumbling about in the piled bones shook itself free and raised a huge stone club. The troggoth brought its weapon smacking down against the ground and pounded a divot in the rock.

'Kill,' Ghroth shouted to his warriors. 'Kill troggoth.' He charged back at the monster as it started for Sorgaas. Attacking the brute from the side, Ghroth's axe raked down the darker scales until it caught on the charred wound from the shaman's spell. The edge of the axe ripped the wound still wider and brought a pained screech from the creature.

Ghroth jumped aside as the troggoth's club swung for him. The blow might have connected had Frang not chosen that moment to release the creature's leg and spring at its arm. The beasthound's fangs stabbed into the monster's wrist, the claws of its legs scratching at its forearm. The troggoth tried to shake Frang loose while its free hand swiped at the ungors to keep them away. Ghroth ducked under the brute's guard to slash at its ribs. The axe bit deep, but even as it was pulled away, the wound regenerated.

'Keep back,' Sorgaas shouted. He did not wait to see if the beast-kin would heed his warning but sent another lance of arcane fire searing into the troggoth. This time his magic struck the brute in its chest, just where it was beginning to close the initial wound Ghroth had dealt it. The flame burned through the grey hide. Smoke rose from the resulting hole, a steam of boiled blood and molten flesh.

The troggoth turned from Ghroth and faced Sorgaas once more. It opened its mouth and spewed a gout of green sludge at the shaman. Ill-aimed, the vomit splashed on the floor several feet away from him. The acidic goo bubbled on the ground, chewing into the rock.

Sorgaas hastily readied another spell as the troggoth's gut heaved and the brute tried to spit another blob of acid at him. This time, when the goo erupted from its mouth, an unseen barrier of arcane energy sent it splashing back into the monster's face. The tough, scaly hide did not suffer from exposure to the acid, but the yellow eyes were not so protected. The troggoth wailed in agony as its own vomit dissolved the vulnerable organs.

'It is blind again,' Sorgaas called out. 'Attack! Attack!'

Tograh lunged at the monster from the side, jabbing the spear between its ribs. Vuluk grabbed an old sword from the pile of bones and hacked away at the troggoth's knee. Frang shifted its weight and the beasthound pulled a long ribbon of flesh away from the brute's arm.

Ghroth came at the monster from behind, determined to get at the spot Sorgaas had initially struck. He leapt onto the brute's back and clamped an arm around its stumpy neck. The troggoth spun around, flailing with its unencumbered arm as it tried to knock the herdchief free. The attempt was useless. Ghroth's axe came hurtling down into the charred wound, each blow striking deeper and deeper into the monster's flesh. Ribs snapped under the chieftain's strikes, shorn by the cleaving blade. Finally a wet, pulsating mass of black tissue was exposed. Ghroth swung one last time. The organ ruptured under his stroke.

The troggoth stumbled on for several moments, its motions increasingly clumsy. The monster's body was reluctant to acknowledge the cleaving of its heart. Only gradually did death steal across its immense frame. The clumsy swings of its arms and the stumbling stamp of its feet became slower and slower until finally they stopped entirely. The troggoth's mouth dropped open in a confused groan and its massive body slammed against the floor with a dolorous echo.

Sorgaas walked towards the monster. At the same time, the ungors backed away from it, uncertain if it would rise again. The shaman gave them a toothy grin. 'Even now its body is regenerating its wounds,' he told them. He laughed at the horror in their eyes, redressing in part their amusement over his uneasiness in the tunnel. 'It will be many days before the troggoth can revive itself from such grievous injuries.'

Ghroth stared at the shaman from atop the monster's back. 'What if Ghroth take head?' he wanted to know, his axe poised for just such a deed.

'It might grow a new one,' Sorgaas told him. 'Or the severed head might generate a new body for itself. Both could happen and there would be two troggoths.' He saw that last possibility was a bit more than Ghroth wanted to think about. The herdchief lowered his axe and climbed down off the monster's back.

The shaman watched Ghroth studying the scorched wound. He could picture the thoughts running through the beastman's mind. He was wondering how much magic Sorgaas could still conjure. Healing the chieftain's wounds had been tiring, but not as greatly as he had let Ghroth believe. The limits of his magic was one secret the herdchief was going to have to keep wondering about.

Tograh and Vuluk showed no interest in the dead monster. The ungors went back to the pile of bones and rummaged through it. Frang joined them, sniffing each one they tossed aside and uttering an annoyed squeal when it failed to find any meat.

From the rubbish, Tograh dragged out a wooden bow adorned with tassels of hair and a quiver fashioned from the hide of some reptile. The ungor scowled at finding no arrows for the quiver, but slung its strap over his neck and shoulder just the same. His frown grew darker when he tested the bow and the string snapped in his hands. He made to throw it away, but reconsidered. He worked the weapon so that it rested in the empty quiver and around his back.

Vuluk picked through the bones for a weapon of his own. Unhappy with the dull sword he had attacked the troggoth with, he tried to find something more formidable. He was still scavenging when Sorgaas walked past him and into the cave.

Sorgaas did not need to ask why the beastkin were hesitant to enter the troggoth's lair. The fug from the scaly monster was heavy, so rank it made his eyes water. The floor was thick with bones and whatever the victims had been carrying that their killer decided was not good to eat. The shaman shone his light across the cave, taking an interest whenever he saw the gleam of metal among the skeletons. The bones belonged to a staggering variety of creatures, both animals and sapient beings. Smashed helms and battered armour evoked an even more impressive array of lands and cultures. Sorgaas saw pieces adorned with the hated twin-tailed comet of Sigmar and others with the skull-rune of Khorne. Indiscriminate in its appetite, the troggoth had claimed all as fodder.

'Troggoth make good trap,' Ghroth stated as he joined Sorgaas in the reeking lair. 'Kill all come inside Beastgrave.'

'That is a reckless assumption,' Sorgaas cautioned Ghroth. 'There may be other ways into the mountain.' He gestured with his glowing staff at the monster's body outside. 'Others may have fought past the troggoth and continued on. Unless it was completely destroyed, its body will regenerate.'

Ghroth gnashed his fangs together. 'None stop Ghroth,' he stated. His eyes were drawn to something lying on the floor. He kicked away the bones around it. Stooping down, he pulled a massive double-headed axe from the morbid litter. 'Beard-jaw make,' he announced as he brought it down into the skull of an orruk. The target shattered into fragments that went spinning across the lair. His clawed hand brushed across the duardin runes etched into the blade.

'Sometimes the beard-jaws put hexes on their things,' Sorgaas advised the chieftain.

'Good axe,' Ghroth said when he shattered a second skull. 'No curse. Curse not stop Ghroth.'

The shaman knew better than to argue with Ghroth. The herd-chief usually laid claim to the biggest weapon he could lay his hands on. It was a visible display of his authority when he did, a reminder to the warherd of who was in charge. For now, that would mean the duardin double-axe. Probably because the trog-goth's stone club was too heavy even for Ghroth to drag along.

'Did you know about this place?' Sorgaas asked. 'Was it part of your vision?'

Ghroth looked uneasy. The swagger of only a moment before left him. He peered intently at the dimensions of the cave, at the jumbled bones around their feet.

'What about the troggoth, or that dark pool outside?' Sorgaas pressed.

'Sorgaas doubt Ghroth?' the herdchief growled.

The shaman shook his head. 'No. I know you had a precognitive vision. I sensed its arcane residue. Yet I am curious if the vision showed you everything. Did you see the troggoth and this cave?'

'No,' Ghroth answered. It was the only answer he was going to give. He turned and stalked out of the cave. Ghroth tossed aside the axe he had killed the troggoth with and laid the double-axe against his shoulder. Vuluk barked in excitement and pounced on the discarded weapon.

It seemed to Sorgaas that Ghroth had gone directly to where the double-axe was lying. As though he had known where it was already. Maybe he had. Maybe finding the weapon had been part of his vision. Maybe the troggoth lying in wait for them had been too. The chieftain had indicated he'd smelled the monster before Sorgaas shone his magical light on it. But none of the other beast-kin had reacted, not even Frang with its sharp nose.

The shaman nodded. Yes, they were peculiar, those circumstances. It led him to think that Ghroth was not taken in by the idea that Sorgaas had rescued him from the tribesmen.

It led him to think that Ghroth might have decided to eliminate Sorgaas. With the chieftain's foreknowledge of what lurked within Beastgrave, that was a possibility that truly put fear in Sorgaas' heart.

Ghroth kneeled beside the dark pool and sucked water into his mouth. He kept one eye on the troggoth's cave as he drank. Sorgaas was clever and Ghroth knew he had made a mistake in picking up the axe. It had made the shaman suspicious. He was not direct in his mind, not like true beastkin. He had the manflesh tendency to plot and scheme. Ghroth could appreciate only too well how good Sorgaas was at such things because he had used them many times for his own benefit.

Sorgaas had made plans that had changed the leaders of the warherd and plans that had changed battles. Ghroth wondered if he had come up with a plan to change the dream from the flames? He had told him it was a vision sent by the gods. If it was true, would Sorgaas – even Sorgaas – try to change Ghroth's destiny?

The herdchief rose from the pool and wiped the moisture from his mouth. He turned to face the cave. The ungors were still prowling through the bone piles, trying to find anything they could use. Frang was still sniffing around for any bit of meat the troggoth had missed. And Sorgaas? Ghroth did not know what the shaman was doing inside the lair. He knew what Sorgaas should be doing, what he had seen the shaman doing in his vision. He should be finding a sword that he would keep for himself and coming out here to look at the troggoth and telling them how soon it would revive from its own death.

All of that was what Sorgaas *should* be doing. But Ghroth was uncertain exactly how precise his vision really was. The nearer to the godbeast's grave they drew, the more distinct his memory of the dream became. Or so he had believed until he had goaded Sorgaas into calling up his magical light in the tunnel. He had seen nothing of those strange walls in his vision. That gap in his presentiment made him less certain of everything else. Finding the troggoth where he expected it to be, taking the axe from where it should have been under the bones – these things had restored some of his confidence, but not all of it.

Something had changed. By some means, Sorgaas had used his spells to change things. Ghroth did not yet know by how much, but he was certain that he knew why. The shaman wanted the godbeast's heart for himself.

As Ghroth watched the mouth of the cave, Sorgaas emerged, a new sword strapped over his cloak and robes. The shaman walked over to the troggoth and studied it. Back in the pattern Ghroth expected.

But for how long, the herdchief wondered. How long before the shaman did something that changed things and threatened Ghroth's destiny?

The chieftain shook his head. He was not smarter than Sorgaas.

His one advantage over the shaman was being unpredictable. If Sorgaas knew more details about the vision than he claimed, and if he was trying to change that vision, the last thing he would expect was for Ghroth to deliberately throw off the sequence on his own.

Ghroth rose and cried out to his followers. 'Go now,' he said. 'Leave bones and scraps. Leave troggoth. Die or heal, it not stop Ghroth.' He felt satisfied when he saw the way the Shaman glanced down at the monster. It seemed obvious to him that Sorgaas expected to stay. Sorgaas knew what was supposed to happen too.

Well, Ghroth would just have to change that. Because no one was going to claim the power he sought. No one was going to steal his destiny from him.

CHAPTER NINE

The tracks left by Ghroth and his warriors led deeper into the mountain. The sylvaneth adjusted to the lack of daylight, the fey glow of their eyes shifting to draw out the detail of their surroundings. The images were cold and grey, but distinct enough to guide Kyra and the others to the opening at the back of the cave, past the mound of skulls.

Kyra felt an ever-increasing unease as they proceeded into the tunnel. Something was all around them, hostile and aware. Something that defied the fey illumination that let the sylvaneth find their way in the darkness. She saw the walls and the ceiling, the floor under their feet, but there was something more that she was missing. With each step she was more convinced that there was a terrible danger lurking close by.

'Stop.' Kyra sent the impulse coursing into the essence of each of her companions. The dryads halted, frozen in place by her command. She felt their bewilderment at her dramatic conquest of their autonomy. 'There is a threat here,' she explained. 'I can feel it close to us.'

Nyiss turned her head from side to side, studying the tunnel ahead of them from every angle. 'I do not see anything.'

'Nor do I,' Eshia apologised. She waved her arm at the ceiling and turned towards the wall. Yanir caught the young dryad and moved her back.

'Wait until Kyra is satisfied before doing anything,' Yanir told Eshia. 'If she feels there is a reason to be wary, we should listen.'

Kyra pressed forward and followed Nyiss' example, studying the tunnel. It ran straight as far as she could see, with no bends or obstructions where the twist-flesh might be lying in wait for them. No, it was a different sort of trap they needed to watch for.

'I can see nothing,' Kyra said to Nyiss. 'But there is something here. I will conjure a light and we will see if it changes our perspective.'

Nyiss closed her long fingers on the branchwraith's arm. 'If you make a light, the Rootcutter might see it.'

The possibility had not been ignored by Kyra, but she had not forgotten the corrupt swine-headed creature that was with the twist-flesh. 'If they do not see us they will smell us,' Kyra reminded the dryad. It was easy for the sylvaneth to forget the hazards of a sense that was so keen in other creatures. 'Should the Rootcutter be near enough to see the light, his warriors have already caught our scent.'

Kyra saw that she had made her point. She took a few more steps ahead of the dryads and raised her hand over her head. She let her companions adjust their eyes for what would follow so they would not be blinded. Kyra drew upon the arcane energies coursing through her wooden body. They gathered in the palm of her hand, bursting from the bark like a bud of sunlight. The brilliant rays washed across the tunnel, exposing not merely cold grey shapes, but the roof and floor in all their colour and detail.

The walls were the feature that immediately captured the attention of the sylvaneth. They were a strange, eerie admixture of bizarre angles, at once seeming both convex and concave. The substance they were shaped from was translucent, almost crystalline in nature and a deep rich gold in colour. Weird glyphs had been cut into them, filing down their faces into vertical columns.

'Keep back from them,' Kyra cautioned the dryads. The subtle motion flowed within the walls, behind their frozen facades. She could liken it to the sluggish crawl of amber bubbling down a tree's trunk. Was this something of a similar nature? The congealing sap of the forests that clothed Beastgrave's slopes, or the frozen blood of the mountain itself? She let just the merest part of her essence reach out to the wall and tried to detect something of its presence.

Hunger was the overwhelming sensation that struck Kyra. A hunger more rapacious than even that of the forest. It groaned and raged, wailing with its need to consume. It reached for her, determined to draw her into its ravenous depths. The hunger was of such vastness that Kyra found herself being smothered by it, crushed down into a meagre spark of identity.

'Take her!' The shout was Eshia's and it forced Kyra back from the depths that reared up to consume her. She felt Eshia's arm pushing against her, then the long talons of Yanir grasped her and pulled her back. She struggled to break free, but as she did Nyiss threw her weight into restraining the branchwraith.

As the siren call from the wall was broken, Kyra looked with wretched horror at Eshia. She had dodged forwards to intercept the branchwraith before she could close on the crystalline surface. Kyra dimly recalled watching this happen. Now she saw in full the grisly aftermath. Eshia was being drawn into the wall, sucked into the amber. She was half inside the wall already, one foot striving desperately to anchor herself to the outside by sinking roots into the floor, her free hand attempting the same by digging at the ceiling.

There were images materialising within the wall. Flame-haired duardin and barbarian marauders, brutish orruk reavers and slinking ratkin – dozens of images trapped behind the walls of the tunnel. Whatever force dominated here was trying to do the same to Eshia, to trap her in its depths like a fly in a blob of amber.

'I am all right,' Kyra snapped at Yanir and Nyiss. 'Take hold of Eshia. Do not let her sink any deeper.'

The dryads released her and hurried to grab Eshia. They dug their own roots into the floor and struggled to retard their companion's descent. Kyra trawled through her arcane knowledge, seeking some way to reverse the hunger that was trying to consume Eshia. The only solution that occurred to her was to expose herself again to the place's ravenous appetite. Her only advantage would be that this time she would know what to expect. She would also know how to entice it.

'I am what you want,' Kyra said. She stretched her arms wide and walked towards the wall some small distance from where Eshia was trapped. She gave Nyiss and Yanir a warning look, imploring them not to interfere. 'I am what you want,' she repeated, projecting a bit more of her essence into the amber depths. She felt it pawing at her, trying to catch her spirit. The walls needed more physical fodder.

Kyra stepped still closer. She saw her reflection on the crystalline facets of its surface. She could also sense its agitation. Such awareness as the place had was being diverted away from Eshia and towards herself. She was the morsel it truly desired.

'She is coming free,' Nyiss cried. Kyra risked one glance at the dryads and saw Eshia's body slowly being drawn out from the wall.

Her ploy was working, if they would only have the time for it to work. Fear hammered inside Kyra's heartwood when she considered this place might be capable of realising the deception.

'Get Eshia loose,' Kyra said. Terror swelled up inside her as she braced herself for what might prove the ultimate sacrifice. Extending her fingers and toe-roots to their fullest, letting the branches on her head stretch away in a broad display, she took the last step and pressed herself against the wall.

The dryads shouted in protest. She could not spare them even the slightest attention. Every speck of her being was focused on the wall and resisting its hungry pull. She felt its oozy clutches gripping her body, trying to suck her into its gelid gut. With all her power, she fought. She fought until she knew she could fight no more.

Kyra screamed in agony and fell back against the floor. She caught just a glimpse of the shape outlined on the wall, the layer of dead bark she had clad herself in before touching the wall. It was drawing that shell into itself, consuming it rapidly. Her essence, still in contact with the place, felt its angry frustration. It had been cheated, baited with crumbs.

'It worked,' Yanir congratulated Kyra. The two dryads were helping Eshia regain her own feet.

'Only too well,' Nyiss said. She pointed at Eshia's arm, or rather where only the stump of an arm should be. The limb was back, not a thing of solid wood and bark, but a golden mass of translucence like some fantastical phantom of her missing arm.

Eshia gazed at the weird limb. As she did, the fingers curled inwards into a fist. 'I can feel it,' she told the others. She reached up with it to the ceiling and scratched at the earth. 'It does what I want it to.'

Kyra looked at Eshia, and then at the sinister walls around them. 'When it spat you loose, it sensed the aura of your severed arm.

In its haste to be rid of you, part of it melded itself to your body to replace what was missing.'

'But it feels like it is part of me,' Eshia said.

'It is also part of that,' Kyra explained, pointing at the wall. 'I can sense its hunger.'

Eshia clamped the amber hand around one of the fingers of her other hand. 'Nothing happened,' she said, hope in her voice.

'These walls do not feed on themselves,' Yanir said. She backed away from Eshia and gave her a wary look.

'Until we know more, be careful,' Kyra told Eshia. 'Touch nothing with that arm unless you have to. You must be cautious until we are sure what has happened to you.'

Eshia bowed her head in acquiescence, a tinge of shame in her voice. 'I will keep my distance until you are sure it is safe for me to rejoin you.'

Kyra was regretful that it was necessary, but to protect all of them they had to know more about what had happened to Eshia and exactly what was the nature of her new arm. She was certain there were dangers enough lurking inside Beastgrave without fostering another one in their very midst.

If Eshia's amber arm became a threat, the sylvaneth would have to leave her behind.

The sylvaneth were no great distance further down the tunnel when a deafening roar swept through the passage. The blood-sap inside Kyra crackled as a blast of heat washed over her. The light she had conjured was blotted out as a mighty wall of flame erupted only a few yards ahead of them. It sprang from both ceiling and floor, a curtain of snarling fire that filled the whole of the tunnel.

Or so it seemed at first glance. Kyra noted the gaps at either side of the curtain – a narrow space between the roaring flames and the amber walls. Just enough room that someone unaware of the peril those walls represented might try to slip past.

'Another illusion?' Nyiss asked. 'Like the one that hid the cave?'

Yanir snapped one of the branches off her head and threw it at the fire curtain. It was set alight the instant it came into contact, flaring up as it was consumed. 'Whatever it is, I do not think we can walk through it like we did the boulder.'

Kyra sensed enough to know the wall of flame was a spell of some sort rather than any natural occurrence. It used magic as its fuel. Whoever had conjured it would have had to set some manner of restriction upon it. The curtain couldn't stand in perpetuity, but there was no way to tell how long it would remain. An hour? A day? Whatever the time span, it was too long to wait. The longer they tarried, the farther ahead Ghroth and his followers would get.

'They intended for us to try to slip around the edges and be consumed by the walls,' Kyra stated. 'This is the work of the twist-flesh. There is a sorcerer with them. He either knows or suspects that we are following and left this to trap us.'

'How can we get through?' Eshia questioned. 'Do we wait for the flames to burn out?'

Kyra grimaced at the suggestion. 'We cannot risk it. We will have to quench the fire ourselves.' She reached up and touched the ceiling with her hands. The fingers stretched out, stabbing into the earth and burrowing forwards. 'Yanir. Nyiss. Help me. I will use my magic to send roots from your fingers through the roof. We must strive to undermine the section above the fire.' She looked back at Eshia. 'Keep guard while we work,' she told her.

The branchwraith's eyes flickered as she divided her power between herself and the two dryads. Their fingers probed deep into the earth. As they reached their limit, little shoots emerged from the fingertips. Quickly they expanded into thin roots and further extended into thousands of tiny rootlets. The fibrous tendrils burrowed into the ceiling, tearing away its integrity. Cracks formed and little streams of dirt spilled into the tunnel.

Kyra exerted a concentrated burst of arcane energy, sending it flaring through the fingers of all three sylvaneth. The surge of power pulsed onwards through the roots and rootlets, but these extensions did not simply channel the branchwraith's magic. They burst apart, and as they exploded they brought a massive shower of earth pouring down from the ceiling.

Though conjured by sorcery, the fiery curtain could not exist in the same space as the cascade of dirt. Like a mundane flame, it was smothered by the collapse, buried under tons of loose earth.

The sylvaneth marched through the clouds of dust and started clawing away at the cave-in. Kyra repeated the same process, sending rootlets from each of her fingers into the mound. This time they did not undermine, but rather spread to form a latticework that would support their labour and keep more dirt from rushing into their excavation.

'If the collapse is no greater on the other side, we can be through in no time,' Yanir said.

Nyiss had a more worrying thought. 'If the twist-flesh heard the collapse, they will know we are here.'

'They may think us destroyed,' Kyra said. 'If they do, they might not waste resources setting other traps behind them.'

'Then let us hope they heard the cave-in,' Yanir said. 'There would be nothing better than to catch the twist-flesh and settle them before they even know what hit them.'

Yanir's words put a thought in Kyra's mind. It was obvious to her that the beastkin knew they were being followed, but that did not mean they knew *who* was following them. That might prove to be something the sylvaneth could use to their advantage.

The amber tunnel with its sinister walls finally reached an end. Kyra felt the change in the air. She sensed water nearby. After leaving the cave-in, she had quenched the arcane light they had been using. Once more they saw their surroundings in shades of grey. As the tunnel expanded into a cavern, the rough irregularity of the walls suggested they were simply some sort of rock. The diminishing of that insistent hunger convinced her that they had put the ravenous amber behind them.

Nyiss gestured to the floor and pointed out the marks of hooves and clawed feet. Ghroth and his warherd had passed this way, leaving their prints in the dust. How far behind the beastkin they were was the next puzzle Kyra needed to solve.

A sharp cracking noise sounded from the darkness ahead of them. Nyiss motioned for the sylvaneth to wait. She started to steal forwards, but Kyra held her back. 'Listen,' she impelled the dryad. They stood rigid as the noises drifted back to them. The cracks were joined by low growls and the gnashing of teeth, the clatter of objects being knocked together and rolling against stone. Kyra had heard such noises before, around wolf dens when the cubs were playing with bones left by their mother.

'Maybe the Rootcutter stopped to eat,' Nyiss whispered.

'Something is ahead of us,' Kyra agreed. 'If we have caught the twist-flesh, remember we still need Ghroth alive. Restrain yourselves.'

The warning given, Kyra gave Nyiss permission to stray ahead of them. The dryad slipped along the cavern and towards a dark opening in the wall. As she approached the opening, Kyra let some of her own essence mingle with the scout's. What Nyiss saw was conveyed back to the branchwraith.

The opening was the mouth of a cave, the interior of which was littered with bones. Skeletons of every description and size were piled inches deep. Nyiss did not look too closely at them.

More important to her were the scraggly creatures that crouched in the midst of all those remains. They were wizened grotesques, with scrawny limbs and hunched bodies. Their heads jutted forwards in a vulture-like manner and their faces were dominated by their wide, fang-ridden mouths. They picked up bones and cracked them against the floor and walls until they split open. Once a bone was broken, the creatures greedily tried to get at the exposed marrow before one of the others could steal it.

Nyiss might have escaped the attention of the squabbling ghouls had she not drawn the interest of the creature lurking outside the cave. Concealed in the deeper shadows beside the pool, a monster twice as large as the bone-eaters sprang at the dryad. The fiend still had shreds of bloodied flesh hanging from its jaws when it attacked. Nyiss saw the carcass of a troggoth lying in the shallows in the split second it took the attacker to slam into her.

The monster knocked Nyiss down and clawed at her with its talons. Like some horrible combination of bat and cat, it scratched and snapped at her, flailing at her with its gangly arms and biting strips of bark with its jagged fangs. The fiend's demented howls brought the ghouls scurrying out from the cave.

Before the hunched creatures could swarm Nyiss, Kyra led the rest of the sylvaneth to their companion's rescue. A burst of bright light erupted from the branchwraith's hand. It sent a shower of flashing sparks dancing before the ghouls, dazzling them as they rushed out of the cave. The reeling scavengers were helpless when Yanir reached them. The old dryad's hands were elongated into raking talons, each finger hardened into a thorny claw. She slashed at one of the pale-skinned ghouls as it staggered away from the fey lights and ripped it open from shoulder to belly. The monster slumped down, shrieking as it pawed at its own exposed guts.

Kyra kept her right arm raised to let the light surge across the battle. One of the ghouls sprang at her, its claws dripping with venom. She swung at the thing with her left hand, clubbing it in the side of the head. The monster was not dissuaded. Its foul claws scratched down her trunk and stripped away layers of bark. Kyra felt the necrotic sting of its poisoned touch searing through her heartwood.

A second ghoul made a lunge for the light-bearing hand. Before it could attack Kyra, a weird mass of translucent gold slammed into it. Caught in mid-air, the ghoul thrashed about in the grip of Eshia's amber hand. Somehow she had sent it stretching across the dozen feet between herself and the monster. The dryad slowly came forwards, as though she were being drawn after the elongated arm. Smoke was boiling off the ghoul as its flesh smouldered in Eshia's grip.

The branchwraith sent her own attacker sprawling with a downward swipe of her arm. The creature flew back into a pile of bones. It shook its head as it regained its feet. The ghoul seized a femur from the jumbled skeletons and, with a feral howl, charged back at Kyra. She let the creature rush at her and directed an intense ray of light into its crazed eyes. The ghoul wailed and threw up its arms to blot out the stinging brilliance. Before it could recover, Kyra closed her hand around its head and brought the wooden fingers together. The creature struggled in her clutch and swatted at her with the leg bone it carried. She only intensified her concentration. The wooden fingers fused together, enfolding the monster's head in a steadily tightening band. As its panting lungs were starved of air, the ghoul's struggles slackened. A final effort by Kyra crushed the creature's skull. She dropped the mangled scavenger and turned back towards Nyiss.

The intervention of the sylvaneth had kept the ghouls away from Nyiss, but she was still beset by her initial foe. Kyra saw at once that it was not like the bone-sucking scavengers she had been fighting. This was much bigger, its body more powerfully built than the lean frames of the ghouls. Its skin was darker, an obsidian black. Scraps of velvet and lace were draped about it, and frilled cuffs encircled the ends of its ape-like arms. The hands were even more abnormal than those of the ghouls, the fingers distorted by dagger-like projections of sharp bone. The fiend's head was squashed and somewhat bat-like in overall shape, with large ears and a wide nose. The mouth was massive and sported a confusion of sharp fangs. The creature's eyes were crimson smears sunk back in the depths of its face. Kyra shuddered when she looked into them, for what she saw there was not merely hostile. It was insane.

The creature had raked Nyiss' neck with its huge claws and stripped away all the bark. A steady trickle of blood-sap bubbled up from the exposed heartwood. The monster leaned forwards and lapped up the stream with its long tongue. After a taste, it reared back, coughing and spitting. With the obsession of madness, it leaned down to drink anew of the dryad's lifeforce.

Kyra felt horror as she drew near to the thing. Unlike the ghouls, there was no discernible aura around Nyiss' attacker. That vital spark that suffused even the most corrupt creature of Chaos was absent. The monster was without a lifeforce, a being from the other side of the grave. In her travels, Kyra had seen ghosts and spectres, but never a physical manifestation of the undead like this. There was a word, one she had heard the quick-blood speak in shuddering whispers.

Vampire.

The undead spat another blob of Nyiss' blood-sap from its mouth. Despite its distaste, the thing leaned down again to suck at the dryad's wound. The ghastly sight spurred Kyra forwards. She thrust her glowing hand towards the bat-like face. The vampire screamed in pain and the outer layers of its skin crackled away in flakes of blackened ash.

Kyra pressed forwards. She thought the vampire would flee

before the light. It lashed out. With its whole body crackling and layers of its skin peeling away, it bore her to the ground. Its fangs snapped above Kyra's face. Its crazed gaze glared down at her.

'Ho, foul witch,' the vampire snarled. The refined, musical voice sounded impossible issuing from the bestial maw. 'Thou wouldst ensorcel yon maiden fair.' It tilted its head back towards Nyiss. 'Dost reckon mine heart so base as to attend such outrage? 'Tis the Count von Dunkelsward who safeguards the virtue of the damsel.'

Kyra let the fingers of her hands extend, stabbing their thorny tips into the vampire's flesh. The Count raked his savage claws down her trunk, gouging deep scratches in her wood.

'Fie, loathly harridan,' the vampire hissed. 'Thinkest thou...'

The vampire kept its weight against the branchwraith's arm, keeping the light in her palm directed away. Kyra shifted the direction of her spell. The light winked out from the trapped hand and reappeared in the opposite palm. She pressed it directly against the undead monster's head. 'I do not think,' she told the monster. 'I *do*.' Brought into direct contact with the vampire, the destructive effects of the light were magnified a hundredfold. The rays seared through the dark flesh, scattering charred flakes and smouldering cinders across the floor. Kyra kept the magical light burning, holding firm while the energy bored clear through the vampire's misshapen skull to erupt from the other side.

Kyra flung the shrieking vampire off her. The Count pitched backwards into the pool and collapsed in the water. Smoke streamed from the monster's scorched head. She turned away from the unmoving creature and hurried to Nyiss. The dryad was still losing much blood-sap from the ragged wound in her throat. The vampire had chewed a big gash in the heartwood of her neck. The glow in Nyiss' eyes was steadily weakening.

'Lie still,' Kyra told Nyiss, though she doubted the dryad could do otherwise. She heard the continued sounds of battle behind her. Yanir and Eshia would have to settle the ghouls on their own. If she left Nyiss now she was certain she would die.

The shimmer of daylight that had struck down the Count faded completely. Kyra channelled a different kind of power into her hands. She apologised to Nyiss before laying those hands on the dryad's neck. 'This will hurt. A lot.'

Nyiss was so weakened by the vampire that only a faint groan escaped her mouth. Her body quivered and trembled under Kyra's hands. The branchwraith refused to be distracted by her companion's spasms. To lose concentration would be to lose a life. She was forcing Nyiss' essence towards the very spot of her pain, drawing her into the full agonies of her wound. It was a torturous manner of healing, but by doing so she compelled the sylvaneth's wooden body to rapidly repair the damage. Nyiss was regenerating her injury so quickly because at the lowest, most primal level of her essence she was trying to make the pain stop.

Kyra was not without empathy. Only the most dire of necessity could have made her compel such suffering on another sylvaneth. It would have been more merciful to let her vital spark fade, but none of them could afford such mercy. There was still Ghroth to stop and the Thornwyld to save.

The wound was just beginning to close when Kyra was suddenly seized from behind. She felt the cold dampness of the brawny arms that closed around her. With an incredible display of strength, she was lifted off the floor. She craned her head around, shifting it completely so she could see what was behind her.

The vampire's hideous visage grinned back at her. Both sides of its head were completely burned through and much of its face was merely raw skull, yet still the undead refused to be destroyed. Its eyes focused upon her, but instead of the rage Kyra expected, there was an abominable tenderness.

'Away, milady. We must away. Yon beasties have routed mine squires and wouldst soon proffer outrage against thee.'

Kyra strove to pull free from the vampire's grasp, but its grip was like coils of steel. Her arms were pinned against her sides, she could not even bring the searing light to play against the Count. She felt the creature's breath against her neck. Its fangs rasped across the bark of her shoulder.

'Let her go, filth!' The shout came from Yanir. The old dryad held a ghoul in either hand. She brought them cracking together in a violent motion and tossed the creatures aside.

Count von Dunkelsward set Kyra back on her feet with elaborate gentility and spun around to confront Yanir. 'Stayest thou behind me. I shall not falter in thy defence.' The vampire's claws screeched as it brought them grinding together.

Freed from the vampire's grasp, Kyra conjured again the light that had seared the undead flesh. She attacked the insane monster from behind, pressing her hand against its back. She felt the flesh melting under her touch. The Count threw back its head in an anguished cry.

Yanir charged the stricken undead. She brought her claws slashing down, the wooden fingers tearing through the muscles of the vampire's arms. The Count lunged at her, trying to bury its fangs in her neck. The dryad brought her hand cracking into the fiend's jaw, splintering several of its fangs. Her fingers punctured the dark skin and sank into the decayed flesh.

Kyra backed away, looking in amazement at the injury she had inflicted on the vampire. A hole had been burned into its back, clean down to the bone. Yet still the monster refused to die. 'I cannot kill it,' she shouted to Yanir.

'You just don't know how,' the old dryad replied. With her fingers gripping the vampire's jaw, she pulled it up off the ground. She ignored the claws that raked her bark, tearing away at her wooden skin. She stared at the Count's exposed breast. Drawing back her other hand, she punched the vampire's chest. The mighty strike smashed through flesh and bone to dig down to the fiend's foul heart.

'The heart is the only vital place in a vampire,' Yanir said. 'Any other hurt done to one will simply heal over time.' She drew her fist from the Count's writhing body. One of the long fingers detached from her hand and remained behind to transfix the creature's heart. 'A shaft of wood in the heart will keep the vampire from rising again.' She let the corpse crash to the ground and stamped her foot on its head, smashing its skull. 'There is nothing lost by added precaution,' she told Kyra.

The handful of ghouls that were still fighting Eshia screamed when they saw the vampire fall. They became a panicked mob as they scurried off into the darkness. Eshia made no move to pursue them. She appeared more concerned with the havoc her amber arm had inflicted than the route of her adversaries. Kyra appreciated the young dryad's misgivings, but there was no time to console her.

Turning from the vanquished vampire, Kyra hurried back to Nyiss. She feared that the abrupt disruption of her magic would undo the dryad's healing. When she looked down at Nyiss, she found the glow in her eyes had returned and the wound on her neck was almost gone entirely. Nyiss started to rise, but Kyra put a restraining hand on her. She evoked a less painful spell to continue the regeneration. She turned her head when she heard Yanir approaching.

'Where did you learn about vampires?' Kyra asked.

Yanir looked down at Nyiss and studied her condition before answering. 'Many winters before you came to the Thornwyld, such a creature was hounded into the forest by the quick-blood. It fell to me to finish the hunt the humans abandoned.' Yanir glanced down at her maimed hand, the stump of her finger still raw and bare. 'Nyiss will recover?' she asked, changing the topic.

'In a little while,' Kyra said. 'The vampire's bite was not so toxic as it would have been to a quick-blood.'

'I am well,' Nyiss protested. 'Let me up and we will look for the trail again.'

Yanir studied the bones piled around the cave. 'This might be the end of the trail,' she said. 'The Rootcutter and his ilk may have found their fate here.'

Eshia marched past the others. Her amber arm glowed with a weird energy. Whatever it had drawn out of the ghouls had strengthened it in some fashion. The dryad pointed to the far side of the pool, the arm flowing outwards as she did so. In its light, a series of hoofprints could be seen on the far shore. 'The path does not end here,' she told the other sylvaneth, a trace of fear in her voice.

'How did you know to look for the trail?' Kyra pressed her.

The glow in Eshia's eyes was strange when she looked back at the branchwraith. 'I cannot say. I only knew to look for it and where.'

Kyra held Eshia's gaze and it came to her why the dryad's eyes were so unsettling.

They had taken on the same glow as her new arm.

CHAPTER TEN

There was light in the tunnel. All the lustre of day, yet Ghroth saw nowhere it could have come from. The ceiling, the walls around him – all were shaped of solid stone. The only markers that distinguished the passage were the strange plinths and the ugly statues that crouched atop them.

Ghroth clenched the duardin axe in both hands. He brought the weapon's double blade cracking against the roof. The impact shuddered through his bones, but inflicted little damage on the rock. Certainly it did nothing to expose the source of the weird light.

The herdchief scowled. He knew there should be light here, but it bothered him that he could not see where it came from. The ambiguity of the vision in the flames was increasingly frustrating to him the nearer he drew to his goal. Why should some things be so clear but others so uncertain in his mind?

The other beastkin stopped. All of them had a worried look in their eyes, even Frang. Ghroth shook his axe at Sorgaas. 'Where light?' he snarled at the shaman.

Sorgaas shook his head. 'I cannot say. There seems to be nothing to cause it, yet here it is. If it is magic, it is of a kind unknown to me.'

Mention of magic made Ghroth's hackles rise. Sorgaas was like a parasite, a tick stuck to the herdchief's fur. He fattened upon Ghroth's power. There was no loyalty in the shaman, only a pragmatic sense of utility. 'Sorgaas follow magic?' Ghroth asked.

The shaman had a ready answer. 'It was you who chose the passage we should follow away from the troggoth's cave. Is this not what you saw in your vision?'

Ghroth rounded on the shaman. Tograh and Vuluk scrambled out of his way as the herdchief marched over to Sorgaas. 'What Ghroth see not tell why Ghroth see it.' He waved the axe at the ceiling. 'Sorgaas think magic. What make magic?'

Sorgaas lost his confident pose as he thought about that. Ghroth could smell the anxiety in the shaman. 'I do not know that it *is* magic,' he finally said. 'We are deep within Beastgrave, a place both sacred and feared by many. Who can say what powers may have gathered inside the mountain?'

'Not Sorgaas,' Ghroth snorted in response. From the scent, he doubted the shaman was lying. He really did not know, and that was something that disturbed him. Ghroth was not entirely displeased. The more worries Sorgaas had the more he would depend on the herdchief's protection.

'Ghroth want Tograh look ahead?' the ungor scout asked. His fingers kept opening and closing around the haft of his spear. There was a sour, frightened tang to his smell, far more pronounced than that of Sorgaas.

'Frang go,' Ghroth decided. At his voice, the beasthound started loping towards him, but when he pointed away down the tunnel, the creature scurried off to check the path ahead of them. 'Tograh stay. Guard herdchief.'

Tograh bowed his head in submission and scowled at the empty quiver hanging off his shoulder. He had uncovered the bow and quiver in the troggoth's lair, but no serviceable arrows. Ghroth thought the ungor would have been a bit more sure of himself if he had some ammunition. Something to keep him away from the scrum of combat.

Ghroth turned from Tograh and regarded the other ungor, Vuluk. He had availed himself of the warchief's axe Ghroth had abandoned. The weapon looked far more formidable in his hands than it had in Ghroth's own. The chieftain felt a spiteful jealousy that Vuluk was using his cast-offs, but a sidewise glance at Sorgaas convinced him to restrain the impulse to snatch it away. That was the kind of bullying reaction the shaman would be expecting to see. Ghroth was still determined to rattle Sorgaas by being unpredictable. He simply gave Vuluk a scowl and looked away.

'There is more here that is strange than just this light,' Sorgaas said. He stepped towards the walls and gave them closer scrutiny.

Remembering the tunnel leading into the mountain, Ghroth watched the shaman with trepidation. He expected ghostly images to appear on the walls, spirits trapped in the rock itself. When no such apparitions manifested, the herdchief breathed a little easier. He was relieved when the shaman's clawed hand brushed across the bare stone and reaffirmed its solidity.

'This is not a natural formation. Neither is it the labour of pick and hammer,' Sorgaas said. He tapped a jagged edge and pointed to a similar place a little lower on the wall. 'It seems as though it has been chewed away.'

The thought of something that could gnaw its way through rock was unpleasant. Even troggoths and gargants didn't like to test their jaws on stone, swallowing such 'grinders' whole. A creature with a bite worse than a gargant was nothing Ghroth wanted to run into.

Sorgaas was of a similar mind. The shaman turned from the gnawed rock to one of the weird plinths. The pedestal rose directly from the floor, and was in fact a part of it, a little projection left behind when the tunnel was excavated. 'This is very old,' he mused. He tapped his finger against the irregular angles all around the plinth. They looked to be miniature repetitions of the scars on the walls – tiny bite marks that had given the structure its shape. Sorgaas stood back and stared up at the summit of the plinth. The roof of the passage was slightly vaulted, allowing the ugly statue to perch high above the floor.

The herdchief did not like to look on the grisly carving. It embodied the worst aspects of chigger and flea, a huge insect with its many arms folded across its body and its long proboscis drooped across its chest. The thing's back legs were curled in reverse, jointed from behind. Two stubby horns protruded just over a set of multifaceted eyes. Immense mandibles stretched outwards from the statue's mouth.

'I cannot see if the statue is cut from the plinth or if it is a separate carving set atop it later,' Sorgaas said. 'It seems to be fashioned from the same stone…'

'Not matter for statues,' Ghroth snapped. 'Sorgaas say they danger, warherd smash.'

'They could be what makes the light,' Sorgaas suggested. 'Or they may serve another purpose. Did you not see them in your vision?'

'Ghroth not remember small things,' the chieftain replied. He shifted the weight of the big axe he carried. 'Ghroth only remember important things.'

Sorgaas waved his hands at the tunnel. 'Even small things may prove important,' he advised. 'It would be wise to tell me everything you saw in the flames.'

An amused snort shook Ghroth's bestial frame. 'If Sorgaas hear then not need Ghroth to show way.'

Ghroth's humour faltered when he noticed something behind them down the passageway. They had passed several of the plinths and he could have sworn each of them had one of the horrible statues squatting at its top. One of the plinths was empty. There was nothing below it to indicate the statue had fallen. It was simply gone.

'We go,' Ghroth barked at the other beastkin. He turned and stalked down the tunnel after Frang. He tried to keep an attitude of confident authority in his speech and manner, but he found his gaze constantly straying to the plinths as he approached them. He watched the bug-like statues, expecting to catch some hint of motion from them.

Ghroth tried to keep Sorgaas' warning from his mind – the caution that small things could be important.

The beastkin reached the end of the strangely illuminated tunnel. Sorgaas directed a last lingering look at the plinths and the weird statues atop them. After his display of bravado, Ghroth had been eager to quit the winding passage. He suspected that, for some reason, the insectile statues were a factor in that decision. The herdchief had taken a more than usual dislike to them. Try as he might, Sorgaas was not able to figure out why. He finally decided to chalk it down to another of the beastman's primitive whims – the erratic choices that made him so difficult to anticipate or manipulate.

The passageway opened into a wider chamber. Nexus was the best word Sorgaas could find to describe the cavernous vault, for the openings of other passageways were everywhere. Some were at the same level as the one from which the warherd had emerged, and others were set higher on the walls, with little elevated ledges connecting them in irregular rings. A few exhibited the same eerie light as the tunnel they had left, and some others had the flicker of firelight glowing inside them. Most were dark, yawning mouths of blackness. Taking in the whole of the nexus, Sorgaas found it recalled to him the honeycomb of an insect colony and he thought again of the weird statues resting on the plinths.

Ghroth prowled ahead of the other beastkin. He studied the passageways, peering intently into each opening. Frang loped along a few paces behind him, dutifully awaiting the command to strike out into one of the tunnels. The ungors kept back, near Sorgaas, less eager than the beasthound to plunge still deeper into the bowels of the mountain. They might have fealty to their herdchief, but it was not enough to entirely overcome their fear.

At last one of the passages attracted Ghroth's attention in full. The chieftain stalked back to its dark mouth and inspected it closely. Finally he swung back around and called to Sorgaas. 'Conjure light,' he ordered and waved the shaman over to him.

Sorgaas evoked a greenish sphere of witchlight and let it suffuse the head of his bray-staff. In its weird glow, the rest of the nexus was thrown into uncanny detail. The walls here had the same chewed appearance as they had seen before. There were also more of the pedestals and the insects crouched on top of them.

'Does it look familiar?' Sorgaas asked as he brought the arcane light closer to the herdchief. Ghroth simply grunted and motioned him closer. Sorgaas felt a notable rise in temperature as he stepped in front of the passageway, a hot breeze wafting from somewhere within. There was a bitter smell as well, a reek he could liken only by its faint similarity to a pool of bubbling pitch.

With the witchlight to aid him, Ghroth scrutinised the tunnel, turning his horned head from one side to the other. When he was content that he had looked at it from every angle, he faced the other beastkin. 'This is way,' he announced.

Sorgaas glanced around at all the other passageways that opened into the nexus. 'You are certain?' he asked.

Ghroth glared at the doubting shaman. 'This what Ghroth see,' he told Sorgaas. 'This way to godbeast.' He pointed at Frang and waved his arm forwards. The beasthound hurried off down the passage. 'Sorgaas follow or Sorgaas stay.' He bared his fangs, leaving no question of what it would mean if Sorgaas did not obey.

'Your vision has led us this far,' Sorgaas said. 'Your vision and my knowledge. It would be unwise to discard either when we are so close to your destiny.' The shaman smiled to see Ghroth's swagger falter. The herdchief was trying to tell himself that Sorgaas was wrong and failing at the attempt.

Finally the chieftain turned back around. 'We go,' he growled. With his axe he motioned Tograh and Vuluk to precede him into the tunnel. He stared expectantly at Sorgaas until the shaman did the same.

'Should you not take the lead?' Sorgaas asked. 'It is you who knows the way, after all.'

Ghroth replied with grim logic. 'Ghroth know much. Only Ghroth know.' He let the edge of his axe slide against the rock wall, the scraping sound echoing through the tunnel. Sorgaas had to strain to hear the chieftain's words. 'Ghroth brave. Ghroth not fool. Not risk losing power now.'

Sorgaas peered more intently at the warriors ahead of them. The ungors were cautiously advancing and Frang was sniffing at the floor just where the witchlight's radius began to fail. Sorgaas thought of the troggoth and how Ghroth had anticipated the brute's ambush. 'We are going to be attacked?'

'Ghroth brave, not fool,' the herdchief replied. 'See others in vision. Many things hunt inside mountain.'

The shaman nodded in agreement. They had all seen the ghostly images caught in the walls at the entrance and the motley variety of bones in the troggoth's lair. It would be foolish to think no one had got past the two menaces as they had, or that there were no other ways to get inside a mountain as gigantic as Beastgrave.

There was one other thought that nagged at Sorgaas. 'Perhaps you have seen enemies ahead of us,' he said, 'but what of enemies behind us? Did your vision show if we are being followed?'

Sorgaas saw the uncertainty his question provoked. When Ghroth answered there was hesitation in his tone. 'Ghroth see none follow.'

Sorgaas knew from Ghroth's glower that he would gain nothing by pressing him further. He had something of an answer, at any rate. The hesitation in Ghroth's voice told him that there *were* deficiencies in the prophetic vision, that not everything within Beastgrave was as he had expected to find it. The shaman's question had placed a new worry in Ghroth's mind. Might one of those gaps be an enemy stalking their trail? Because he had seen no such foe, could he be certain one did not exist?

The shaman had his own worries in the same vein. He was not forgetting the magic that had freed Ghroth. And he was not so arrogant of his own abilities to discount the chance that whoever the wizard was, they could have slipped past his trap in the tunnel.

Let Ghroth keep his attention on the path ahead. Sorgaas was going to keep one eye on the trail the beastkin left behind.

The heat in the tunnel steadily increased as the beastkin pressed onwards. Ghroth's mouth hung open as he tried to cool off. He noted with annoyance that Sorgaas was sweating, another of the turnskin's human traits.

He kept sniffing the air, but aside from the scents of the other beastkin, there was only the strong burning smell. Ghroth knew what that smell belonged to. He had seen it in his vision. Briefly he thought about telling Sorgaas but decided against it. If the shaman was so wise he could figure it out for himself.

The tunnel was much like the one that had opened into the nexus. Ghroth still found himself giving the ugly statues careful scrutiny. None of them moved while he was looking at them, at least, but he remained convinced they could do so. The idea of pulling one of them down and taking a closer look at it was terrifying, for no reason he could explain even to himself.

Marks in the dirt along the passageway took Ghroth's mind away from the insectile statues. He noted the long, thin footprints of grots. There were bigger tracks that resembled those of a human wearing shoes, but sunk to such a depth and were of such size that he reasoned the man was very large and clad in armour. He found the prints of panthers and tracks even bigger and deeper than those of the armoured warrior. The tracks of wolves made him lift his head and sniff at the air again. He cocked his head to one side and listened intently for a stray sound.

Frang, loping along at the front of their group, had a far sharper nose than any of them. Ghroth knew the beasthound would detect any odd scent before he could. But would the animalistic Frang know how to interpret what it smelled? That was the riddle that kept the herdchief alert.

Several times the beastmen stopped and waited for their herdchief. Side branches were the reason for these pauses, Ghroth's warriors awaiting his decision on which tunnel they should follow. Always he made a careful inspection, matching the evidence of his eyes to the images in his mind. When he was satisfied, only then did he motion the group to proceed along the course he chose.

At last, with the heat grown towards the nigh intolerable, Ghroth's warherd reached the landmark he had been expecting them to find. A mephitic odour slammed into them as they emerged from the tunnel into a tremendous chamber.

There was no need here for the shaman's witchlight and Sorgaas dispelled the glow. All the illumination the beastkin could want was provided by a hellish red pulse that cast its rays across them. The chamber they had emerged into was a great chimney, soaring far into the lofty heights of Beastgrave. The ledge they stood upon fell away after a few yards, plunging down into the depths far below.

Against one side of the chimney was the cause of the pulsating crimson light – a fiery cataract that slithered up through the mountain, and a river of molten magma that bubbled and churned as it crawled up the wall in defiance of the rule of gravity. While the river itself was suspended in its impossible course, as it seethed it threw off blazing fragments that hurtled downwards in a steady drizzle of fire. When the fragments struck solid rock, gouts of smoke billowed away.

'Where do we go from here?' Sorgaas asked Ghroth.

The herdchief stepped away from the ledge and cast his gaze across the chimney. Scores of other tunnels were opening into the flume. Some of these were joined by causeways and bridges, spans of rock that stretched across the black depths. His interest was in a tunnel at roughly the same level as the one from which they had emerged.

'There. There is path,' Ghroth said, and pointed his axe at the tunnel.

The shaman scowled. 'There is no bridge here. We will have to go back and find a higher approach if we would cross here.'

Ghroth fixed Sorgaas with a scowl of his own. 'Sorgaas say great shaman. Sorgaas say gods listen to Sorgaas.' He pointed up at a distant span. The chimney was wider there than it was at their own level and the bridge was an enormous mass of stone. 'We not find bridge. Sorgaas bring bridge here.'

Sorgaas blinked in dismay at what the herdchief was asking of him. 'I cannot snap my fingers and bring the bridge down here,' he protested. 'There are limits to magic. One does not test the favour of the gods...'

Before Sorgaas could react, Ghroth seized him by the neck. He spun around and held the shaman over the edge. 'Ghroth strong,' he boasted, jostling Sorgaas with the single hand that had hold of him. His voice dropped to a hiss. 'How long Ghroth be strong?'

The shaman clenched his eyes tight and strange words tumbled across his fangs. Ghroth felt the air turn cold around him as Sorgaas hastily conjured a spell. He was sure that whatever enchantment the turnskin was making, it would not be anything targeted against him. It would take far mightier magic than he had yet seen from Sorgaas to strike the herdchief before he could drop the shaman into the pit.

A crackle of energy suddenly leapt from the bray-staff. Like a flash of lightning it streaked upwards to slash into the span. The energy sheared through the rock that anchored the bridge at one side. As its foundation crumbled away, the arch snapped free from the other end. Tons of stone was sent hurtling downwards. The smaller bridges in its path were obliterated, smashed to rubble as the plummeting hulk swept through them.

'Back to tunnel,' Ghroth shouted at the beastkin. He flung Sorgaas into the passageway. Hurrying after the shaman, he was barely within its protection when the avalanche came roaring down. Clouds of dust rushed into the tunnel while a violent tremor shook the mountain. There was a deafening clamour, a grinding cacophony that shivered through the herdchief's bones.

The monstrous quake was over in a moment. Only faint echoes of rocks bouncing off walls reached Ghroth's ears. He did not wait for the dust to completely settle. Clenching his axe in both hands, he marched out from the passageway.

The ledge on which he had stood before was gone. In its place was a mass of twisted stone that reached across the pit to the tunnel on the other side. Narrower at this point than it was higher up, the chimney's walls had stopped the bridge as it fell, pressing it tight in its new position. The position in which Ghroth had seen it in his vision.

Sorgaas crept forwards and joined Ghroth at the mouth of the passageway. He was filled with awe and his body trembled at the magnitude of what his magic had done.

'Now cross,' Ghroth told him. 'Sorgaas magic do this. Bring bridge where Ghroth want.'

The shaman leaned on his staff and continued to shake. The charms and talismans clattered against his horns. Ghroth drew a deep breath. He could smell the weakness in Sorgaas' scent. The shaman had told the truth about the limits to his magic, the source of all that made him strong. Sorgaas would need time to recover from this feat. Right now he was good for little.

'Vuluk,' Ghroth barked. He pointed at the fallen bridge when the ungor emerged from the passageway. 'Cross,' he ordered. 'Find if bridge strong or weak.'

'Vuluk fall,' the ungor objected.

Ghroth's fur bristled with aggravation. 'Vuluk fall here or Vuluk fall from bridge.' He stepped towards the ungor. 'Vuluk choose.'

The ungor circled around Ghroth and stepped out onto the bridge. Carefully he picked his way across the span. As Vuluk moved, bits of rock were dislodged and sent careening into the pit. Each time he froze and glanced back.

Ghroth and the other beastkin spectated from the mouth of the passage. Tograh was especially attentive to Vuluk's progress. The scout was very aware that if the other ungor fell, it would be his turn next.

When Vuluk finally picked his way to the other side and was framed in the dark opening of the far tunnel, Ghroth called to him to wait. Now that he was convinced the bridge would hold, he waved the rest of his warherd across. He was relieved when they were all on the other side.

Ghroth would need every warrior he had for what was ahead of them.

Fatigue dragged at every muscle in Sorgaas' body as he marched down the darkened tunnel. He was almost grateful Ghroth had not demanded he renew the witchlight after they left the chimney. As tired as he was, even such a minor conjuration felt like it would be beyond his ability. The beastmen had fashioned crude torches from strips of the shaman's cloak and blobs of burning stone cast down by the magma streams. He was too weary to question the weird way the fiery stone simply smouldered when wrapped in cloth while it reacted with caustic violence when splashed against the rock walls of the chimney. Sorgaas decided it was simply another of the uncanny mysteries that permeated Beastgrave.

The corridor they followed was markedly different from the strange passageways with their chewed walls and weird statues. Here they were surrounded by a rough, porous rock that had a yellowish cast to it. The ceiling was low and uneven, forcing Ghroth to crouch down at several points and causing Sorgaas to hold his staff at an awkward angle as he trudged along. Little trickles of water dripped down from the roof, turning the floor into an unpleasant mash of dirt and dust. The shaman could make no sense of the disordered prints caught there but he knew that something had used this tunnel in the past.

Gradually the burnt smell from the chimney lessened and the air began to lose its heat. Sorgaas saw Frang stop ahead, the beast-hound's snout raised as it snuffled. It was not long before the creature was moving again, the ungors following a bit behind it. Sorgaas was next in the line, but when he reached the spot where Frang had stopped he could discern nothing that explained its interest.

'Frang smell new smell,' Ghroth told Sorgaas. The gor sucked a deep breath into his lungs. He grinned at the shaman. 'Sorgaas not find smell?' He motioned him onwards, regardless of what he did or did not understand.

It was many minutes before Sorgaas detected the odour that Ghroth was speaking of. A raw, heady smell, that of soil kicked up from below the surface. There was more – a rich scent of roots and tubers. There was a wary and expectant attitude about the herdchief, something not explained by these smells on their own. What else was it Ghroth expected them to find?

The beastkin entered a wide, grotto-like cavity. The ceiling here was dozens of feet high and from it descended a wild variety of roots. Clumps of soil clung to the largest of them and the floor itself was heaped with black mounds of earth. Little fingers of daylight filtered down along with the roots, strange to see after the peculiar glows and flickers the beastkin had experienced.

'We must be near to the surface,' Sorgaas told Ghroth. The herdchief didn't seem to pay him any attention. There was an unaccountable intensity about Ghroth as he slowly marched into the grotto. His eyes kept roving around the room. His hands gripped the duardin axe with such an excess of anticipation that Sorgaas saw the haft bending.

The shaman was certain that Ghroth had seen this chamber in his vision. More than that, he knew what they could expect from this place. Sorgaas matched the herdchief's wariness, his gaze prying into every corner and cranny. He looked up at the ledges which circled the room but could find no hint of a cave or tunnel. Then he happened upon one of the earthen mounds. Clear in the loose soil was the print of a huge wolf.

Before Sorgaas could draw Ghroth's attention to his find, Frang snarled. The beasthound was near the far end of the grotto where the mouth of another passageway gaped. Tograh and Vuluk started forwards to see what Frang had found, but Ghroth stayed where he was. Sorgaas was convinced the herdchief already knew what was coming.

Frang scrambled back into the grotto. Where it had been standing, an arrow struck the floor and went spinning away. More arrows came streaking out from the darkened tunnel. In response, the two ungors hurried into cover.

The howls of wolves thundered through the grotto as three grey-furred animals charged out from the tunnel. The huge creatures had saddles strapped to their backs and each of them carried a wiry rider. These were lean, wizened beings, with hairless green skins. They wore rough jerkins of fur and leather with wooden quivers slung across their backs. An assortment of leather caps and metal helms covered their heads, but the faces beneath were all of similar cast – pinched and hungry with beady little eyes and long sharp noses above a fanged giggle of a mouth.

Sorgaas knew the horrible archers to be grots, a malicious greenskin breed that infested many places in Ghur. He knew something else. If there was one thing a grot shunned, it was a fair fight.

'Ghroth. This is only a distraction. The real attack...'

Even as the shaman was speaking, the earthen mound where he had spotted the track exploded outwards. From the loose earth an enormous wolf sprang at him, the canine's jaws stretched wide. A grot scurried out from the same concealment, spitting dirt while charging at Sorgaas with a spiked mace.

Before either of the hidden foes could reach Sorgaas, Ghroth intercepted them. The duardin double-headed axe flashed out and hit the wolf in mid-leap. The animal spun through the air, its ribs cracked and one foreleg shorn entirely. The grot beside it froze in shock, spattered with the wolf's blood. Still spitting dirt, it tried to blink the gore from its face while it turned and fled.

Other ambushers emerged from the piles of earth. Two more

wolves and an equal number of grots. Rather than plunging straight for the beastkin, these attackers swung up into the saddles on their steeds before trying to confront the warherd.

Ghroth charged one of the wolfriders as the grot reached its saddle. The savage steed lunged for the herdchief and snapped at him with its fangs. The gor twisted away and the wolf's teeth only caught a bit of fur. The huge axe in Ghroth's hands took a far more vicious toll on the grot in the saddle. The greenskin shrieked as it crashed down into his fur cap. With the chieftain's brawn behind the blow, the blade cleaved through the rider's skull and to its waist. The butchered grot sagged obscenely against the wolf's hindquarters as the animal darted onwards.

Sorgaas did not have the liberty to watch Ghroth and the now riderless wolf. The other hidden wolfrider was bolting towards him, intent on easier prey than the furious chieftain. The shaman managed to throw himself aside as the canine leapt at him. Its claws raked across his cloak and the scimitar carried by its rider cracked against the head of his bray-staff.

Sorgaas scrambled away from his attacker as the wolf turned and made another rush at him. The animal's fangs snapped at his leg while the grot took a swing at his head. More from panic than skill, the shaman spun the bray-staff around. Again he blocked the grot's blow with the head of his staff. The butt-end he brought cracking down on the wolf's head. The animal whimpered and stumbled away. Dazed, it resisted the frantic efforts of the grot to get back into the fray.

Sorgaas ripped one of the talismans from his nasal horn and held it aloft in a clenched fist. He shouted at the grot, hurling at him a tirade of arcane gibberish. Visibly shaken, it redoubled its efforts to get the wolf moving, fumbling desperately at the belt which kept it in the saddle. Sorgaas took a step towards the panicked greenskin and threw the talisman at it.

A squeal of absolute terror rang out. Desperate, the grot stabbed the tip of his scimitar into the wolf's flank to snap the canine from its daze. The animal snarled in anger and swung its body around to try to bite whatever had struck it. The reaction only made the grot more frantic, and it chopped the edge of its scimitar against the wolf's head, severing its ear.

Utterly enraged, the wolf dropped to the ground and rolled onto its back. It shifted back and forth, grinding the trapped grot against the floor. When the grot's shrieks stopped, the wolf rose to its feet and pulled the dead rider off its back. The greenskin hanging from its jaws, the animal quickly trotted away.

Sorgaas limped forwards and recovered the talisman from the floor. The sounds of battle were fading. He looked across the grotto as one of the grot archers went riding back down the tunnel. A riderless wolf hurried after, a big gash running down the animal's flank. The rest of the wolves and grots were dead. Vuluk was prying a dead grot from his axe while Tograh was scavenging arrows from the corpse of another. Frang had its jaws locked around the throat of a dead wolf, stubbornly worrying the carcass from side to side.

An agonised yelp rang out from behind him. Sorgaas turned to see Ghroth standing over the body of the last wolf. The herdchief pulled a bit of bloodied flesh off his axe. He sniffed it warily and tossed it aside.

'Bad eat grots,' Ghroth stated. 'Wolves same. Smell of mushrooms. Bad eat.'

Sorgaas nodded at the statement. His magic would make him immune to the risk, but for the other beastkin it would be best to defer to Ghroth. Grots were known to eat many things that would poison anything else. Perhaps they had conditioned their mounts to do the same.

'The other attackers have fled,' Sorgaas told Ghroth. 'It does not look like we suffered any casualties. Your anticipation of the ambush made the difference. Now if you had…'

Ghroth looked away before Sorgaas could make another appeal to him about disclosing all the details of his vision. The herd-chief turned to Frang and ordered the beasthound to leave the wolf carcass alone.

'Fight not over,' Ghroth told Sorgaas. 'More enemy come.' He gestured with his axe at the far tunnel and up at the ledges. 'Fight here. Better here.' It was as much information as the herdchief was going to give him. Slinging his axe over his shoulder, Ghroth marched off to give orders to the other beastkin.

Sorgaas resisted the urge to rush after Ghroth. There were things he needed to know, such as what kind of enemies the herdchief knew were coming and how long they had to prepare for them. He knew it would do no good to ask. Ghroth was capricious enough to keep such details from the shaman simply because he *did* ask.

CHAPTER ELEVEN

The trail left by Ghroth led the sylvaneth through the winding passageways. Nyiss had recovered enough from the vampire's bite that Kyra was comfortable letting her take the lead again. More comfortable than letting Eshia guide them through the mountain. Nyiss' capabilities were founded on skill and experience, things that could be quantified. Eshia's sudden affinity was more mysterious. Even she was troubled by the uncanny impressions that came to her.

As they moved through the tunnels, Eshia stopped and directed Kyra's attention to the stone plinths that jutted from the walls and the evil-looking statues that squatted on top of them. 'They dwelt in Beastgrave in another age,' she confided to the branchwraith. 'Long before the quick-blood and the sylvaneth first came to the mountain. Perhaps in another age they shall dwell here again.'

The young dryad shook her head. Kyra felt the fear and confusion rife within her essence. 'I do not know why I said that,' she apologised.

Yanir gave Eshia a wary look. 'I wish that you hadn't,' she said. 'We have enough to worry about without wondering about these statues.'

Kyra shifted her attention between the plinth and Eshia. 'It is Beastgrave,' she told Eshia. She pointed to the amber arm. 'When you were saved from the mountain's hunger, a bit of it melded with your spirit as well as your body.'

'What can I do?' Eshia implored.

'Remain who you are,' Kyra said. 'When we passed through the forest on Beastgrave's slopes, I felt a malicious presence. When I tried to draw upon my magic and connect with the trees I felt that presence rushing into me, trying to smother me in its malevolence. I thought it was the awful spirit of the forest, but I think it was Beastgrave itself. There is an awareness within the mountain, a force as alive as the Thornwyld, only vicious and dark.

'But it *can* be fought. If you resist you can fend it off, keep it from polluting your essence.' Kyra gestured at the statue on the plinth. 'When the mountain whispers to you, be resolute. Do not let it drown your spirit. If it seeks to flood you with its presence you have to hold it back. Control the flow. Preserve who you are.'

Eshia bowed. 'I will try,' she said. 'I will not forget why I am here and what I must do.' She raised her eyes to look up at the statues. 'Perhaps that is what happened to them. Perhaps they lost so much of themselves to Beastgrave that finally there was nothing left and they became part of the mountain.'

'We will not stay here that long,' Yanir vowed. 'We will find the Rootcutter, pluck his head from his shoulders and destroy the relic he is hunting. A simple task. We will be gone from Beastgrave long before it can do more than whisper to you.'

The old dryad's reassuring words rang hollow in the twisted tunnel. The walls echoed Yanir's voice, distorting their meaning into something rife with menace. Kyra was certain the effect was more than mere coincidence. Until that moment, there had been no echo in the winding corridors.

Beastgrave whispers to you. The echo had an almost gloating quality about it. Kyra was reminded of a young fox she had seen toying with a vole it had caught. It was a far from pleasant comparison.

Eshia added another problem to Kyra's worries. She raised her amber arm, the viscous limb changing shape ever so slightly. 'If I am in part with the mountain, what will happen to me when we leave?'

Kyra was afraid to give an answer. She was afraid that she already knew. 'We will do what can be done for you, Eshia,' she said. The branchwraith could imagine the scene that would unfold. The sylvaneth would have to leave her behind.

'I understand,' Eshia said. 'But I can still help to save the Thornwyld. Even if I can never walk under its trees again, I can still save our home.'

'I will not leave you,' Nyiss told her.

Eshia frowned and a sigh rustled through her branches. 'Yes, you will. Do you think I want any of you to be lost as well?' She turned back to Kyra. 'You have felt what the call of the mountain is like. How long do you think it can really be resisted? How long before you become too tired to fight it any more? Eventually whoever I am will be worn away. I will be something else. Something I do not want any of you to become.'

There was earnestness in Eshia's voice. Kyra could not refute the dire prediction the dryad made. Beastgrave would wear them down given time. In the forest she had experienced some hint of what that would mean.

Because she could not contradict Eshia's warning, Kyra could only make a grim promise to her. 'We will not leave you to wander the mountain alone.' Eshia's essence swelled with a vibrancy she knew to be gratitude. The other dryads looked away.

'The Rootcutter's trail is clear,' Nyiss said, waving her hand at the floor. 'Let us hurry and run him to ground. Then all that we have sacrificed will not have been in vain.'

With many turns and diversions the trail left by Ghroth and his followers wound its way down the passageways. For what must have been hours Nyiss pursued their tracks, always wary lest the twist-flesh were nearer than she expected them to be. Sometimes other prints showed in the dirt, but none were newer than those of the beastkin.

At least not until the trail went past an ugly-looking side-tunnel. Nyiss stopped as she neared the dark opening. Her long fingers pointed at the dirt, tracing the tracks she had been following in the air. She glanced back at the side-tunnel and hurriedly rejoined the other sylvaneth.

'Something else has come into this passage,' Nyiss reported to Kyra. 'They came out of that tunnel and into this one. I cannot tell how many they might be, but certainly there are more than three.'

'What sort of prints are they?' Yanir asked. Her bark was already thickening in anticipation of a fight.

'Strange ones,' Nyiss said. 'They could be the tracks of mice, but hundreds of times larger. There are marks where tails were dragged across the floor.'

'Do you think they are following Ghroth?' Kyra asked. 'Or did they just happen into the tunnel?'

'I cannot tell,' Nyiss confessed. 'Whatever they are, they might be hunting the twist-flesh.'

'We will have to assume so,' Kyra decided. It was better to be cautious than to make wishful assumptions. She went forward with Nyiss and examined the side-tunnel. It was different from the passageway with the plinths, somehow rougher in its construction. It also looked much more recent. None of the sylvaneth could offer any idea as to who or what might have gouged such a burrow. Neither could they tell how far it might descend into the mountain.

'The twist-flesh did not go this way.' Kyra moved from the side-tunnel and looked ahead along the main passage. 'Eshia, keep an eye on the path behind us in case anything comes out of there and takes up our trail.'

The sylvaneth pressed on. They had not gone far before Eshia hissed a warning to her companions. 'I hear something scurrying behind us.'

Yanir moved back to join the young dryad. 'Whatever it is, it isn't going to be happy when it catches up.' She stretched her hands out, her fingers tightening into talons of thorn.

'Keep watch ahead of us,' Kyra told Nyiss. The branchwraith moved back too in case the others needed her magic to help them against their pursuers.

The furtive scurrying sounds grew steadily louder. A few excited squeaks rang out and from around the last bend in the passage the sylvaneth saw several furry creatures bounding towards them. Crook-backed, their bodies covered in brown fur and long naked tails dragging behind them, the things bore a general resemblance to the wood-rats that prowled the Thornwyld. These were hideously enlarged, however, bigger than foxes and with ghastly fangs jutting from their mouths. The vermin hugged the walls, keeping close enough for their wiry whiskers to maintain contact.

As the giant rats moved closer, Eshia flung her amber arm towards them. The limb projected outwards several feet and the fingers closed around one of the animals. The vermin squealed as smoke boiled off it.

The rest of the rats chittered angrily and came swarming onwards. Eshia released the first animal and seized another, but half a dozen more avoided her and rushed towards the sylvaneth. Yanir swept her claws across them as they leapt at her. Two were thrown back, their bodies raked by the rending talons. Others sprang at the dryads, their chisel-like fangs gnawing into their bark. One darted between the dryads to launch itself at Kyra.

Kyra hit the leaping rat with her hand, batting it back down the passageway. She sent an invigorating rush of arcane energy surging through Yanir and Eshia. The rats gnawing on them were shocked by the influx. Squeaking in pain, they dropped to the floor and hurriedly retreated.

Yanir looked down at her leg and pulled a gnawed strip of bark free. 'That was not so bad,' she stated.

The retreating rats turned around the corner. Their frightened squeaks were soon lost, drowned out by a loud and vengeful chittering. Kyra looked at Yanir. 'You should not have said that.'

The sylvaneth backed away as the sounds grew louder and more intense. From around the bend a great brown mass of rodents flooded towards them, beady eyes glittering with malice. Where before there had been only a handful of rats, now they were confronted by scores, even hundreds of the vermin.

'Too many to fight here,' Kyra told her companions. Having seen the way the giant rats had bitten into the dryads, she had no illusions about how long they could stand against an entire horde of the creatures. 'Run!' she ordered the other sylvaneth. While the dryads hurried past her, Kyra raised her hand and evoked a flash of fey light. The dazzling brilliance blinded the swarm and a bedlam of anger and confusion sounded from the rats.

Kyra knew it would only be a temporary measure. She turned and joined the others in retreat. Behind them, the din of scurrying feet announced that the rats were back on the move. When they sounded too close, Kyra turned and blinded them with another flare of light. The vermin were faster than the sylvaneth. The chase would come down to a matter of which gave out first – her magic or their ravening persistence.

'The tunnel opens out ahead,' Nyiss shouted. The dryad led the way into a larger chamber. Kyra sent a final flash of light to blind the rat horde and ran. She hoped they would find some kind of advantage once they were out of the passageway.

The advantage they found was one that benefited the rats. The passageway opened out into a wide chamber with a high ceiling. It was a confluence of several tunnels that opened into the cavern from an assortment of heights and directions. Many of the corridors were alive with vermin, far more than the horde that had chased after the sylvaneth. Kyra realised that the rodents had driven them into an ambush.

A deeper squeaking drew Kyra's attention to a passageway across the chamber. Standing among the giant rats was a grotesque creature. It reminded her in some ways of the twist-flesh, but this was a merging of human and rat. The thing wore a smock-like garment over its hunched body and a metal helmet covered its elongated head. The ratkin's hands gripped a long whip, and when its red eyes turned towards the branchwraith it cracked the lash in the air.

The swarms of rodents surged out into the central chamber, chittering angrily. Kyra raised her arms and conjured a flash of light greater than those she had used in the tunnel. The vermin squealed against the stinging glow, but the continued cracking of the whip made it clear to her that their monstrous overlord was not going to let them slink back into the tunnels.

'They are all around us,' Nyiss shouted to Kyra. 'They are blocking all the passages.'

Kyra gestured up at the higher tunnels. 'Not all of them,' she told the dryads. 'Climb!'

The sylvaneth ran to the wall, crushing blinded vermin under their feet. They sank their thorny claws into the rock, forcing handholds as they climbed. Each of them had rats climbing up to their bodies, gnawing at their bark. As they ascended, rodents would drop away, often with a sliver of wood clenched in their fangs. Blood-sap seeped from the bites and dripped down onto the horde.

Kyra paused in her climb and glanced down. The floor of the cavern was a seething carpet of rats. The animals were crushing each other as they tried to reach the wall and pursue the sylvaneth. The sheer press of vermin was creating a pyramid against the wall, rising higher and higher with each passing moment.

As she watched, the ratkin cracked its lash and squeaked at the horde, goading the animals to frenzied effort. Kyra ignored the rats gnawing at her wooden body to focus her concentration on the creature. She pointed her finger at the ratkin and a sliver of wood went shooting across the chamber at it.

Her concentration faltered at the last moment. Instead of the missile skewering the whipmaster's heart, it struck the ratkin's shoulder. The creature yelped and leapt into the air. Before Kyra could try to target the creature with another spell, it had scrambled back into the shelter of a tunnel.

'It was worth a try,' Yanir consoled Kyra. Despite the rats clinging to her own body, the old dryad had dropped back to swat vermin off the branchwraith.

'Maybe it will buy us the time we need,' Kyra said.

Without the whipmaster, the rats below seemed less frantic than they had been. Then her attention was drawn back towards the tunnel the ratkin had ducked into. A huge shadow loomed there now. A massive brute squeezed its bulk through the opening. It was a gigantic beast with a naked, muscular torso and long, powerful arms. The thing's head was that of a colossal rat with fangs as long as daggers. The claws that tipped its huge paws were as big as swords. The monster stared stupidly around the chamber, indifferent to the swarming rats or the sylvaneth, at least until the injured whipmaster appeared beside it. The ratkin pointed its whip up at Kyra and squeaked angrily.

Kyra did not need to know the ratkin's shrill language to understand what it had told the huge monster. The indifference faded from its dull gaze, replaced by a raw fury. The creature stormed across the chamber, smashing dozens of rats under its feet.

'Don't be foolish,' Yanir scolded Kyra when she pointed her hand towards the charging brute. The dryad pulled at her, impelling her upwards. Kyra submitted to her direction. Any spell she threw at the rat-beast would have to fell it instantly. There would be no time for a second chance.

Nyiss and Eshia were above them, standing at the mouth of a tunnel and plucking rats from their bodies. Kyra saw desperation in their faces. A moment later a thudding impact shook through the wall. She glanced over her shoulder and saw the rat-beast climbing up after them.

'Look out!' Eshia cried. She moved to the edge and thrust her amber arm at the rat-beast. The elongated limb struck the monster in one of its hands. The thing howled in pain as smoke boiled from the burned flesh. It dropped back to the cavern floor, smashing scores of rats under its bulk.

Kyra and Yanir hurried upwards. They had not quite reached the top when they felt the wall shake again and knew the rat-beast was climbing after them again.

'This way,' Nyiss said as she started off down the tunnel. Kyra plucked the last rat out of her branches and ran after the dryad. As she followed Nyiss, the temperature grew notably warmer. There was a glow at the far end of the passageway, a dull red light that offset the gloom.

Kyra heard the rat-beast pursuing them into the tunnel. Other squeaks and squeals told her at least some of the giant vermin were with the monster. Whatever was ahead of them, whatever was causing the red light and the savage heat, she knew it could be no worse than what was behind them.

Nyiss came up short at the far end of the tunnel. She turned and shouted back to the other sylvaneth. 'We're trapped. There's nowhere to go.'

Kyra and the other dryads joined Nyiss. A gigantic cavern lay before them, molten magma glowing along one of its walls. There were dozens of tunnels and passageways at every side, some of them joined by stone bridges and archways. But not this tunnel. Ahead was nothing but a yawning pit.

Behind them, the tunnel echoed with the hungry clamour of vermin.

'Over the side,' Kyra told the dryads. The rock walls of the pit were of the same character as those in the nexus where the rats had ambushed them. The sylvaneth could sink their claws into them, use their toe-roots to find support. If they could ascend before, certainly they could descend here. If they could just reach one of the other tunnels they might yet cheat the vermin.

The weird river of magma was flowing upwards, but as Kyra swung out over the ledge there was a spray of molten rock as one of the loamy bubbles on its surface burst. Fiery flecks spattered across the chimney, scorching the stone wherever they lighted. One of the embers seared into her body, scorching through the bark and deep into the wood beneath. Only a desperate investment of magical energy was able to quench the flame as it threatened to set her entire body alight. Kyra's essence screamed in agony as she did her best to minimise the damage. Should she submit even as much as a moment to the torment it would be too much. She would lose her grip and plummet from the wall.

There was no need to warn the dryads of the peril. Each of them felt Kyra's pain pulse back into their own spirits. To linger in the tunnel was not an option. The rat-beast and the lesser vermin would overwhelm them if they remained where they were.

Better the comparatively quick and clean death offered by the abyss and the magma spray than to be gnawed to splinters by rats.

'We descend to the next passageway,' Kyra shouted. The branch-wraith kept her concentration divided between the climb and mitigating the damage done to her by the ember. The effort made it difficult to climb down. Nyiss and Yanir soon passed her while Eshia deliberately resumed her role as rearguard, hanging back so that Kyra would be at less risk.

'It is no good,' Nyiss cried out.

Kyra stopped and looked down. The tunnel she had chosen for them to make their escape was choked with giant rats. The whip-master was there as well. The ratkin glared back at her and gnashed its fangs. It was simple enough to see the creature's scheme. The rat-kin intended to catch the sylvaneth between two hordes of vermin.

Dirt and pebbles pelted down on Kyra's head. She glanced back up to see the rat-beast stabbing its claws into the rock so it could follow them down. Eshia struck at it with her amber arm, but the burning touch only enraged the monster even more.

Another bubble burst on the magma flow. None of the fiery spray hit the sylvaneth, but it came near enough that Kyra knew their reprieve was only temporary.

'The big one is herding us to the others,' Yanir growled.

'Circle around the chimney,' Kyra said. It was a command given in utter desperation. Circling the chimney would expose them to the falling embers for much longer. It was likely all of them would be burned off the walls before they could circle over to another tunnel. But climbing down to the swarms of rats was certain destruction for them.

The dryads started to climb sideways when still another hazard presented itself. Kyra saw something pale and sleek go streaking up from below. She had only a fleeting glimpse of it, but when her gaze strayed down in the direction from which it had come, she saw that it was not alone. A cave or tunnel several hundred yards lower in the chimney and on the opposite side of the abyss had three more sinister creatures standing on its ledge. They were slender in build, with white skins and lean limbs. The legs were scaly and clawed like those of an eagle, but they had manlike arms and visages that could only be described as something of the aelves. One of the creatures threw itself into the abyss. At once great black pinions snapped out from the being's back, lifting it upwards on bat-like wings.

The flying creature darted up towards Kyra, its powerful claws striking so close to her that they drew sparks from the wall beside her head. That beautiful aelf-like face pulled back in a monstrous snarl, displaying rows of needle-like fangs. It spun away and climbed higher up the chimney.

'Harpies!' Kyra called out to the dryads, applying to the horrible fliers a name she had known only from her mystical learning. 'Guard yourselves.'

How she would defend herself against the harpies was more than Kyra could say. It was difficult enough trying to keep the ember's fire from burning through her. She could not divert even a morsel of her magic to driving them away and it took all her strength to keep her hold on the rock. When she spotted another harpy rising, she knew there was nothing she could do to stop it from attacking her.

The harpy did indeed come screaming upwards, the fearsome talons on its feet splayed to their widest extent. Before it could slam into her a stream of golden semi-liquid struck the creature. Its shrieks altered from anger to agony as a pale arm and a black wing boiled in the acidic grip of Eshia. The amber fingers loosed their hold after only a moment and the mangled harpy went plummeting into the abyss.

Eshia's intervention was not bought without consequence. By

diverting her attention to helping Kyra, the young dryad faltered in her race with the rat-beast. The delay imposed by smiting the harpy let the descending monster close the gap between them. Retaining its hold on the rock with one claw, the rat-beast swung the other at Eshia. Its enormous talons ripped into her wooden body, cracking through the bark and splitting open her trunk.

'No!' Kyra screamed as Eshia lost her grasp and went hurtling down into the depths.

She was given no opportunity to mourn the loss of Eshia. Flush with its opportunistic victory, the rat-beast squealed in excitement and descended even more swiftly towards Kyra. At the same time, the ratkin whipmaster was compelling scores of vermin to climb up the chimney to get at the sylvaneth. Many lost their hold and went tumbling off into the darkness, but dozens more maintained their grip. Soon a brown, seething mass was surging up towards them.

The rat-beast was near enough that it took a swipe at Kyra. The brute's heavy claws drew sparks from the rock just above her head. A feral snarl rumbled from its massive chest. It shifted its body to position itself better and raised its arm for another strike. At that instant, a winged harpy dived down. Kyra did not know if the flying enemy was intent on her still, but if it was, the rat-beast got in the way. As the hulking beast started to swing its arm at her, the harpy's talons tore into its flesh.

A sharp, keening squeal rose from the rat-beast as the talons ripped into it. Black blood gushed from the wound, spraying down on Kyra. The harpy tried to pull away, but as it did the huge vermin instinctively struck at the winged monster – struck at it with the clawed hand that had been gripping the wall. The clumsy swing missed the harpy, but it doomed the creature. The rat-beast's grip on the wall was broken, its feet unable to maintain any kind of hold. It pitched outwards into the abyss. The harpy, its talons still embedded in the vermin's arm, was unable to fly free and hurtled into the darkness with its victim. The bat-like wings desperately beat at the air as the two went plummeting to their destruction.

The falling harpy screamed as it plunged down the chimney. The cries alerted the rest of the flock. The trio circled around the sylvaneth and made renewed assaults on them. They did not seek a bold strike as their fallen comrade had, but would sweep past and rake their claws against the dryads. The sharp talons tore long gashes in their bark and ugly cuts that brought blood-sap bubbling up from their heartwood.

The swarms of rats were thrown into panic each time the harpies came flying past them. In their desperation, the rodents climbed over each other, the added weight breaking the hold of those gripping the wall. Clumps of squeaking vermin dropped off and spun away into the chimney. The whipmaster, viewing the panic of its animals, tried to drive off the harpies. The ratkin's whip licked out, snaring one of the fliers around its leg. It tried to pull its catch down to the tunnel, but the harpy's strength was much greater. It dragged the ratman out from the passage and into the open air. The whipmaster clung to its whip and dangled off the creature's leg. With the ratkin's added weight, the harpy was unable to climb. It slowly descended, despite the frantic beating of its wings. Kyra soon lost track of the embattled enemies as they dropped from view.

The remaining harpies circled away, ready for another dive. One bore a deep cut where Yanir's claws had managed to rake it. The wounded harpy turned for Kyra and made ready to attack. Before the winged enemy could start its descent though, there was a loud burbling from the molten river. A bubble larger than any Kyra had seen before swelled and burst. The spray of fiery embers spattered across the huge cavern. Several of them struck the harpy. The delicate membranes of the wing were pitted with smouldering holes. The creature screamed as it went careening down the chasm. It smacked against the wall before bouncing away again, its body a broken mass of bloodied rags. The mangled remnant was soon lost to the darkness of the pit.

The last harpy lost heart for the battle after the loss of its brood. Hissing hatefully at the sylvaneth, it swung away and retreated into the yawning mouth of a tunnel. Kyra looked downwards and saw that Nyiss and Yanir were swatting away the rest of the vermin climbing up the walls. The dryads bled freely from their feet where the rats had caught them, scores of little bites in the comparatively soft fibres of their toe-roots.

Kyra dared to think they might make it to the tunnel when she saw a larger rat-like face appear. It was another of the ratkin whipmasters and, like its vanished compatriot, it exerted a hideous command over the other vermin. Shrieking angrily, it used a spiked goad to force fresh streams of rats out onto the wall.

'We cannot endure this,' Nyiss cried. Kyra felt the desperate weariness in the dryad's spirit.

'If we fall, the Thornwyld falls with us,' Yanir shouted. One of her clawed hands swept across the giant rats and sent a clutch of them pitching downwards.

Kyra saw something more than the falling rats. There was a new light there, one that was far different from the glow of the magma river and the flickers that shone from some of the tunnels. This was a golden light, and as she watched it grew larger. Closer. Bursting upwards with a bizarre series of hops. There was a familiarity to that light and she did not dare to hope. As the gold light came still nearer Kyra saw the pair of fey flickers that were rising with it.

'Eshia,' Kyra yelled to the dryads. 'She is still alive.' The other sylvaneth added their own exclamations of jubilant relief at the news. They risked glances past the swarming vermin to spot the steadily advancing shape of their companion.

Eshia climbed the wall in a peculiar fashion. The amber arm would essentially meld into the rock and fling the rest of her body upwards. The claws and roots of her other limbs would stab into the wall and she would retreat the squamous arm to repeat the process. Her progress was rapid. In a matter of minutes she grew from the faint light Kyra had first spotted to a clearly distinguished dryad shape clutching the wall. It was not long before she was below the level of the passage the rats were swarming from.

The ratkin was too fixated on the enemies above to notice the menace approaching from below. The first it was aware of its peril was when Eshia's acidic hand boiled over the ledge and incinerated a swathe of vermin. The ratman turned to run, but the dryad was faster. Her fingers locked around its head and seared it down to the bone. With a backwards fling, she tossed the ratkin's carcass into the pit.

The loss of the second whipmaster was too much for the giant rats. Those in the tunnel fled deeper into the mountain. The ones climbing the wall were thrown into such a panic that many of them did not need the weight of terrified vermin to make them loose their hold. Scores of the rats simply sprang away from the wall and threw themselves into the abyss.

'The way is clear for us,' Nyiss cried out. She started to adjust her angle of descent, moving back to their initial goal.

'No,' Eshia called. 'We must go still lower. I have found a bridge the Rootcutter used to cross.'

'How do you know?' asked Kyra.

The young dryad turned her head to her amber arm. 'Do not ask me how,' she said, 'but I do. Trust me.'

Kyra felt coldness well up inside her. She did trust Eshia. That was not the problem. Could she trust whatever force was revealing these things to her?

Could she trust Beastgrave?

CHAPTER TWELVE

Ghroth stood in the middle of the cavern and faced the tunnel down which the wolves had fled. The double-bladed duardin axe was before him, its head resting on the ground and the beastman's hands leaning on the butt of the weapon. The herdchief's body was tense with expectation as he gazed into the dark passageway.

On the ledges that ringed the cavern were Ghroth's followers. The beastkin were spread out to gain the best advantage over the foes he expected them to soon encounter. Tograh, his quiver filled with grot arrows, was positioned in the middle of the chamber. Sorgaas was off to the opposite side. The shaman had feasted on the hearts and brains of the dead wolves, sustenance he claimed would replenish his magic and his connection to the Dark Gods. Ghroth hoped the turnskin was speaking the truth for he would need that spellcraft in the coming conflict.

Near to the entrance, flanking the tunnel, Vuluk and Frang were poised. The ungor had a spear looted from the wolfriders as well as the axe Ghroth had discarded at the troggoth's cave.

The beasthound had its claws and teeth, but more importantly its keen sense of smell. Frang would detect the enemy before anyone. Such warning as could be given would come from the swine-headed mutant.

Time was the uncertainty in Ghroth's vision. The fight with the wolfriders and the cavern in which it occurred were clear enough. So too was the fray to come, when enemies would emerge from the tunnel. He knew the nature of those enemies, though he had kept the knowledge from Sorgaas and the others lest they lose courage and go slinking off to safety. What he did not know was when the enemy would show itself. Or how the battle would be resolved.

There was no question that Ghroth would endure. He had seen the cyclopean vault within which the godbeast lay entombed. He had seen himself, flush with triumph, standing upon the monster's breast, shreds of its heart hanging from his fangs. He knew he would be victorious. At least so long as events remained true to those he had seen in the flames.

Magic could interpret prophecies, but it could also change them. The shaman's power was both boon and bane. Unlike the rest of his followers, Sorgaas did not obey out of submission and fear. He held to Ghroth's banner because it suited his own strange inclinations, arcane purposes the herdchief could neither understand nor anticipate. It was reckless to trust too greatly in things one did not understand.

The visions had shown Ghroth that Sorgaas would be here, loosing his spells upon their foes. Afterwards, in that black crypt, there had only been the chieftain. What had befallen his followers was unrevealed… leaving Ghroth to his own judgement and devices, to weigh the benefit of Sorgaas' powers against the shaman's threat.

Ghroth turned back to the tunnel, his muscles shivering with anticipation. The battle was enough for now. He would meet the enemy head on and he would prevail. The further the warherd delved into Beastgrave, the more clarity he felt, the more confidence he had in his visions. He could not fall here. His destiny was elsewhere within the mountain. All the obstacles cast into his path only served to make him stronger. Worthy of his victory in the godbeast's grave.

A low snarl from Frang drew Ghroth's attention to the ledge where the beasthound crouched. Its hackles were raised, its fur bristled. The white of fangs glistened as it growled. The creature was fixated on the tunnel, as alert as Ghroth had ever seen it. He took a deep breath, trying to draw the scent Frang had caught. It did not matter that he could smell nothing; he already knew what was coming. There was no need to warn the rest of his followers. All of them were watching for Frang's alarm.

It was some minutes later when the first enemy emerged from the tunnel. Ghroth smelt the fear in the grot's scent. One of the wolfriders, absent of his steed, came creeping forwards. The greenskin had a vindictive expression on its sharp face. It actually smiled when it spotted the herdchief leaning on his axe. The grot motioned with one of its fingers as though slitting a throat.

Ghroth's lips curled back, displaying his fangs. He felt gratified when the grot lost its grin and anxiously darted a look over its shoulder. It babbled something in its shrill voice. Before it could run off, Tograh returned one of the grot arrows to the wolfrider. The feathered shaft struck it between the shoulders, the impact spinning the greenskin around. It fumbled at the barbed arrowhead protruding from its chest and sank to its knees.

The next instant the grot was crushed against the floor. Two massive creatures came bounding into the cavern. Nearly twice as large as the wolves, they were sleek and powerful in build, every inch of rippling muscles and corded sinew designed for speed and strength. The long bodies were covered in white fur dappled with black spots. The four powerful legs ended in broad feet with heavy pads. A striped tail flicked behind the charging animals. Ahead of the hunched shoulders each had a leonine head, long tufts of black fur stretching away from the ears and sword-like tusks jutting from each cat's lower jaw.

The tigers charged over the dying wolfrider and rushed for Ghroth. Intent on the prey they could see, their feline caution diminished by the smell of fresh blood, the cats failed to detect the ambush that waited for them. From the ledge, Frang leapt upon one animal. The beasthound's claws ripped into the cat's hide while its swinish jaws snapped at the creature's neck. The tiger tried to whip around and sink its fangs into its attacker, but all it managed to do was lose its balance and crash to the floor. Cat and beasthound were soon a blur of snarling bodies rolling across the ground, each trying to gain the advantage that would bring swift death to its opponent.

The second tiger was hit in its side by one of Tograh's arrows. Vuluk cast his spear at the cat, but the animal turned aside and the implement clattered against the cavern floor. Spinning around, it sprang at the ledge he was standing on. The tiger's jump was short, but the sharp claws hidden in its toes found purchase on the wall. Growling with fury, the cat climbed after the ungor. Another arrow from Tograh jounced off the tiger's shoulder, deflected by the thick bones beneath its fur.

Ghroth made no motion to enter the fray. His followers would have to deal with the tigers. He would have enough work for his axe when their master entered the fight.

A deafening shout boomed from the tunnel. The floor shivered as a huge weight ploughed through the darkness. The rank odour of the tigers' master was thick with the smell of death and blood, of offal and butchery. When she emerged into the light she presented an appearance that equalled the horrid scent. Nearly as tall as the troggoth, the ogor huntress had a greater resemblance to humans in her shape. Massive in stature, her heavily built frame was draped in the rough hides of bears and mammoths. A brassiere fashioned from ox skulls circled her chest while a gut-plate made from the bull-like head of a bovigor covered her pro-digious belly. A crude cloak cut from a gargant's scalp hung across her back.

The ogor glanced at the embattled tigers, but settled upon the defiant image of Ghroth leaning upon his axe. She bellowed in her thunderous voice. There was a huge stone club clenched in her fist, steel studs projecting from its sides. The huntress let this weapon drop and tore a lance-like spear from a sheath on her back. Holding it overhand, she aimed at the herdchief.

Ghroth called out a command to Sorgaas. 'Ogor throw spear, Sorgaas throw spell.'

The next instant, the immense spear was thrown across the cav-ern by the huntress, flying straight for Ghroth's chest.

Sorgaas heard Ghroth's shout. He saw the enormous spear speed-ing for the chieftain. For an instant the thought flashed through his mind to let the ogor's attack succeed. The spear had been cast with such force that it could have pierced the armour of a dragon. Ghroth would be spitted like a shank of manflesh when it connected.

The shaman let the temptation pass. He was still uncertain if Ghroth was essential to wresting the godbeast's power from the mountain. Without the confidence to do without him, Sorgaas was compelled to safeguard the herdchief.

Sorgaas raised his bray-staff and called upon the sorceries of Chaos. His breath turned cold as his body channelled the magic of his spell-prayer. A flare of energy rocketed from the head of the staff as he held it towards the flying spear. The weapon was encompassed in purple flames that consumed it so rapidly that when it reached Ghroth it was no more than a charred image, a shadow that collapsed into ash when it hit the gor.

The ogor shook her head in disbelief when the spear was disintegrated. Ghroth seized upon her shock. He lifted his axe and charged the huntress before she could pull a second spear from the sheath on her back. She recovered her senses enough to grab her club and meet the herdchief's attack. The cavern echoed with the clamorous impact of the duardin axe smacking against the stone club. The ogor staggered back a pace from the jarring impact. Ghroth was knocked away as though he had hit a solid wall.

'Your arrogance will be your undoing,' Sorgaas hissed as Ghroth rushed at the huntress a second time. Whatever the chieftain thought he knew about his vision, there was one rule all practitioners of magic soon appreciated about prophecy. The gods did not suffer those who tempted the inevitability of their future.

Sorgaas hurried to conjure another spell. He turned his braystaff towards Ghroth. The energy he evoked coursed into the goat-headed champion. There was no visible change in the herdchief, but he was changed just the same. For a brief moment in time his strength was augmented by sorcery.

Ogors were mighty in brawn, but slow in their reactions. The huntress was no exception to this aspect of her kind. Ghroth returned to the attack before she decided to adjust her own tactics. When he lunged at her with his axe, she met the assault with a swipe of her club.

Sorgaas focused on the fight and maintained the energies that coursed through Ghroth's muscles. There was a far different reaction when the duardin axe struck the stone club this time. A loud crack rang through the chamber as the club was split. Fragments of the broken weapon pelted the walls and bounced from the roof.

The ogor continued with her swing. The half of the club that retained its shape slammed into Ghroth. The chieftain was sent sprawling, the double-axe knocked from his grasp. Pieces of the shattered club pattered across the floor. The huntress stared at the truncated remnants of her weapon, little more than the grip she held in her thick fingers. Grunting in annoyance, she threw the remains away and reached to her quiver for another massive spear.

'Get up, you fool!' Sorgaas shouted at Ghroth. The strengthening energies were all that had preserved the herdchief from serious harm when the stone club smacked into him. Sorgaas could not maintain that spell while he diverted his concentration to new magic. Ghroth would have to fend for himself for a few deadly seconds.

The ogor did not cast her spear at the fallen beastman, but took a few lumbering steps towards him. Gripping the spear in both massive hands, she stabbed the weapon down at Ghroth and tried to pin him to the floor. At the last possible moment he rolled aside, letting the stone tip of the weapon strike up sparks as it scraped across the ground.

Sorgaas waved the bray-staff overhead, spinning it in a wide circle before pointing it at the huntress. The ogor was ready to take another stab as Ghroth crawled away from her. The spear in her hands responded to the shaman's spell. The wooden shaft glowed with heat and scorched her fingers. Bellowing in pain and surprise, the ogor dropped the weapon and turned towards the ledge where Sorgaas stood.

What primitive instinct directed the ogor's attention to the source of the spell Sorgaas did not know. He was confident that he was safe from retaliation. 'What are you going to do about it?' he taunted the bellowing huntress.

The answer came as quick as it was unexpected. The ogor's huge maw was open, her bellow growing more enraged with each heartbeat. More than simple frustration was in that roar. Sorgaas felt the air around him grow chill. Before he could conjure a defensive barrier, frost formed on his fur and he heard the creaking groan of his staff as ice burrowed into its cracks. The biting cold was such that concentration was impossible. The blood slowed in his veins and there was no magic he could evoke to save himself.

'Help me,' Sorgaas brayed through shivering teeth. He was uncertain if his appeal was for mortal or divine ears. In his distress, rescue from any quarter would be welcomed.

'Sorgaas belong Ghroth.' The fierce cry rang out as Ghroth charged the ogor. The duardin axe slashed deep into her arm and drew a great gout of blood. The icy bellow of the huntress vanished in a snarl of pain. She rounded on Ghroth, kicking out with an enormous boot and delivering a strike that would have shattered a lesser warrior. The herdchief replied in kind and chopped toes from the ogor's foot.

The shaman fought to recover from the effects of the frozen breath. He struggled through his shivering agonies to conjure an inner flame that would dissipate the vicious frost. While he recovered, he could only watch the battle raging across the cavern. Frang and one of the tigers scrabbled across the floor, claws and teeth ripping into each other. The second tiger had pursued Vuluk up to a ledge near the ceiling. The ungor was managing to keep the cat at bay with swipes of his axe. Tograh continued to loose arrows into the animal with varying results. Some of the missiles went wide; others failed to pierce the tiger's thick hide. Four had struck true, their feathered shafts embedded in the creature's body.

The battlers backed away from one another, glowering with pure hate – a brief respite before they returned to the fray. Ghroth clenched his axe tight, his body tensed for a burst of violent action.

A change came upon the herdchief. The hate vanished from his eyes and in its place there was an expression of intense surprise.

Ghroth was not looking at the ogor huntress, but past her, at something back down the passage through which the beastkin had entered the cavern. Sorgaas turned his head and looked for what had provoked such a reaction from Ghroth.

Striding out from the passage was a group of strange wooden creatures cast in the roughest of human shape. Tree-fiends such as the warherd had fought when trying to penetrate certain taboo forests. Sorgaas did not know how or why these creatures were inside Beastgrave, but there was one thing he was certain of. From Ghroth's reaction, the appearance of these tree-fiends was something his prophetic vision had not warned him to expect.

The sounds of battle rang down into the darkened tunnel. Kyra indicated to the other sylvaneth to be cautious. All of them sensed the presence of growing things nearby – life of root and stem. If they were so near to the surface it might mean there was another entrance into Beastgrave here. Huntsmen might have found their way into the mountain to avenge their witch doctor, or some other malefic force might have taken up pursuit of the Rootcutter and the abominable relic he sought. Kyra wanted to be certain what was ahead of them before they rushed into some new conflict.

She discerned a familiar voice shouting out from the turmoil of battle. 'That was Ghroth,' Kyra told the others.

'He sounds injured,' Nyiss said. The concern in the dryad's voice was genuine. 'If he dies we may never find the godbeast.'

'Unless what is ahead of us is the godbeast's tomb,' Yanir suggested.

Kyra considered that reasoning, but rejected it. There was too much at risk if they were wrong. 'We have to intercede and make sure Ghroth lives.'

'There could be another way,' Eshia said. She pressed her amber hand to the wall of the tunnel. 'If I try hard enough, if I put my spirit into sympathy with the mountain, perhaps I can find the way...'

A shiver rippled through Kyra's branches just hearing the idea. Places had their own presence, some strong and undeniable, others soft and barely felt. The presence around Beastgrave was as powerful as anything she had ever known, greater even than the wyldwoods. It was also more malignant. 'The danger is too great,' she said. 'You would expose yourself to great risk for something we could not trust.'

'Eshia found the twist-flesh's trail after we lost it,' Yanir said.

'There was no choice,' Kyra stated. 'Now there is.' Her bark darkened as she willed her body into an armoured, martial aspect. 'We will use Ghroth to guide us, not forces we do not understand.'

The discussion was ended. Following the branchwraith's lead, the dryads hardened their trunks and lengthened their claws. The hollows of their faces warped into gnarled, fearsome visages, war masks to strike fear into their foes. They strode boldly down the tunnel towards the fighting and emerged into a cavern with a high roof. Masses of roots dangled from the ceiling and in spots narrow slivers of daylight streamed downwards. Heaps of thick, dark soil lay strewn about the chamber, and the walls were characterised by shelf-like ledges.

Kyra drew in the details of the cavern, then her attention focused on the battle raging before her. A white panther-like animal was trying to reach a small twist-flesh with an axe high on one of the ledges while another twist-flesh loosed arrows into it from across the chamber. On the floor, tumbling about the corpses of grots and wolves, were another of the panthers and the many-legged mutant they had trailed from the Thornwyld. Of immediate interest to the sylvaneth were the two combatants closest to them – one of the gigantic quick-blooded creatures Kyra knew as copse-breakers, and her enemy, the goat-headed Ghroth himself.

The hulking huntress turned, startled by the appearance of the sylvaneth. Her powerful arm drew back and cast the stone-tipped spear she held. The weapon flew through the cavern and smashed into Kyra's body. Such was the hideous power of the ogor's strength that despite the thickened bark that covered her body, the branch-wraith was pierced by the spear. It struck with a sickening crunch, splinters of wood spraying away from the wound as it punched into the heartwood. The stone tip emerged from her back with several inches of the haft behind it.

'Kyra!' Eshia yelled. She rushed to the stricken branchwraith and tried to support her reeling frame with her one good arm.

Yanir uttered a groaning rumble that shuddered across the cavern. She charged for the huntress, slashing at the ogor with her claws before she could drag another spear from the quiver on her back. The thorny talons tore through the hides she wore and ripped into the copse-breaker's flesh. Bloody ribbons of skin clung to her claws as Yanir raked them across the ogor's face and scratched deep furrows in the brutal features. The huntress howled in pain and wrapped her brawny arms around the dryad. A creaking groan sounded from Yanir as her foe tried to crush her in a bear hug.

Nyiss moved in to help Yanir, but before she could reach the ogor, the tiger on the ledge sprang at her. The animal's claws cut across the dryad's body as it struck her, digging long scratches into her side. Landing behind Nyiss, the cat quickly circled around her, hissing and spitting as it put itself between the dryad and its mistress. She lashed out at the tiger, her claws ripping fresh injuries in its arrow-pierced hide. It snarled and spun as she struck, sinking its long fangs into her arm. Wood splintered under the power-ful bite and Nyiss felt an icy cold pulsating from the cat's jaws, a cold that caused crystals of frost to crackle around her wound. She brought her other hand against the tiger's neck and tried to pull the animal off, but the more she tugged at it the deeper it clenched its fangs.

'Get Ghroth,' Kyra cried out as she wilted against Eshia. Bloodsap was spurting from her wound, pain throbbing through her being, but foremost in her thoughts was fear. Fear that the Rootcutter would escape them and reach the terrible prize he sought.

Eshia laid Kyra against the ground. The young dryad rushed towards Ghroth. The beastman stood with his axe at the ready but had made no effort to interfere with the clash of sylvaneth and ogor. Perhaps he intended to wait and fight the winner. Eshia was going to change that plan.

Ghroth turned to meet Eshia's charge. He lifted his double-headed axe in both hands and ran towards her. Before he could come within reach, Eshia's amber arm shot out, its acidic touch wrapping about the head of the axe. The weapon sizzled under that grip, steam bubbling up into the air. The beastman brayed in alarm and threw his weapon aside. He tried to brush away the drops of molten metal that had fallen onto his hands.

'Alive,' Kyra called to Eshia. 'We need him alive.' Before entering Beastgrave, the young dryad had been reluctant to kill anything but now she was not so certain that the mountain's ferocity had not set roots in Eshia's essence. It was perhaps this reminder that caused Eshia to draw back her amber arm and try to get closer to Ghroth.

Kyra suddenly sensed powerful magic at work. She turned her gaze up to the ledges above the cavern. For the first time she noticed a cloaked twist-flesh with a lupine head. Dark energies swirled around him as he conjured his spell. 'The twist-flesh sorcerer,' she shouted in warning to Eshia and the others. It was all she could do for the moment. The ogor spear that transfixed her made any deeper concentration impossible. She could only watch in disgust as the wolf-headed shaman bit off his own finger.

Black blood sprayed from the shaman's wound, but it did not remain blood for long. It assumed a thick, smoky quality. Instead of falling to the floor, it drifted through the air. Quickly it took a form, a shape like that of some daemonic bull. Only the head and forequarters of the animal assumed any real definition, but those were enough. At the shaman's gesture, the black apparition flew across the cavern. One of the soil heaps burst apart as the spell swept through it, cast aside as though an avalanche had struck it. The bull barrelled into its true target. Eshia was smashed by the spell, hurled across the chamber as though smacked by the tail of a dragon. Her body spun through the air and sped straight for the opposite wall. There was a loud crack as the dryad struck. She dropped to the ground and remained unmoving.

Absolute desperation seized Kyra. She felt the twisted presence of Beastgrave's forests just above the roof of the cavern, a source of power she loathed to open herself to but the only resource the branchwraith had left to draw upon. She thought of the Thornwyld and all that depended upon their success in stopping Ghroth and destroying the godbeast's heart. Whatever sacrifice she made, it was a small price to pay.

The glow in Kyra's eyes flickered as she reached out with her essence. Her spirit flowed up into the roots hanging from the ceiling and into the trees they fed. She allowed some of their hungry presence to seep back into her, lending her the energy she needed to block out her pain and focus upon her magic. At her command the roots swayed and reached down in ropey tendrils. Her control over them was sluggish at first. When she directed the coils against the twist-flesh sorcerer, the cloaked villain was able to avoid them and leap down to the cavern floor. The smaller beastkin hurried to follow his example, clambering down from their perches to escape the writhing roots.

Kyra raised her hand and pointed towards Ghroth. The beastman was ensnared by a spiral of constricting roots and lifted off the floor. Savage delight throbbed through her mind as she found the enemy in her grip. She could crush him like a berry, watch his corrupt blood seep into the soil. She could rend his body to gory fragments and scatter them through the vastness of Beastgrave. Not a speck of the chieftain would be left intact...

The violent desires flared through Kyra, shivering to the deepest parts of her essence. Already the roots were tightening, ravaging Ghroth's body. Blood bubbled from his mouth as he tried to scream with such breath as was still in his lungs. Panic seized the branchwraith. They still needed Ghroth alive to find the crypt. Only then could they ensure the safety of the Thornwyld.

Horrified by the passions goading her to destroy Ghroth, Kyra focused all her will against the aroused bloodlust of the roots. She was unable to mitigate their violence, so she forced them to release the herdchief. He slopped to the ground, gasping for air. The other twist-flesh hurried to him. They lifted him from the floor and carried him away to the tunnel on the other side of the cavern. The swine-headed beasthound stopped worrying at the throat of the tiger it had killed to follow the rest of the retreating warherd.

Kyra felt panic again as the twist-flesh entered the darkened tunnel. They could not lose the Rootcutter again. Not now. Not when he might be close to his goal. The turmoil of her agony reached out and connected to the essences of the dryads. 'We cannot fail,' she told them. 'But to succeed will cost us dearly.'

The dryads understood her meaning. Kyra felt their consent as she let her magic flow into them – magic rife with the vicious taint of Beastgrave's forests. New strength pulsed into the dryads, invigorating their savaged bodies and fatigued spirits.

Nyiss stabbed her claw into one of the tiger's arrow wounds and sent an extension of her talon tearing deep into the animal's flesh. The cat opened its jaws in an agonised yowl and collapsed at her feet.

Yanir used her bolstered power to break free of the ogor's grip by snapping one of the copse-breaker's arms, cracking the thick limb as though it were a brittle branch. The huntress stumbled back, gawping at the havoc wrought against her. Yanir did not relent in her attack. She seized the ogor's face and savagely tore her lower jaw free. An anguished gurgle was the only sound the ogor made before she crashed to the ground.

Kyra rose to her feet. She was appalled by the brutal delight she sensed in all of them. Even Yanir had never taken such pleasure from killing. She hurriedly tried to shut off the flow of energy between herself and the forest. More than before, she found the process arduous. It was an ordeal for which she was not prepared. It was more than the resistance from Beastgrave's forest, it was her own resistance that confounded her. Whatever part of her wanted to remain pure, it was not equal to the part that wanted to share the mountain's hunger.

Dimly Kyra realised that Eshia was approaching her. The young dryad's trunk was split, cracked by her brutal impact with the wall. She moved slowly, but with each step her gait was less wobbly. Kyra felt the sympathy in Eshia's essence, and a kind of anxious regret. As the dryad came closer she began to speak.

'Pain will block the flow,' Eshia said.

'Do it,' Kyra told her.

Eshia reached for the spear embedded in Kyra's body. The invigorating flow of magic had caused the wound to close. The dryad opened it again when she forced the spear all the way through.

Kyra's essence screamed in torment as the spear was forced through her. But she retained enough concentration to take advantage of the agony. The connection with the forest was disrupted and while it was broken she was able to close it off. Not entirely.

Not completely. For there was within each of them a residue of the mountain's savagery.

'Even when we have found the crypt and destroyed both Ghroth and the godbeast, we will be unfit to return to the Thornwyld,' Kyra said. 'This place is inside us. We cannot bring it away into the wyldwood.'

Nyiss and Yanir bowed their heads in agreement. 'The Rootcutter had to be stopped,' Nyiss said. 'Whatever the price.'

'So long as we succeed, we will be content,' Yanir added. 'To guard the Thornwyld and punish those who trespass within has always been my purpose.'

Kyra gestured to the tunnel. 'Nyiss, pick up their trail. They may make it more difficult for you now that they know they're being followed.'

'I will not lose them,' Nyiss vowed.

'No,' Kyra said. 'Whatever we must do, we will keep after the Rootcutter to the very end.'

CHAPTER THIRTEEN

Ghroth drew great ragged breaths into his lungs. Even though he knew he was free of the constricting roots, his body refused to accept the reality. His skin felt tight against his bones, his muscles constrained so that every effort to move was an act of will.

Only one thing gave Ghroth any sense of comfort. The tunnel down which Tograh and Vuluk were carrying him felt familiar. The strangely corroded texture of the rock walls, the toppled plinths that sometimes lay across the floor – these were things that evoked his vision. That alone caused his heart to stir and his blood to race. He was certain they were again on the path that would lead to his destiny.

'Not carry Ghroth,' the chieftain snarled at his warriors. He shook himself free from the ungors. Unsteady on his legs, he pressed one hand to the wall to support himself. It had a strange clamminess about it. He drew another breath and detected the smell of mould. A pale scum of the growth covered everything. He sniffed at what had come off on his fingers. There was a necrotic quality about it that was far from his liking and he tried to brush it off.

Sorgaas crept forwards and inspected the wall. His hand was wrapped in a bandage torn from his cloak and he used this covering to dab at the mould. The shaman scowled at the pallid substance. 'You must be careful what you touch from here,' he warned. 'This is carrion-rot.' He shifted his bray-staff under his arm and used his claw to peel away the tainted bandage and toss it into the darkness. He held up the ugly stump of his finger so Ghroth could see. 'The mould thrives on dead flesh, but if it gets into a wound it is worse than deadly. It will bring a slow contamination that will turn the victim into one of the undead.'

'Vuluk,' Ghroth snapped. The ungor walked to him. When he was close, the chieftain took away his steel axe and held the hand which had touched the wall out to him. 'Clean Ghroth hand,' he ordered. He looked at the burned spots that marred the fur on its back. He lifted his new axe and gave Vuluk a further warning to be careful.

Sorgaas was still looking at the walls, surprised to see so much of the mould. 'This should not be here,' he muttered. 'In a cemetery or on a battlefield, perhaps, but to grow in such abundance on raw stone would need considerable magic to...' His eyes widened with alarm. He swung back to Ghroth. 'In your vision, was there anything that made you think of a gateway or a window? Some kind of opening between Ghur and Shyish?'

Ghroth could only follow part of what Sorgaas was saying. He did not know about gateways and openings, much less the intricacies of magic. But there was one thing that the shaman's questions did make him wonder about. How far could he trust what he had seen? The certainty that had been growing inside him had suffered drastically when the tree-fiends attacked them. There had been no warning of them in the prophecy and because of them he had lost the axe he had seen himself carrying into the godbeast's grave. If those things could change, what else could?

Yet there were still signs that supported the veracity of Ghroth's vision. 'Ghroth see this tunnel,' he told the shaman. 'Ghroth see path to godbeast. Close. Soon.'

Sorgaas gave him a sharp look. 'And what is it that you have not seen?'

Ghroth bared his fangs. A thought had come to him when the tree-fiends made the roots fall upon him. He had seen their magic before when the warherd tried to claim their forest as a new hunting ground. He wondered if he had also seen that same magic at work when he was saved from being sacrificed. He stepped towards Sorgaas and raised his axe. 'Tree-fiends track warherd. Maybe track Ghroth long. Maybe free Ghroth with tree-magic.'

Sorgaas did not mistake the accusation. He backed away from Ghroth and shifted his bray-staff back into his clawed hand. He held the other before him, displaying the missing finger. 'I bit my own finger off to save you,' he protested. 'If I wanted you dead, would I maim myself to help you?'

Before Ghroth could make his mind up, Frang came loping out of the darkness to rejoin the beastkin. It was visibly excited, its fur bristling and a low snarl rumbling from its throat. The beasthound turned and faced back the way it had come.

'Tree-fiends,' Ghroth growled. He looked at the walls, slick with the carrion-rot mould. 'Tree-fiends hurt by fight. Much wounds.'

'The mould feeds on flesh,' Sorgaas reminded him. 'Their wooden bodies offer nothing for the carrion-rot.'

Ghroth stamped his hoof against the floor. His idea had been to fight their pursuers here and use the mould to gain an advantage. 'Go,' he snarled at the others. 'Not fight here. Fight better place.'

A kick of Ghroth's hoof sent Frang rushing ahead of them down the tunnel. He let the beasthound get a good distance away before he followed. The rest of the warherd came after, placing themselves between Ghroth and the tree-fiends. Ghroth was certain his goal was close as they pushed deeper into the mountain. Every twist and turn revealed by Sorgaas' light was familiar to him – he knew instantly which passageway to take. Their only hesitation was to call Frang back when the beasthound set out down the wrong corridor.

Ghroth kept his senses keen for any sign the tree-fiends were closing in. Any stray sound or wayward scent that could warn him. He dreaded to see even the hint of a root splitting the rock. The tree-fiends were at their most dangerous when they could use their magic to animate other plants. Now he knew that included tangles of roots underground as well as cursed forests on the surface.

While watching for anything that could help the tree-fiends, Ghroth noticed that the thickness of the mould was becoming more pronounced. The carrion-rot was taking on a translucent quality, casting its own ghostly glow. 'Sorgaas no light,' he told the shaman. When the spell faded the orangish glow from the mould was still bright enough to see by.

'Use mould-glow,' Ghroth told the others.

'Scent bad,' Tograh said. 'Dead smell.' The raider had an arrow drawn from his quiver and was ready to nock it to his bow. Vuluk stood close to him, a sharp splinter from one of the fallen plinths gripped in his hands.

Ghroth paused. He did not need to draw a breath to know what Tograh was speaking of. There was a rankness to the air. Not the kind of deathly odour from corpses – that at least would be a familiar scent. This was something else, an impression of stagnation. Something locked away too long. Not like spoiled fruit or rotten meat. It was a staleness that went far beyond putrefaction.

'Frang!' Ghroth shouted. The beasthound's keen senses should have warned them of bad air. He intended to impress on the creature the hazards of laxity.

'Frang does not sense this,' Sorgaas told Ghroth as the beast-hound came loping back. 'It hasn't a brain big enough to know what is wrong.' There was an excitement in the shaman's voice, a mix of dread and anticipation. 'There is a saturation of death ahead of us, a concentration of those dark energies that make the carrion-rot thrive on bare stone.' He nodded his lupine head. 'Yes, I think it must be the godbeast's tomb. We are close.'

Ghroth coughed and tried to spit the taste of the air from his mouth. 'Tree-fiends follow,' he reminded the shaman. 'Ghroth take heart, take power. Fight tree-fiends then.'

Again, Sorgaas nodded. 'It will all be for nothing if we are caught by our enemies.'

The beastkin pressed on into the eerily glowing depths of Beastgrave. Sorgaas thought the luminescence of the mould lent everything a decayed sheen. It was an effect that well suited the hideous tang in the air. He knew enough about the different winds of magic to recognise the baleful emanations of Shyish. Whatever Ghroth had said or seen, he was convinced there was some kind of portal open to the haunted realm. Perhaps it was close, perhaps far, but the shaman was certain there was some connection. Near or distant, the dark magic was being pulled down into this tunnel and drawn onwards.

The other beastkin advanced ahead of Sorgaas. Certain he was unobserved, he brought the head of his bray-staff scraping against one of the walls. It was fairly caked in mould – he was impressed by how much of the glowing encrustation he removed. He was even more impressed by what he found underneath. Ghroth had pressed onwards thinking what lay under the mould was just the same rock as before. The herdchief was wrong.

What Sorgaas had exposed was a section of rock as smooth as plaster. Images were picked out on that surface, pictures of incalculable age. They were abominably suggestive of the insectile statues he had seen before. These were depicted carrying large reptiles to what must be a huge basin. The insects butchered these lizards in unspeakable fashion and filled the bowl with their dismembered bodies.

Intrigued as much as he was disgusted, Sorgaas swept the braystaff down another section, revealing another picture. There was a gargantuan creature sitting on the other side of the basin. It was a great black shape, shaggy and brutish, with long arms and massive jaws. It was plucking bits of the lizards from the bowl and devouring them. Even as a simple image, the shaman sensed the awesome power of the creature the insects were feeding. It was strange that only now did it occur to him that a godbeast would certainly have its devoted worshippers.

'Sorgaas follow,' Ghroth barked from further down the tunnel.

Sorgaas considered the image. Its presence here meant they were likely close to where the godbeast was entombed. The long hunt was almost over. He would have to decide what to do about Ghroth. If not for the menace of the tree-fiends pursuing them, he would make his move the instant they were in the crypt. Not knowing how far behind their hunters might be put a different perspective on things. He might even have to let Ghroth claim the heart and be content to serve the new beastlord. Distasteful but better than being torn to ribbons by tree-fiends.

There was a notable downward slope to the tunnel. The air if anything became still more rank. There was an increasing coldness to the atmosphere. To the others these changes might be enigmatic, but Sorgaas knew they were provoked by the accumulation of Shyish. There was a big conglomeration of that deathly energy close.

Frang howled in distress, the sound echoing down the tunnel. Sorgaas hurried forward to see the beasthound cringing at Ghroth's feet. The herdchief was exultant, waving his arms at two colossal doors that closed the end of the tunnel. Each of the portals looked to be shaped from some dark and lustreless ore, banded with straps of metal. The combination must have weighed many tons, for each door was a dozen feet high and eight feet wide.

'Here,' Ghroth shouted to the ungors. 'Here is what Ghroth see. Here is where Ghroth find destiny.'

Sorgaas was not so certain. 'We must get past the doors first. Whoever put them here may have laid hexes and traps on them.' He set his staff so it pointed towards the obstruction and drew on his magic. There would be no time for subtlety with the tree-fiends on their trail. He raised his hand to his mouth.

Ghroth struck the shaman's hand away. 'No need. Ghroth see doors. Ghroth see doors open.' Boldly, with arrogant surety, the chieftain strode forwards.

'Traps! Hexes!' Sorgaas called after the swaggering herdchief. Ghroth ignored him and kept going.

The tunnel shook and rolled. Rocks and dirt pattered down from the roof. The floor jumped under Sorgaas' feet and knocked him to the ground. Tograh and Vuluk shrieked in terror while Frang cowered down on its belly. Ghroth managed to keep standing and continued towards the doors.

Sorgaas was certain the chieftain's arrogance had triggered some spell or mechanism that would bring the whole mountain down around their heads. The thought of being squashed like a bug beneath an avalanche of rock rushed through his mind. He wailed to the Dark Gods to redeem him from his plight.

Amazingly the next few moments did not see the mountain falling down about Sorgaas' horns. He watched in wonder as the huge doors parted before Ghroth's approach. Dust and dirt spilled down from the ancient portals as they moved. The creaking groan that sounded from them sliced through the air. A powerful wind rushed down the corridor, carrying with it a confusion of musty smells and a decayed reek. There was a sound, wavering between a strident hum and a soft whisper.

Ghroth stood in the opening, his bestial figure framed by the green glow that shone from the place beyond the doors. The herd-chief was exultant. 'Ghroth destiny. Here find godbeast power.' He gestured with his axe to his followers and motioned them to join him as he stepped through the doorway.

Sorgaas hurried after the chieftain, stumbling as the tunnel continued to shudder around them. Beyond the doors the ground was firm, devoid of even a trace of the agitation that beset the corridor outside. The portals opened into a vast cavern, so tremendous in scope that the shaman was awed by the enormity. It seemed to stretch away to the very limits of sight, all illuminated by the glowing mould. Great spans of solid stone reared up to brace the roof, each one more bloated and misshapen with mineral encrustations than the next. Stalactites and stalagmites of every size jutted from the floor and ceiling like the teeth of Beastgrave itself, a gigantic maw that could never be filled.

Lying amid the fields of mineral growths were colossal blocks of worked stone. Sorgaas could not begin to conceive how such constructions could have been raised without the mightiest of sorceries. Their scale was cyclopean and from a distance they seemed to be cut from individual slabs. From somewhere the notion came to him that maybe the blocks had not been cut at all, but had in some fantastical way been *grown* into their desired shapes and positions.

The beastkin stalked deeper into the cavern. The ungors warily inspected every shadow they passed, sharp with fear. Frang lingered back with the rest of them and refused to stray ahead as it had done before. For his part, Sorgaas conjured wards to defend him against ancient curses and unquiet spirits. In his spellcraft, the shaman kept one eye on Ghroth. There was no hesitance about the herdchief. It was obvious from the way he marched through the cavern that he was following a path he had expected to find. The path foretold to him in his vision.

The decayed smell grew stronger as the beastkin moved further, as did the sighing-humming sound. Sorgaas felt dwarfed by the megalithic pillars they crawled across, the full enormity of the ruins blotted out by the aeons of minerals that had seeped down. At times the shaman could almost detect a faded glyph or image on the blocks, but they seemed to evaporate before his eyes when he tried to make any kind of closer study.

The stink became so pungent it could almost be tasted. The sound became so powerful that Sorgaas felt it as a dull vibration in his bones. Ghroth became more eager than ever, striking out well ahead of them all. The shaman saw him clambering over a mound of rubble that reared up from the floor. The chieftain reached the top and threw his head back in a triumphal howl.

The sight instilled courage in the ungors and Frang. They dashed forwards to join Ghroth in his victory. Sorgaas saw something else. There was a shape to the rubble, definition that had not been obliterated by the minerals that encased it. Because of the size, he wanted to reject the idea that had taken hold in his mind. When he scrambled forwards and climbed to the top he did not continue onwards as the others had. Ghroth was leading them over a toppled column that lay deeper in the ruins. Sorgaas turned to the wide hollow at the middle of the rubble.

The bottom of the hollow was a jumble of debris, thick with the mineral build-up. Yet a few objects were clear enough for Sorgaas to pick out despite the patina that encrusted them. A clawed limb. A saurian skull. The hollow was filled with ancient bones.

The rubble over which they had climbed was part of a huge basin, a bowl big enough to hold the carcass of a mammoth. Sorgaas thought of the pictures on the wall and the hulking creature that had been receiving sacrifices in such a bowl.

Sorgaas scrambled away from the basin. His first instinct was to flee, to escape the dreadful implications. The impulse held him for only a moment before it was beaten into abeyance by his will. One great desire had kept Sorgaas alive, given him a purpose when his mutations caused him to be cast out by his family and left alone in the forest. That was the obsession for power. Not power as crude chieftains like Ghroth reckoned such things. The power Sorgaas sought was that which was locked away inside all knowledge. To learn and understand a thing was to possess it always, be it the hidden ambition of a gor warrior or the secret intonations of a spell. Once a thing was known it became power. Even as his body urged him to run, Sorgaas knew he could not. He had to know. Suspicion was not enough. He had to see and know.

The state of the basin and its contents gave Sorgaas reassurance. After the epochs of time needed to wreak such damage, the thing that had once fed from that bowl would be little more than a fossil itself. It would be amusing to watch Ghroth try to gnaw his way through a rock to consume its power.

Sorgaas climbed across the fallen pillar. Beyond it stood a forest-like maze of stalagmites. There were sharp teeth of stone in every size and dimension, some short enough to step over, others so wide across that he had difficulty moving around them. After a short time among the stalagmites, he became disoriented. He had lost sight of the others. The overwhelming stench of the cavern had grown to such excess that he could no longer pick the scent of the beastkin from the air. The humming sigh had risen to such a volume that there was no chance of hearing anything so meagre as the rap of a hoof against the floor.

The shaman cupped his clawed hand before him and spat on the scaly palm. With his other hand he reached into his mouth and worked one of his fangs loose. He barked in pain as it came free and blood dripped down his muzzle. Sorgaas focused on the needs of his spell and strove to ignore the dull throbbing of his gums. He slapped the removed fang into the little speck of spittle and waved his fingers across it in a series of arcane passes. A few blood-flecked words and the feat was accomplished. The fang spun around in his hand, circling rapidly until it settled in a firm position, pointing between his thumb and the first claw. It held there until he moved, when it adjusted itself so that it indicated the same direction it had been pointing in before.

Sorgaas was satisfied that his spell would lead him in the right direction. The magic he had evoked would lead him to Ghroth, and the chieftain, in turn, would lead him to the godbeast's remains. Though he was certain Ghroth's vision of his destiny was impossible, there might yet be some sort of power that could be wrested from the fossil. Whichever god or daemon had sent the prophecy to the herdchief was showing him things in a way he could understand, not the literal reality ahead of him. Already there had been disruptions and variations in what Ghroth had expected to experience in Beastgrave. The end of his hunt would simply be another change the herdchief would have to accept.

The glow of the mould lessened as Sorgaas pressed on. Where before the morbid growth had been everywhere, now he found that it was displaced on the stalagmites by wiry clumps of moss. Creeping vines circled many of the stones and hung between them in a latticework of stalks and leaves. The floor became soft, mushy with decayed vegetation. The material squelched under his feet as he moved through it. Once, he stepped into a weak spot and sank up to his knee in rotten leaves and dead moss. The fall caused him to lose the guiding talisman he had created as he sought to brace himself against one of the stalagmites. The enchanted fang was sent flying into the darkness.

Using his bray-staff, Sorgaas pulled himself out of the hole. He cursed the loss of his talisman and debated creating another. A loud howl that rang out from somewhere directly ahead gave him hope that such magic would be unnecessary. He struck out in that direction, recognising the sound as coming from Frang. The beasthound continued to bay for some time, giving voice to its fright. Sorgaas was grateful for the sound, but also surprised that Ghroth allowed it to persist so long. The same noise that was leading him through the stalagmites could also lead others.

The shaman pressed on. The glow from the carrion-rot mould had diminished significantly, creating a strange green twilight of deep shadows. He saw a huge block of worked stone ahead of him. Climbing to its top, he found that the cavern ahead was lit more brightly than the forest of stalagmites. He could see far enough into the distance to observe many more gigantic pillars and walls, some fallen, some upright but partly entombed in minerals. He did not give the ruins much scrutiny, for there were things much closer to him that demanded his full attention.

Frang was a little below Sorgaas, halfway down the inside face of the fallen pillar. The beasthound had its swinish head raised and was howling its fright. It had reason to be afraid.

Beyond the pillar was a deep recess, a cavity in the floor. The fissure was not empty. A gargantuan bulk reposed there. At an estimate, Sorgaas judged it to be fifty feet from the top of its scaly head to the bottom of its splayed feet. The thing was not much less than thirty feet across at its broad shoulders. Long arms with enormous claws hung from those shoulders, each of the hands big enough to crush a troggoth in them. The chest was broad and wide, tapering down to a narrow waist and comparatively short but thick legs. The head was set directly on the shoulders with only the stumpiest of necks. The godbeast's hulk was partly covered in dark hair. The head, chest and undersides of the arms and hands were hairless, given over to a rough, scaly hide. The giant lay sprawled on its side and a row of jagged spikes stuck up from its hairy back.

Sorgaas knew he looked upon the godbeast. Any doubt was banished when he saw its face. Partly covered by moss and vines like the rest of the body, partly dissolved by decay, what remained still evoked an impression of terrifying power. It was a squashed, pushed-in face, with heavy brows and long jaws. The nose was short with wide nostrils. Sharp fangs jutted out from the mouth. The eyes were sunk deep into the skull, coated in some leathery membrane.

The awe that gripped Sorgaas as he gazed on the godbeast's corpse was greater than anything he had ever felt. There could be no doubt that the titan was dead. In many places the skin and hair was split open. Bones protruded through the meat and muscle. Ribs stood exposed along the upturned side of the body. The mandible along one jaw was completely devoid of flesh. Yet despite that patina of rot and ruin, the prodigious strength of the godbeast remained.

'Sorgaas see now,' Ghroth shouted to the shaman. The gor chieftain and his ungor minions stood on the other side of the godbeast's body, poised on another of the toppled pillars. He gestured with his axe at the titan's chest. 'Sorgaas watch. See Ghroth take godbeast power. See Ghroth be beastlord.'

Ghroth was ready to leap down onto the huge body. The godbeast lay on its left side, so to reach the heart the herdchief would have to hack through several feet of flesh and bone. It was a task he appeared unwilling to trust to anyone but himself.

Before Ghroth could jump down, the frightened baying of Frang was replaced by loud snarling. Sorgaas turned around just in time to see the beasthound lunge at a figure that had appeared at the top of the pillar. The foe that had provoked the already agitated Frang to attack was one of the tree-fiends. The mutant's jaws clamped tight around the creature's arm as she swung at it. There was a crunching sound as the fangs splintered wood. Frang's claws raked at its foe's body, digging deep scratches in the bark.

'Ghroth. We are attacked,' Sorgaas shouted even as he hurried down from the side of the pillar. Other tree-fiends were cresting the pillar, no doubt drawn, as he had feared, by Frang's howls. The shaman had no intention of facing such enemies up close. That was the forte of mighty champions like Ghroth.

The herdchief glowered down at the godbeast's corpse. There was not time enough to cut his way to his prize. He had no choice about it. He had to rout these enemies before anything else. Ghroth pointed his axe up at the interlopers. 'Tree-fiends. Ghroth will break tree-fiends. Ghroth will chop and burn all tree-fiends.'

Ghroth and the ungors charged towards the pillar to meet their foes. Sorgaas let them sweep past him and focused his mind on crafting a spell that would bolster their attack. He did not have the energy to muster the phantasmal bull again, but he thought there was something that might serve as well. As he drew aetheric power from the winds, he felt the air grow heavier around him. Sorgaas turned back towards the godbeast's corpse. A wave of fascinated horror surged through him.

Sorgaas recalled something he had read in the grimoire of a sorcerer. *Death comes slow to a god.*

'Kill. Kill tree-fiends.' Ghroth lunged up the side of the pillar towards the wooden creatures. He saw the amber-armed foe who had melted his weapon in their previous battle. He chose her as his immediate target and left her long-clawed companion to the ungors.

The tree-fiends were rushing down to confront the beastkin

with savage eagerness. It was his enemy's urge to enter the fray that Ghroth exploited when he attacked. He hurled himself up the sloping side of the pillar and struck low. His nose filled with the scent of singed fur and charred horn as his foe lashed out at him, the acidic brush with the bubbling amber scorching the top of his head. He kept beneath the angle of attack and barrelled into the wooden creature.

Ghroth's axe flashed out, crunching into the tree-fiend's leg, splitting it down to the heartwood. She had been stepping towards him and her full weight pressed down on the wounded limb. The wood fractured and flew into splinters, unable to support the tree-fiend further. A moaning wail rose from the tree-fiend as she lost any semblance of balance and went pitching over the side of the pillar. Ghroth rubbed his hand across his bleeding scalp and flicked a blob of gore after his enemy.

'All tree-fiend fall,' Ghroth shouted down at the toppled creature. In her plunge, she had landed on the sharp stalagmites below and several had punched through her body. She writhed on the stone spikes, splinters and sap dripping from her wounds.

'Rootcutter,' a furious voice roared at Ghroth. He turned from his fallen adversary to face this new one. The speaker was thinner than the other tree-fiends, with sections of pale heartwood showing where the darker bark was absent. The knots that shaped her face had a fierce intensity about them, a hostility that would brook no quarter and suffer no compromise. Here was an enemy that could not simply be driven off. To be rid of her, Ghroth would have to destroy her.

'Rootcutter and branch-burner,' Ghroth snarled at the tree-fiend. He made a show of drawing a deep breath even though the stench of the godbeast made it impossible to smell anything else. 'Carry Thornwyld scent. Good. Ghroth know where lead great brayherd first.'

The tree-fiend's face contorted into a vicious snarl, splintered fangs elongating in her mouth. 'You will never leave Beastgrave. You or the power you crave.'

Ghroth barked with laughter. Frang was tearing into one tree-fiend. Another was bleeding from several of Tograh's arrows and had Vuluk pounding her legs with his club. Then, of course, there was the creature he had pushed off the pillar to impale herself on the stones below. 'Tree-fiends not stop Ghroth. Tree-fiends only...'

Ghroth's words faltered. The herdchief felt a terrible pain inside him. Blood bubbled from his mouth. Beyond the pain he felt a crawling, slithering undulation beneath his skin. He looked down and found that his body had been pierced by animated vines. He glared at the tree-fiend. He knew it had been her magic that had rescued him from the huntsmen. She was calling on that magic again, only this time it was not to save him but to destroy him. While she bandied words with Ghroth, she had been weaving her spell.

Rage gripped Ghroth. Reckless of the damage wrought on his own body, he sprang at the wood-witch. Blood spurted from his ruptured skin as the piercing vines were torn free, shreds of flesh clinging to their thorns. The havoc they wrought on his body was considerable but Ghroth champed down on his torment. He had been used, exploited by these tree-fiends. He would return their manipulation with the most hideous revenge he could imagine.

But first he was going to chop this wood-witch into kindling.

Ghroth's axe flashed towards the tree-fiend's snarling face. Before the blade could cut down into her, an invisible force pressed back against him. Ghroth struggled on, pushing his body to its limits to reach his foe. It was like marching against a mighty wind. Each inch gained threatened to knock him three inches back. But the herdchief would not be stopped. He would prevail. He was prevailing. He glared down into the fey lights of the wood-witch's eyes. He would see those lights when they faltered and faded into darkness.

'Kyra!' The shriek rose from one of the other tree-fiends. Ghroth shifted his gaze just enough to see the creature that had been fighting the ungors. She had caught Vuluk and was holding him in her fist. She swung around and hurled her captive towards the melee. The mangled body of a beastman made for an inaccurate missile. It slammed into both its intended target and the wood-witch. Both were sent sprawling by the impact.

Ghroth was the first to regain his feet. He threw Vuluk's body off him and sent the broken-necked ungor rolling down the side of the pillar. He retrieved his axe and stalked over to the fallen wood-witch, holding back when he saw masses of vines slithering towards her. Ghroth wondered if her pose of vulnerability was bait to lure him into a witch's trap.

All thoughts of tree-fiends and magic were routed from Ghroth's mind suddenly. The steady hum-and-sigh noise that had filled the cavern abruptly stopped. In its place was an imposing silence.

A silence that exploded in an earth-shaking roar.

Sorgaas gawped in terrified wonder, afraid to believe the evidence of his eyes. Yet there was no question. There had been motion. The shiver of a leg muscle beneath those layers of hair and scale. As he looked on, another spasm rippled through the chest. A quiver of animation flickered through the jaw. The leathery caul slid back from one of the eyes.

The godbeast lived.

'My magic,' Sorgaas muttered in amazement. 'Can it be my conjuring has broken its slumber?' Half-mad with fear, half-insane with excitement, the shaman tore at his injured finger. Blood dripped from the reopened wound, blood that he hastily used to draw more energy into himself. Now that he was aware of it, he could feel some of that power fleeing from him and being drawn into the gargantuan bulk of the godbeast.

Sorgaas looked upwards at the pillar where Ghroth and his followers fought the tree-fiends. It seemed such a petty conflict to him. Everything about Ghroth was petty, from his brutal simplicity to the puerile vision that had driven the chieftain to Beastgrave. A vision that, Sorgaas reminded himself, was not so precise as the herdchief claimed. How could it be? How could something as wretched as Ghroth claim the might of a god?

'My magic,' Sorgaas crowed as he saw more motion rush through the godbeast's bulk. In ancient times the insects had placated this monster with offerings and sacrifices. They had communed with its awesome power. What the insectile creatures had done, Sorgaas would exceed.

'My magic awakens you,' Sorgaas told the stirring titan. 'It is my power that revives you. I shall be your priest. Your hierophant. I will serve your awesome power. You will be my patron, my great and mighty lord.'

The shaman's pulse raced with rapturous adulation. That he could have been content to bask in the afterglow of a mere beast-lord, to feed off the position and authority of a mere mortal, was absurd to him. Here was true power. Immortal power. The power of a god. He would serve that power and so become a reflection of its terror and glory.

'Yes. Yes! Rise, my master!' Sorgaas howled in triumph as he watched one of the clawed hands flex and set itself against the floor. The other eye was open, staring up at the roof with a distant gaze. The chest was expanding as the godbeast drew breath into its long-dormant lungs.

The steady hum and sigh that had risen to a deafening volume abruptly stopped. Sorgaas experienced a surge of horror when the godbeast rose. Strands of vine and moss fell from the giant as it stood upright. The scaly, somehow simian head pivoted upwards and its mouth opened with a deafening roar.

Sorgaas felt the sound vibrate through his bones. He clapped his hands to his ears and stared up at the arisen colossus. 'Live, my master. Live again and let the kingdoms of Ghur tremble before your power.'

The godbeast ceased its bellowing. It turned its head and fixed its deep-set eyes on Sorgaas. The shaman lifted his bray-staff and called to the titan. 'Let me serve you. Let me worship you. I shall show you lands to conquer. Tribes and kingdoms that will bow before your might. All will bow before us, master, or they will be destroyed!'

The godbeast's eyes narrowed. A scowl pulled at its fanged jaws. Before Sorgaas knew what was happening, the colossus raised one gargantuan foot and brought it stamping down on the shaman. His last sensation before his spirit fled his flesh was that of his body being ground to paste under the godbeast's heel.

CHAPTER FOURTEEN

Kyra trembled with terrified awe as the godbeast rose to its feet. The monster brought its foot stamping down on the twist-flesh mystic who grovelled before it. The wolf-headed shaman was pulverised, flattened by the godbeast's crushing weight. When the titan lifted its foot again, there was nothing but a crimson mire smeared across the floor.

'The godbeast lives,' Kyra called to the other sylvaneth. It was a foolish thing to do. It was impossible that any of them could have failed to see the colossus rise from its grave or hear its thunderous roar. Indeed, for the moment, the battle between the beastkin and dryads was forgotten as all of the combatants stared at the gargantuan monstrosity.

A brooding silence filled the cavern as the godbeast's gaze roved across the fighters. The monster's eyes bore down on them with such power that Kyra felt as though it were staring through her wooden body to see the soul within.

A howl of mad defiance rang out. Ghroth hurled himself down

the side of the pillar and rushed towards the godbeast. Hooves squelched in the mush of rotten leaves and dead moss, but the chieftain maintained his momentum. He threw himself at the hulking monster and his steel axe sank into the huge knee.

The godbeast struck out with its clawed hand, trying to pluck Ghroth away from its leg. The beastman ripped his axe free and dropped away just ahead of the swiping claws. When the herdchief landed he instantly swung around and hacked at the monster's other hand as it reached for him. Dark blood erupted and the titan jerked its hand back in pain.

It can be hurt, Kyra realised. If the godbeast was vulnerable, there was a chance Ghroth could kill it. Kill it and claim the hideous prize he was after. 'The Rootcutter. Stop him,' Kyra told the dryads. Her fear of the godbeast was nothing beside her fear of what Ghroth would do with its power.

Yanir swung around and charged down towards the chieftain. The twisted archer that had been harrying her fled at her approach, scurrying away to a new vantage. The old dryad ignored him and kept on for Ghroth. Kyra let her own essence flow into Yanir, fortifying her and pouring new energy into her. The branchwraith did not worry about the toll the transference would have on her own body. What mattered was stopping Ghroth.

Ghroth had ducked behind the stalagmites and was using the stone teeth to shield him from the godbeast's anger. The huge claws struck out, shattering stalagmites to rubble, but always too late to catch the chieftain. The Rootcutter darted forwards and lunged at the titan. The axe bit down into its arm, shearing through the hairy hide to split the flesh beneath. Then the beastman was dodging away, back among the stalagmites, to avoid the monster's wrath.

Yanir confronted Ghroth as he tried to slip away. Quickened by Kyra's essence, the dryad slashed at him. Kyra guided the thorn-tipped fingers, steering them at the chieftain as he tried to duck the blow. The flashing talons raked his back, digging new wounds into his already bloodied hide. Ghroth stumbled, fell to his knees. He struck out with his axe, but Yanir set her arm in its path and let the blow smash down into her limb.

'Now, Yanir. Finish it,' Kyra's essence enjoined the old dryad.

Yanir raised her arm to deal the killing blow, but before she could strike, a great shadow loomed over her. Kyra shared the dryad's agony as a huge hand closed around her and pulled her up into the air. The godbeast held her where its sunken eyes could inspect its catch. Its hand tightened. The shriek of wood splintering, of the dryad's body being crushed into pulp, wailed through Kyra's senses. She felt Yanir's torture as her body ruptured, as the blood-sap exploded from her veins. In that red hell of suffering, Kyra's essence was flung back into her own body. From her own eyes she saw Yanir's husk crumble in the godbeast's grip.

The branchwraith tried to struggle to her feet. Ghroth, wounded but very much alive, was slinking among the stalagmites, watching for his chance to strike again. If Kyra could stop him, if at least that much of the vision could be thwarted, the Thornwyld might send others to deal with the godbeast. There might be time enough to do that.

Below Kyra, Nyiss was still fighting the loathsome beasthound. She had been raked and ravaged by the creature's claws and fangs to a horrible degree. Long strips of bark had been torn from her body. The heartwood beneath was slashed and scarred. Blood-sap drooled from scores of cuts and gashes, yet the dryad refused to relent. She swatted and slapped at the tormenting beast, trying to rend it with her talons. The beasthound was too agile for Nyiss, scrambling away from her gripping hand with spastic jerks of its body.

'Nyiss, I will help you,' Kyra told the embattled dryad. She did not have the stamina to project her essence as she had when bolstering Yanir, but Kyra still had some power. She reached out with her magic and stirred the hanging vines into motion. She felt once more the awful hunger and maliciousness of the mountain flowing into her. She tried to be quick so not too much would get inside her.

Long tendrils of vine spooled down from the stalactites overhead. They fell upon the beasthound, coiling around the creature and restricting its movement. Nyiss seized the constrained enemy. Her hand closed around one of its legs and with a savagery more befitting a crazed spite-revenant than one of the Thornwyld's dryads, she wrenched the limb from the beasthound's body. The creature yowled in agony and struggled to twist free. Kyra's vines held it fast. There was no escape for it when Nyiss grabbed another leg and tore it loose.

Kyra limped down the side of the pillar to join Nyiss. The godbeast was still trying to find Ghroth among the stalagmites. The chieftain was being helped by the twist-flesh archer. When the colossus came too close to Ghroth, the smaller beastman would pop out from behind a rock to loose an arrow into the monster. The titan turned to swat at this new tormentor, but when it did the herdchief sprang out from hiding and gashed its leg with his axe. The godbeast snapped around and tried to catch Ghroth, but he was already ducking back into the forest of stones. The archer took the opportunity to send another arrow slamming into the behemoth's back.

The branchwraith reached Nyiss as the dryad was freeing herself from the mangled beasthound. She had removed four of its legs and shredded the thing's hide down to the bone along its back. The quivering wreckage flopped against the pillar and rolled down to the floor of the cavern.

Nyiss regarded the gore that coated her claws. 'It escaped from me in the Thornwyld. It did not escape this time.'

Kyra shivered at the ferocity in Nyiss' tone. It was too much like listening to one of the feral outcasts that existed at the edge of sylvaneth enclaves, crazed wretches who heard only the war song. She was more appalled because there was a part of her that shared the dryad's delight. It was the mountain Beastgrave's malice stealing into them as it had all things that drew life from its blighted soil.

'The Rootcutter,' Kyra reminded Nyiss. 'We must stop him. It is only the two of us left to do it.'

Nyiss stared at the splintered husk of Yanir strewn about the floor. 'The Rootcutter, then the monster,' she hissed. The dryad stole forwards, her bark taking on the hue of the vines and leaf-litter. 'I will come upon him from the left. If he shows himself, try to force him towards me.' Nyiss headed through the stalagmites, only the exposed heartwood from the beasthound's attack betraying her presence as she moved.

Kyra lifted herself onto one of the stalagmites and waited for her chance at Ghroth. If she could fell the chieftain with her magic there would be no need to drive him to Nyiss' claws. Even if she simply injured him, slowed him enough that he couldn't slip away from the godbeast's grip, it would mean victory. Whatever was needed to end the Rootcutter and his murderous dream.

Kyra let her awareness seep out into the vines and other growths that infested the godbeast's lair. It was not simply her own essence she exposed to the malignant call of Beastgrave but that sacred centre within all sylvaneth, that place within which the harmonies of the goddess Alarielle were enshrined. Terror more complete and horrible than anything she had ever known raced within her as the divine Spirit Song that reached across the Mortal Realms to every child of the Radiant Queen grew soft and indistinct. In its place there was a primal cacophony, the rage and malice of Beastgrave. Strength and madness shuddered through her. Spiky growths erupted from her body, unconscious manifestations of the viciousness that promised to overwhelm her.

'No,' Kyra hissed. Desperately she repressed the wild urges, the bloodthirsty visions that swelled inside her. She forced the energies she had drawn into her to obey. Magic streamed from her, the magic of Ghyran that resonated within all growing things. The ugly vines reared up, undulating around her like the tentacles of some oceanic leviathan.

Kyra spotted Ghroth as he slipped around the side of a stalagmite and prepared to attack the godbeast once more. She lifted her hand. The masses of vines spiralling around her snapped like whips. With each crack they dislodged their thorns and sent them flying at the chieftain. Several of the darts hit Ghroth and peppered his hide with fresh wounds. Some glanced off the rocks around him. Others struck the colossal godbeast.

Ghroth retreated back into the rocks, narrowly escaping the huge fist the godbeast slammed into the floor. The monster swung around, searching for where the stabbing thorns had come from. The scaly, simian head curled into an enraged snarl and the cavern boomed with the monster's furious howl. In rapid strides, it stormed towards the rock on which Kyra stood.

The branchwraith threw up her arms as the gargantuan horror came for her. In her desperation, Kyra conjured another spray of thorns from the vines. The godbeast roared again as the fusillade struck it and the sharp needles stabbed into its flesh. A tremor rolled through the cavern and the ground bucked and swayed. Shrill creaks and moans rumbled from overhead. Kyra saw some of the stalactites swaying above the godbeast. One came loose and hurtled downwards. The jagged piece of stone smashed down into the monster's body, shattering across its broad shoulders.

The impact staggered the godbeast, driving it down to one knee. It shook its head, apparently stunned by the blow. From the ceiling, a second stalactite came smashing downwards. This one cracked against the titan's arm. Kyra felt the vibration from the collision resonate through the rock she stood upon.

More of the stalactites were swaying above the godbeast. Through the fog of maliciousness that clouded her senses, Kyra realised that only the stones directly over the colossus were agitated, as though the mountain had been roused to strike at the monster. Understanding slammed into her with the impact of an avalanche. She had directed the vines against the godbeast, vines that were bound to Beastgrave as much as the sylvaneth were bound to their Spirit Song. In doing so, she had focused the mountain's malice against the titan.

In trying to stop Ghroth from killing the godbeast, Kyra's own actions were going to kill it for him.

Kyra exerted the utmost of her willpower and forced the snarling malevolence of Beastgrave out from her. She felt a searing pain as the Spirit Song surged back into distinction and she was once again a part of the ethereal melody. As she cut herself off from the mountain, the vines around her drooped and withered. She saw another change as well. The stalactites on the ceiling were no longer only swaying directly above the godbeast. Others across the cavern were agitated and moving, plummeting down from where they hung to shatter on the floor. It struck Kyra that she had been acting as the focus for Beastgrave's malignance. Without her to guide that wrath, the mountain was blindly lashing out. There was no direction to its violence.

The godbeast was more focused. It had not forgotten the branchwraith. Shaking the rubble from its battered hulk, the monster lumbered towards Kyra. She leapt from the rock just as the colossus reached for her. Its vengeful grip pulverised the stone and Kyra was slashed by the fragments that exploded from the crushed stalagmite. The godbeast reared back, searching for her. Its grisly gaze spotted Kyra and it swung its clawed hand towards her.

At that instant a mangled figure lurched into view. Kyra was shocked to see Eshia emerge to confront the godbeast. The young dryad's wooden body was splintered and pitted by the stalagmites that had ripped into her. A mixture of blood-sap and glowing amber streamed from her wounds. The lights in the hollows of her face were the merest embers. Her spirit was quickly fading, but even as death reached out to take her, Eshia refused to abandon her companions.

'Run.' Eshia's voice rang through Kyra's essence. She lifted her amber arm and sent it stretching out to strike the godbeast's leg. Flesh and hair sizzled under the acidic clutch. The huge monster spun around.

Eshia drew back as the monster came at her. The amber arm struck at the godbeast's face, burning across one cheek and up towards the sunken eye. The titanic fist came smashing down into the dryad. Eshia's body exploded under the impact, splinters of her heartwood pelting the stalagmites. The amber arm lost consistency and dripped away from the wreckage of the dryad in an oozing puddle.

'Eshia,' Kyra whispered, mourning the valiant dryad who had given everything for their quest. There was no time to respect her sacrifice. To linger would be to throw away the chance Kyra had been given.

Ghroth was back in the maze of stone somewhere. If Kyra could keep after him, she was certain she could drive the chieftain towards Nyiss. Together they would end his threat. They would avenge their fallen companions and kill the godbeast.

The cavern was still quaking as she moved between the stalagmites. Stalactites continued to fall from the roof, crashing down among the cyclopean ruins, the noise of their impact shuddering across the subterranean vastness. The godbeast was raging about the stone forest, seeking its enemies.

An anguished scream was the token of the monster's success. Kyra looked back through the gaps between the stones and saw the godbeast lift a shrieking figure from among the stalagmites. It was the twist-flesh archer. The small beastman flailed about in the titan's grip, his legs caught between the immense fingers. The titan reached around with his other hand and clutched the archer's torso. The ghastly sound of tearing flesh shuddered through the air as the godbeast pulled its victim apart. The colossus licked the gore from its fingers and began searching for the rest of its foes.

Kyra quickened her pace. She was desperate to find Ghroth before the godbeast found her. The urge to reach out with her magic and use the mountain's tainted plants to locate the chieftain nagged at her. It would be easy to find him with that method, for the vines and moss were all around them. To do so, however, would be to reconnect with the foul influence of Beastgrave and refocus its attention on the godbeast. Kyra could not risk that. The sylvaneth had to dispose of Ghroth on their own.

She spotted Nyiss before she found Ghroth. The scars from the beasthound had left patches of exposed heartwood the dryad was unable to camouflage. Kyra felt a new dread when she saw Nyiss lying in ambush ahead of her. It meant that Ghroth had slipped past, that their enemy had circumvented them both.

Motion close to Nyiss gave Kyra a new reason to feel fear. Stealthily approaching the dryad was the mangled beasthound. The vindictive mutant was not quite dead and with the last of its strength it was stalking Nyiss.

'Behind you.' Kyra placed the words in the dryad's mind and warned her of the danger.

Nyiss turned towards the crawling beasthound. The creature snarled at her and did its best to quicken its pace. The dryad lunged forwards and stamped down on the mutant's swinish head.

Her weight crushed its skull and the creature perished with a low squeal.

The dryad's action brought an immediate reaction. From behind one of the stalagmites, Ghroth charged into view. The chieftain must have detected Nyiss and his crippled beasthound. At his vantage point he had been watching them, biding his time until the opportune moment to strike. While Nyiss was distracted by the beasthound, Ghroth attacked her from behind.

'The Rootcutter,' Kyra shouted at Nyiss, but the warning was too late. Ghroth's axe was already striking the dryad as she leaned over the beasthound. The steel edge smashed down through Nyiss' head, cleaving through her face. She turned and tried to rake him with her claws, but already the lights were fleeing from her eyes. The dryad crashed to the floor beside the dead beasthound.

'You will suffer for that,' Kyra snarled at Ghroth as the beastman ripped his axe from Nyiss' face. The anger that burned through her essence was more than the righteous determination to protect the Thornwyld from this villain. There was a raw, savage hate there, something of the mountain's ferocity. With Nyiss gone, Kyra was alone, a solitary echo of the sylvaneth. That feeling of isolation fed her rage and dulled her reason. She threw her arms wide and cast aside all reserve.

'Tree-fiend,' Ghroth growled at her. He shambled forwards, Nyiss' blood-sap still dripping from his axe. Before he could take more than a few steps, the vines around him sprang into violent animation. Enthralled by Kyra's magic, thick bands of thorny tendrils wrapped themselves around the goat-headed warlord. His arms were pinioned to his sides, his legs pulled together as the thick cords encircled him. Ghroth gnashed his fangs in rage as the thorns dug into his fur and slashed into his flesh.

Kyra had her enemy. A thought would destroy him. But it was not enough, not enough to sate the savage cruelty the mountain demanded. 'You will suffer for what you have done,' Kyra promised her captive, 'and all that you would have done given the chance.'

The branchwraith focused her wrath into the vines. They shifted and shuddered, slow at first and then steadily increasing in speed. Ghroth cried out as blood streamed from his ravaged body. There was no pity in Kyra when she heard the shrieks. Mercy was an alien concept, something locked away in the soft murmur of the Spirit Song that was being drowned by the roar of Beastgrave. Ghroth was her enemy and he would suffer until the last speck of life bled out of him. Kyra directed the vines to move faster as they sawed into the beastman's flesh.

The crash of toppling stalagmites and the thunder of giant feet drew Kyra's gaze away from Ghroth. The godbeast loomed over the scene. Kyra might have been deaf to Ghroth's screams, but the colossus was not. Still hunting for enemies among the stones, the titan was drawn by the chieftain's cries. It reached down and seized the snared beastman. The monster lifted him from the ground, tearing the vines loose as it did so.

'No!' Kyra shouted at the hulking colossus. 'You will not take him from me!' Such was the wild lust for revenge that raged inside her that she leapt from her place of hiding and pounced on the monster's leg. Her sharp claws dug into the godbeast's hide, tearing handholds in its flesh as she climbed up its body.

The godbeast howled and roared, stamping its leg and swatting at Kyra with its hand in an effort to knock her loose. She withdrew her claws and flung herself to the side. Her move carried her upwards and she again stabbed her claws into the monster's flesh. She was ascending the creature's hairy back, a place where the huge arms could not reach.

Kyra remained focused on the captive in the godbeast's grip. With fanatical determination she moved steadily upwards. She thought if she could just gain the right vantage she could direct a spell at the chieftain that would kill him outright. Obsession had its talons in her mind. All she could think of was that the god-beast would steal her revenge from her.

Stalactites from the ceiling crashed down around the godbeast. They were not so scattered and random as before, but shifted and stirred wherever the monster turned. When it stopped moving to try to pull Kyra from its back, one of the stalactites crashed into its shoulder and knocked it to the ground.

Kyra dug her claws in deeper to keep from being sent flying when the monster fell. As it hit the ground, the godbeast's hold on Ghroth loosened. The chieftain pulled his axe free and brought the weapon chopping across the titan's thumb. The monster's hand snapped open as pain shot through it. Ghroth dropped to the ground and staggered towards the godbeast's body, his gaze intent on the chest and the heart that beat within.

Panic seized Kyra. The mad drive for revenge that she had allowed to overwhelm her threatened to destroy everything. Ghroth was within reach of his prize, the power that would make him beast-lord and draw to him such armies that the Thornwyld would be crushed under his hooves.

The branchwraith withdrew her claws and fought to focus her concentration, to evoke some spell that would prevent the disaster unfolding. The effort had her mind reeling as a dozen ideas came to her at once and she could not channel her magic to a single purpose.

Ghroth lifted his axe, a brutal sneer of triumph on his face. The godbeast was staring at him with one baleful eye. Before the chieftain could bring his weapon hacking down into the titan's chest, one of the colossal arms whipped out and swatted him with the back of its hand. The Rootcutter was flung across the cavern as though shot from a catapult. His body smacked into one of the gigantic pillars. Ghroth tumbled to the floor with a boneless fluidity that bespoke of ruptured organs and a shattered skeleton.

Relief raced through Kyra. The Rootcutter was dead, his threat to the Thornwyld ended.

More stalactites cracked and fell. Flecks of stone slashed into Kyra and dashed any sense of victory. Ghroth's menace was over, but the godbeast remained.

The monster rose back to its feet. It lifted its face to the roof and roared at the ceiling. It seemed to Kyra as if the godbeast were raging against the mountain itself – and that the mountain was returning its enmity. More stalactites fell, forcing the titan back. It could be no coincidence, Kyra knew. The positioning of the stones that fell loose was too deliberate. It was as if Beastgrave itself were conspiring to kill the godbeast. The idea sounded absurd, but after all Kyra had seen and experienced, she did not dismiss it. But if the mountain wanted to kill the colossus, why didn't it?

The answer was one Kyra knew only too well. Focus. Beastgrave was an enormous mountain with who knew how many miles of caves and tunnels worming through its depths. Whatever presence there was that held sway here, how could it be expected to fixate upon any one thing for long? It was simply too vast to diminish itself for so narrow a chore as killing a single creature, even something as gargantuan as the godbeast. That work was for others to accomplish.

Kyra felt the truth of the idea. Maybe that was why the vision had come to her. She had been drawn to Beastgrave not to simply stop Ghroth but to destroy the godbeast as well. A purpose the mountain, not the Sylvan Conclave alone, demanded of her.

Alone and exhausted, her body racked by the seemingly continual series of battles the sylvaneth had fought since entering Beastgrave, Kyra made a final prayer to Alarielle. She knew it was doubtful anything of her would find its way back to the Thornwyld or any other enclave. Her experiences and memories would be lost. There would be no seed of essence to be cultivated in a new soul pod. This would be the last of her. Only her accomplishments would linger on in the Spirit Song of the sylvaneth.

Kyra did not draw upon the ferocious powers of the mountain. She did not expose her essence anew to the hungry malice of the things that grew in Beastgrave. It was a different energy she called upon to work her final magic. The power of Ghyran, the spark that resonated within every sylvaneth and gave them life.

Still clinging to the godbeast's back, Kyra poured arcane energies into her hands and feet, into every part of her wooden body. Roots exploded from her bark and ripped down into the titan's flesh. The monster howled and raged, but still its hands could not reach her. In desperation it knelt beside one of the fallen pillars and tried to scrape the branchwraith from its body. Kyra felt her left leg crushed to splinters, but before the colossus could inflict more damage, a stalactite smashed down on its head and pitched it to the floor.

Deeper and deeper Kyra's rootlets dug into the godbeast's hulk. They carved paths through meat and sinew, past veins and bones, all being guided by her will to a single goal. The stunned monster shook its scaly head and rose to its hands and knees. A rumble of fury rose from its fanged maw.

The rumble exploded into a bellow of pain. Kyra's rootlets had reached their target, slicing into the monster's pounding heart. The lights in Kyra's face dimmed as she turned her entire power to what she needed to do. She diverted the blood-sap inside her own body into the rootlets. Dozens of tendrils filled with the sap, holding it poised until each was at its capacity. Kyra kept the merest residue to maintain herself. It would not support her for long, but she knew it would be long enough.

The godbeast was clutching at its back again, trying to catch hold of Kyra. Its fingers brushed across one of her arms, almost snaring her. Kyra waited no longer. In perfect synchronisation, the dozens of rootlets pumped the branchwraith's blood-sap straight into the monster's heart.

The godbeast reared up and shrieked once. Kyra felt the colossal heart burst from the flood she sent flowing into it, unable to contain both the monster's blood and her blood-sap. She dropped away, her dried claws cracking off as she fell from the titan's back. She landed hard on the ground, further fracturing her brittle body. From the floor she watched the godbeast take a few staggering steps and slam down onto its side. The monster's gaze was dull, its breath ragged. Gore cascaded from the left side of its chest, bubbling away from the exploded heart.

'Eshia, Nyiss, Yanir.' Kyra sent the thought drifting through the cavern, hoping to touch the spirits of her fallen companions. It was important to her that they knew. 'We won.'

Kyra lay upon the ground, her body splintered and shattered. She felt her spirit fading away, her essence draining out of her. With the death of the godbeast, the cavern had fallen into absolute silence. Even the rumbling of the mountain had drifted away. No more stalactites fell from the ceiling to crash against the stalagmites below.

When a sound did intrude upon the silence, it took Kyra's drooping awareness several moments before she could make sense of the sound. A feeling of dread pulsed through her. She struggled to raise herself up with her fractured arms. The sound was repeated. Growing louder. Growing closer.

It was the sound of hoofed feet walking across the bare patches of rock between the dead moss and leaf litter. Kyra wondered if there were already more twist-flesh seeking the prize Ghroth had tried to claim. Then she saw the source of the footfalls and her dread intensified.

The creature that strode across the cavern wasn't some pretender to the Rootcutter's infamies. It was Ghroth himself, his body intact without a hint of broken bones or ruptured organs. His pelt was whole and intact, without the cuts and gashes of recent battle. It was as though the chieftain had escaped his fights with the sylvaneth and the godbeast without suffering a single blemish.

Ghroth gripped his axe and approached the dead bulk of the godbeast. He peered at the exploded chest and the burst heart within. The chieftain howled and raged in frustration, lashing out with his axe and cleaving ribbons of flesh from the slain monster. In the midst of his fury, Ghroth spotted Kyra.

Kyra lay helpless as the beastman stalked towards her, unable to do anything but watch her enemy draw near. Ghroth kicked his hoof against her body. The rough impact further splintered her already cracked and brittle bark. Ghroth leaned down over her and stared into the dying light of her eyes.

The chieftain stood up again and barked in cruel amusement. He shouldered his axe and turned away. Kyra watched him as he vanished into the maze of stalagmites. Her gaze dimmed into darkness.

Kyra felt the last of her essence ebb away...

Some time later, vision returned to Kyra. A kind of awed wonder resonated within her – shock that she was still alive. Before she appreciated what she was doing, she rose to her feet. Only when she was standing did Kyra stare down at herself in amazement. Her broken hands were whole again, the leg that had been crushed by the godbeast intact once more. Impossibly, she was healed. In some amazing fashion, she had regenerated from her grievous wounds.

A dark cloud boiled through Kyra's mind as she recalled the same transformation restoring Ghroth. She wanted to dismiss the memory as a nightmare, some horrible imagining as she had felt herself dying. When she turned to where she had seen Ghroth's body land after being flung away by the godbeast, she knew it was no dream. There was no broken corpse lying there.

Kyra looked at her surroundings. The carcass of the godbeast was there, but other victims of the battle were not. The crimson smear where the wolf-faced mystic had been killed was gone. So too were the torn halves of the twist-flesh archer. The fact of her own miraculous regeneration turned sour when she considered that Ghroth and his warherd had also been revived. Perhaps because they were a kind of quick-blood, the process had worked faster on them. Whatever the reason, the brutes of Chaos were gone.

The dour belief that her enemies had been revived was set aside when Kyra felt familiar spirits resonating within her essence. She turned from where the beastkin had fallen to gaze upon a far more pleasing miracle. Yanir was walking out from among the stalagmites. Eshia too, her amber arm congealed around her shoulder. A few moments later and Nyiss joined them too, the scars from her fight with the beasthound vanished.

'Kyra, how can this be?' Eshia asked. 'We... we were dead.'

The branchwraith walked over to the dryads. 'All of this has been the doing of Beastgrave,' she said. It was the only thing that felt true to Kyra. 'The mountain drew us all here, both Ghroth and ourselves, in order to kill the godbeast.' She gestured to the hulking carcass. Thus far it had shown no sign that it too was regenerating.

'But if the mountain lured us here, why restore us when we were...' Nyiss pressed her hand to her head, as though feeling for where Ghroth's axe had struck her.

Kyra felt there was an answer to that too. Perhaps the godbeast was not as dead as it seemed. Just as the twist-flesh had revived more speedily than the sylvaneth, maybe the process would work slower with the titan. Maybe the colossus was regenerating without the intention of Beastgrave. Maybe the mountain simply wanted to keep the monster dormant until some awful time of its own choosing. She tried to explain these thoughts to the dryads.

'We are simply more invaders trapped inside the mountain,' Yanir said. 'Doomed to prowl these tunnels looking for prey.'

'Beastgrave keeps us here in case the godbeast rises before its time,' Kyra said. 'To ensure we remain, the mountain has restored Ghroth and his warriors. We cannot leave while they are alive.' She pointed at the dead colossus. 'Not while there is any chance the Rootcutter could still claim the power he craves.'

The sylvaneth shared a solemn look. They might never see the Thornwyld again, never escape from Beastgrave. The expression in their eyes took on a feral light, the angry hunger of the mountain shining in their gaze.

So long as there were enemies of the sylvaneth to hunt, this was where they would remain.

Not doom, but rather destiny.

Beastgrave was part of them. This was where they belonged.

ABOUT THE AUTHOR

C L Werner's Black Library credits include the Age of Sigmar novels *Overlords of the Iron Dragon*, *Profit's Ruin*, *The Tainted Heart* and *Beastgrave*, the novella 'Scion of the Storm' in *Hammers of Sigmar*, and the Warhammer Horror novel *Castle of Blood*. For Warhammer he has written the novels *Deathblade*, *Mathias Thulmann: Witch Hunter*, *Runefang* and *Brunner the Bounty Hunter*, the Thanquol and Boneripper series and Warhammer Chronicles: The Black Plague series. For Warhammer 40,000 he has written the Space Marine Battles novel *The Siege of Castellax*. Currently living in the American south-west, he continues to write stories of mayhem and madness set in the Warhammer worlds.

YOUR
NEXT READ

WARHAMMER AGE OF SIGMAR

OATHS & CONQUESTS

DAVID GUYMER • WILLIAM KING • EVAN DICKEN
AND MANY MORE

OATHS AND CONQUESTS
by various authors

War rages in the Mortal Realms. The heroes of Order stand against the darkness of Chaos,
the fury of Destruction and the sinister chill of Death in thirteen tales that lay bare the
oaths of the righteous and the conquests of the damned.
